T0147671

BETWEEN HEAVEN AND HELL

INTO THE ABYSS

SHORT STORIES BY:
JAMES L. WHITMER

iUniverse, Inc.
Bloomington

BETWEEN HEAVEN AND HELL
Into the Abyss

iUniverse books may be ordered through booksellers or by contacting:

iUniverse
1663 Liberty Drive
Bloomington, IN 47403
www.iuniverse.com
1-800-Authors (1-800-288-4677)

ISBN: 978-1-4759-5845-4 (sc)
ISBN: 978-1-4759-5846-1 (ebk)

Printed in the United States of America

iUniverse rev. date: 11/20/2012

Cover design by Carla Scornavacco, C-S designs, Chicago, Illinois

BETWEEN
HEAVEN
AND HELL

TABLE OF CONTENTS

THE 13TH FLOOR

By James L. Whitmer

CHAPTER 1

"Took me twenty years. Depends on what you've done," said the man.

"What am I going to do for the next twenty years?"

"Soul searching would be a good place to start," said the man, kicking off his elevator shoes and rising from the three-legged stool that he had occupied for the past twenty years. Exiting floor number 13 into the white light that failed to penetrate the elevator car, he threw his nametag to the other man. On it in small letters was simply printed the name *Jimmie*.

Then the door closed and the red light on the elevator panel lit up, as the elevator began its descent. His eyes were now focused on the only other numbered floor on the panel, floor number one. The elevator softly settled to a stop, the light from the panel dimly illuminating floor number one like the sign of a cheap motel. The door opened and a gentle rush of air from behind him hastened his exit. He was outside now, watching the flow of foot traffic toward the elevator bank that he had used for thirty some years in this very same building.

People began looking at him and waving. *Hi, Jimmie*, he heard several say. *Jimmie?* Then, *C'mon, Jimmie, we'll be late*, as the throng of people at the other elevator bank began to multiply. There had to be six or seven people there now. He looked down at his shoes, the kind he wore when he was eighteen. He then noticed the keys jingling on the clip he wore on his belt. *Let's go, Jimmie, got a big meeting.* Inexplicably he was soon at the elevator at the opposite end from where he had emerged, opening the door with the big elevator key from his clip. The people poured in. *Hey, just another day of ups and downs. Don't know how you do it, but keep at it.* He looked at the front corner of the elevator, its only occupant an empty stool, and then forlornly sat down. Somehow he knew at which floor to stop for each of the passengers. *See ya, at lunchtime, Jimmie. Jimmie* resonated in the middle of his head as the last occupant exited. He was alone now as the elevator began its descent to the first floor. *Jimmie?* He felt his face, soft, no beard, and no eyeglasses. As the door opened he rushed out and found the nearest men's room. Looking in the mirror he realized that he looked eighteen years old. Dead at forty-eight and now eighteen. That means thirty years in . . . Limbo.

CHAPTER 2

It was a lost art, sitting on a three-legged stool all day and going up and down. But that was Jimmie's job now. And he seemed to be getting very good at it.

"Hey, Jimmie, how do you do it?" asked his first customer of the day.

He was a tall, slender man, and was dressed as a banker. He always exited at the twelfth floor.

"Oh, you just get used to it," said Jimmie, pressing the required buttons on the elevator panel.

"Hey, and how come there's no 13th floor? Are people around here superstitious?" asked the banker.

Jimmie looked at the panel in front of him. There was no button for a 13th floor. Why hadn't he recognized that before? It went directly form twelve to fourteen. But . . .

"See ya later, Jimmie," said the banker, as the elevator doors opened, and the banker exited with a grin that looked like dollar signs.

CHAPTER 3

Time was irrelevant to Jimmie now. Time just didn't matter much at all anymore. When his shift was over, and the building was closed for the night, he simply remained in his elevator. The night custodians and maids never noticed him. It was as if he became invisible as soon as his shift ended. It wasn't as if Jimmie didn't try to attract their attention. Screaming at the top of his lungs simply made no difference. No one heard him and no one saw him. He was a non-entity, for all intents and purposes, until the morning throng of elevator riders converged on his car. And then he was simply *Jimmie* again. Yes, time didn't matter much, except in the calculation of how long Jimmie would have to wait in Limbo before he got the chance to ride that other elevator, at the other end of the building, to floor number 13, like the other Jimmie had. But that would be a very long time, as Jimmie calculated, almost thirty years. No, Jimmie could simply not face thirty years of soul searching. There must be another way. What if he simply just sauntered on down to that other elevator bank in the morning and just rode that car up to the 13th floor and got off? Yes, what if he did just that?

CHAPTER 4

It was just before 7:00 a.m. The morning commuters would be arriving soon. Lester, the night custodian, was at the front of the building getting ready to unlock the double set of glass doors that would allow the throng of daily workers and visitors to enter. Lester was jingling his set of brass keys and whistling a disco tune of sorts as he stopped for a moment and bent down to tie his shoes. Seeing the opening, Jimmie stepped out of his elevator prison and bolted toward the opposite end of the building where the elevator that would take him to the 13th floor stood in eerie silence.

The door was open and Jimmie stepped inside. The elevator was empty, except for the worn stool that occupied the front corner like a wary sentinel. As he began to sit down, he noticed that the top of the stool had etchings of sorts deeply cut into it. Probably the work of the other *Jimmie* or the several other *Jimmies* that had preceded him, he thought. He looked closer to try to make out the meanings of the etchings, which appeared to have been made with a small penknife or a key. *Do your time*, was roughly scratched next to the number *13*. Well, Jimmie was surely *not* going to do his time. Thirty years in an elevator, going up and down, up and down . . . no, that just wouldn't cut it. He sat down on the small stool, looked up at the elevator panel, and pressed the only button on the panel. The red light for floor number 13 lit up, splaying Jimmie's face with an odd red glow, the color one would observe from the embers of a dying campfire. The glow on his face was warm, and seemed to be getting slightly warmer as he felt the elevator begin its ascent to his final destination, floor 13, and escape from this hellhole of an existence.

CHAPTER 5

The air in the elevator was heating up, and the red glow on Jimmie's face was increasing in intensity. It didn't exactly burn, but the sensation of heat upon his skin was apparent. He raised his hand in front of his face to shield the glow from the elevator button, but the red light went right through it, and continued to bathe his face in a now deeper reddish color, the color of drying blood. His shoes began to emit faint wisps of smoke, as he felt heat surge through his toes and up into his ankles. His shoelaces were now burning and the smoke that emanated from below him began to rise and attack his face. The heat on his face was becoming increasingly uncomfortable, and his eyebrows began to twitch, as they too became victims of the unrelenting intensity of the heat.

Then the elevator door abruptly stopped in its ascent, and jolted Jimmie from the stool. He was on the floor, breathing in smoke, choking, and seeking refuge from the merciless glow of the red elevator button that fully massaged the interior of the elevator like an old friend. Jimmie struggled to his feet, searching amidst the smoke and heat for the *open door* button on the elevator panel. He found it, right next to the button for floor 13, which now was pulsating like a ticking heartbeat. Desperate and singed hands came down hard on the button and the door slowly opened to floor 13.

CHAPTER 6

"Who are you?" Jimmie panted out, as the heat surrounded him in layers, the stench of burning flesh assaulting his swollen face.

"I am Ardanari Iswara. And you have attempted to enter a realm where you are not welcome."

"Let me off. Just like the other *Jimmie*. Floor 13. That's where he left me. It wasn't supposed to be like this," he said, waving frantically as the smoke engulfed him.

Ardanari Iswara floated stoically in mid-air, the smoke and the heat of no concern to the hermaphrodite.

"You spoke of the other *Jimmie*. There have been many *Jimmies*. You are simply just another. Unfortunately for you, however, you will not enter into the light like the others. You simply did not abide by the rules and *do your time*. You will not pass. No, Jimmie, unlike the others who abided their time in Limbo with the patience of saints, you chose to try to circumvent the rules by selfishly seeking the 13th floor when you were told to indulge yourself in soul searching, which you have apparently abandoned."

"30 years!" screamed Jimmie, his eyebrows burned to cinders and the lobes of his ears beginning to melt into fatty drops of liquid flesh.

"Others have endured more. You chose the self-serving, selfish route, just like in your real life. Now you will realize the consequences."

"Who are you?" screamed Jimmie, his face pooling in thick, hot liquid.

"I've already told you my name. I am a hermaphrodite. I symbolize the essential idea in life, that all pairs of opposites can eventually be integrated into oneness. Evil and good, being opposites, can eventually be integrated into oneness. That was your fate. Your evil life plus 30 years of soul searching would eventually have been integrated into oneness in the afterlife. But you chose a different path. As a result, you thwarted oneness and you have sealed your fate to dwell in eternity with the others who are unworthy of final redemption. Behold your fate!"

Adnari Iswara, holding a delicate lotus flower in one hand, bathed in the light of eternal peacefulness; and raising her other hand to the darkness and smoke of the charred elevator, a hand upon which a slithering serpent was coiled, floated in midair, and condemned Jimmie to eternal damnation. As the elevator door to floor number 13 closed with a vengeance, it sealed the fate of the disbeliever to an eternity of soul scarching for the totality of the integration of opposites.

THE
SEDUCTION
OF INDIA

By James L. Whitmer

CHAPTER 1

Her name was India. But she wasn't from India. In fact, she wasn't from anywhere associated with a particular country's name. But she was from somewhere and that *somewhere* proved to be the most distinctive aspect of our relationship. Yes, there was a relationship, and I stress *was*, between India and myself. And that relationship started with a seduction. Whether it was the seduction *by* India or the seduction *of* India, I will defer to you, reader, to determine for yourself. Because in the most intense of human physical encounters where hormones rule the day, there always *is* a seduction of some kind involved. And as this chronicle slowly plays itself out like a tired record, scratched and dusty, and is laid before you like the sweet tasting chardonnay at a romantic midnight encounter, the myriad elements of that very seduction will be yours to analyze, and to assemble into a mosaic of love or lust, or whatever synonym or antonym thereof you decide fits nicely into the equation. And so back to that midnight encounter where blossoming lilacs at the top of weather-worn branches slow-dancing in the breeze effervesced their luxuriant fragrance of enticement around me, as I sat forlornly alone, staring at the flickering candle on a table shared only by an empty chair and myself. It was then that she entered and the seduction began. In the beginning I deemed it the seduction of India. But in the end . . . well, I will leave that to your judgment to determine the true nature of that initial encounter.

CHAPTER 2

What exactly I was pondering over at the time eludes me. But the soft light from the flickering candle was falling on my face, a face that was held upwards by trembling hands. And that's where the conversation began.

She was seated across from me as I looked up. Her countenance appeared angelic, as the orange-yellow glow of the lone sentinel massaged her face, as a masseuse at an expensive spa was wont to do. We were bathed in a gentle luminosity that signaled a harbinger of innocent romance devoid of conceit and false promises. Our eyes met, mine swollen from misery, hers bright and gaily dancing and overflowing in an incandescent mist of possibilities. And then she spoke.

"Is it really that bad?" she had asked, her hair falling onto her shoulders in a playful and erotic sort of way.

It was hair envied by countesses, and sought after by pretenders.

That bad? I held that thought in my mind like a magician concealing cards. Yes, it was that bad. And yet she was there, seated right across from me, flicking her cigarette ashes onto the cobblestone floor of the quaint outdoor café where we found ourselves staring at each other. And somehow the thoughts of misery receded, and the delicate flavor of her words absorbed my despair.

The waiter was soon pouring champagne into our glasses, and the music from the old guitarist in the corner was floating over us in gentle waves, as if we could reach out and touch them. Her smile beheld secrets, secrets that tempted to be discovered, secrets born of midnight encounters in clandestine and exotic places. She wore those secrets on her face and in the coolness of her eyes. They were mine to be discerned, to be dissected once discovered, and yet an invisible wall kept me out, and the stark coldness of her hypnotizing countenance contrasted with the gaiety in her eyes; black eyes, onyx-like and shiny, as if fairies polished them with silken cloths.

"You are quite handsome," she had said, her onyx-like eyes seeking attention, as a flamenco dancer seeks to capture the essence of the human spirit in every bodily movement and gesture.

After wiping the cold, damp sweat from my brow, and readjusting the clumsy knot in my tie, I had looked deeply into those eyes. They were eyes that had seen much suffering, yet they were eyes that twinkled with the glow of new beginnings. And a new beginning was the exact prescription that I needed, a prescription to be scribbled out on invisible paper, with a signature unreadable and erotic in its loops and swirls, and ending abruptly with undotted *i*'s and uncrossed *t*'s, mysteriously communicating a message that would unencrypt the tangle of mistakes and bad decisions that defined my very being, and save me from entering deeper into the abyss in which I was trapped. And as the conversation flowed indiscriminately between us like the gentle air from hummingbird's wings on an early spring's day, I imagined floating in midair that very same remedy, authored by her, and mine for the taking. And so I grasped at nothingness, attempting to secure my salvation, and was only met with simple laughter.

"What in heaven's name are you reaching for?" she had asked me, giggling like a school girl between sips of champagne, and then reaching into her cigarette case. But a cigarette case is a small flat case for holding cigarettes, which can be carried in a purse or pocket. But she held no purse near her, and her dress was pocketless. This simple mystery of her cigarette case should have been a signal to me that this melodious and enticing creature of the night was no mere mortal seeking a vapid and soon-to-be-forgotten sexual tryst with a stranger, but an essence from another place and another time, where beauty dispatched her docents as mere skirmishers seeking out the picket lines of soon-to-be romantic co-conspirators.

And so I returned my hand to its resting place on the table and humbly excused myself for the error in my judgment, white-washing it as a mindless habit of mine when sitting in the presence of such unadorned beauty.

"Unadorned?" Her voice was as melodious in its tenor, as her eyes were as dark as the deepest night.

Had I embarrassed her with the simple word *unadorned*? I searched for an answer, and then I looked again at her cigarette case, which she had placed on the table next to her empty glass. As the waiter refilled it, I read the inscription in cursive lettering that was slightly raised on its cover, as if it were branded there. *India* in neat, gold-plated lettering met my glance. *India*, what an odd sort of name, I had whispered.

"Yes, my name is India," she had said, reaching for another cigarette from her case and then reaching over to the candle to light it.

The shallow glow of the burning tobacco was focused on the pinpoints of my eyes as I read again the word *India*, holding it within me, as if to let it go would result in her desertion. I then clumsily asked her if she was from India, and as soon as the words came out, I wanted to suck them back in, as her skin was neither dark nor tanned, but of an alabaster tone that rivaled the color of Egyptian vases.

She looked quite curiously at me, as if seeking an understanding of a deep mathematical problem. She then exhaled softly and the gray-white smoke surrounded me, as if an abbot were placing sacred vestments upon me.

"I have never been to India," she had stated, as if reciting a lesson from a hand-held chalk slate. "I am really from nowhere, but you will soon learn that later, my prince."

She clapped her delicate hands and the waiter returned. Her fingers played a melody of anticipation on her glass as it was refilled. And then mine was next, and I watched as the waiter, with the steadfastness of a connoisseur of fine wines, poured. The infinitesimally small bubbles slowly escaped from the opaque liquid, as I watched the level of the liquor rise to its resting place. India's reflection was floating on the surface as the bubbles effervesced to nothingness. Her eyes, midnight black, beckoned me to drink, somehow assuring me that to do so would waylay my fears and release my inner soul to her for the taking. I lifted my glass and sought hers for a toast to our destiny. But the bubbles were no more, and she was gone.

CHAPTER 3

That evening, as I lay in my bed, thoughts of India pounded incessantly on my brain, as wide-awake, I stared at the ceiling. The stale light from the crescent moon seeped into my chamber through tattered curtains, depicting incoherent images above me that begged for translation. But only thoughts of India persisted and the shadowy moonlight message, undeciphered, quilted the ceiling above me.

India, India, India, who was this mysterious denizen of the evening, this creature of celestial beauty, mysterious as the Seven Wonders of the World, and as elusive as the interpretation of Jungian shapes? I looked again at the ceiling above me and the jumble of shaded images and intersecting lines now depicted a cross, black and ominous, a cross which I imagined symbolized, as Jung had predicted, inner urges, yet opposite in nature. But what were India's inner urges, as I now was attempting to come to grips with my own inner urges? Urges that focused on her, on India, a name that to me was ensconced in unadorned beauty and profound mystery. *India,* I held that thought deep inside of me, in a place protected from intruders, from name thieves, from those who would shatter my world, our world, mine and India's. But was there such a place? Had I invented it all to compensate for my nagging misery and despair?

I looked again upwards and the cross was no longer a cross, but had been replaced by a simple square, exact in dimensions, and obeying every law of ancient geometry that Euclid had ever imagined. It was wonderfully perfect. It defined her. And within the confines of that perfectly symmetrical shape her image dwelled. And there, within that very image, Jung's interpretation of the square as a symbol for the horizon merged with my desire for her. And so I closed my eyes slowly, as thoughts of a once sun-soaked distant horizon now foggily aglow with the fainted violet hues of diminishing twilight beckoned me, and upon which India, arms outstretched, took me prisoner.

CHAPTER 4

I had known misery before. And I had surely known depression. But none compared with the feelings that were struggling within me as I searched frantically to find her. Evening after evening I had returned to the place of our initial encounter, to that small, quaint outdoor café with a cobblestone patio where we had met and where the lone, old guitarist strummed softly on an ancient guitar, as notes of sadness floated past me. His name was Salvadore and, like India, he had confided in me that he really was from nowhere. He was part gypsy, knowing not where he was born, nor where he would spend his final days. And he fervently played each evening at the café, afterwards retiring to a small room located above a tavern that was adjacent to the indoor part of the café where wealthy patrons wiled away the hours sipping expensive wines and listening to the crackling embers of burning driftwood.

Though Salvadore was of no help to me in my search for India, we did, in fact, become friends. And as I sat alone each evening, the chair opposite of mine empty, and the flickering candle casting its shadow on beauty lost, he would approach, and with the silence of a lost lamb, massage the strings of his guitar so that only I could hear. It was a gypsy melody I did not recognize, but it was a melody that inextricably reminded me of her, of gypsy caravans, of golden earrings and skin as white as unblemished snow.

As the softness of the old guitarist's tune fell on me night after night, I began to imagine India as a high priestess, as Isis, the goddess of the night. Yes, she was from the night. We had met at midnight and her eyes were as dark as any night had ever been or would be. I imagined that, despite the alabaster nature of her skin, she was born of the evening and dwelt in its inner darkness. And also of the night, of the deepest, darkest night, her tiara resembled a lunar crescent, and signified to me the predominance of femininity. Yes, she *was* the essence of femininity, and yet being passive in nature, she dominated my existence. The throne upon which I envisioned her sitting was situated between two columns, and the entrance to her throne was veiled in transparent silk. The colors of the columns were blue and red, and I soon understood her true nature from those very colors. Blue denoted the lunar aspect of her personality, her nightly meanderings, and her dark nature; while red stood for fire, and the very nature of her enticing sexual machinations. The floor upon which her throne stood was checkered, with alternating black and white tiles; the whiteness a testament to her skin and the blackness an avenue to her inner mysteries; and all an enduring testament to the laws of chance and the concept of opposites. Yes, our meeting was the result of pure chance, and yet the concept of opposites was yet to be defined, as I had envisioned us as one. But maybe we were, in fact, opposites, or was there simply no one else with whom to be compared? I looked again at the empty chair opposite me, and then back at Salvadore sitting quietly in the corner eating crabs from soft shells and drinking cheap, red wine, and wondered aloud, *did she really exist?*

CHAPTER 5

It was November now and the outside portion of the café was closed. I now made my home away from home in a neat little corner of the indoor café, nestled between a crackling fire and a bevy of ostentatious patrons. Night after night, I stared into the sizzling embers, searching for her visage, for remnants of our past encounter. And all the while, Salvadore, meandering among the guests, strummed on his ancient guitar and softly sang gypsy ballads.

Hypnotized by the elusive colors emanating from the hearth, I occasionally was brought back to reality by the simple absence of guitar music. And so I looked to the opposite corner of the café and found Salvadore tuning his guitar, and smiling softly at me, a dish of crab shells at his feet, and a half-empty carafe of cheap, red wine neatly secreted underneath his stool. And on and on it went, night after night, and then near midnight on the last day of November, when the winds outside were howling with the vengeance of lost souls, a voice awoke me from my musings.

"I was out of the country," she had said. "India, to be specific. I had never been there before, and decided to go."

She appeared as before, perfect in every dimension, with eyes that sought the beauty of nature, yet restricted onlookers to the outskirts of her inner self. Her hair was longer, and flowed freely on bare shoulders. And, as before, her stare was mysterious and undefined.

"Take this," I had said, offering her my jacket. "You must be cold."

"I burn with desire. I burn with life itself. Keep your jacket, my prince, and tell me what you have been thinking about," she had said, placing her cigarette case on the table in front of her, the inscription *India* beckoning me toward her, and then reaching inside she removed a slender, ivory-colored cigarette.

I focused on the name *India* on her cigarette case. I repeated it in my mind, as if to brand it there forever, never to be lost again, never to be shared with another human being. *India*, I whispered softly.

"Yes, India. I was abroad tending to some personal business."

"But you had said that you were not from India."

"I am from nowhere. I am from everywhere. But my roots are in India. My mother was of gypsy blood," she had said, looking at Salvadore methodically tuning his guitar. "Like him."

"And your father?"

"A military man from Britain, or so I've been told. I never met him. Ran away, I suppose. But it is of no matter. I am half-gypsy and half whatever he was. It was a long time ago."

"But your name? *India?*"

"Oh, that? I invented it. Don't people invent things just to keep from going insane? Hm, don't they? Somewhere deep down inside of me the essence of gypsy blood mingles with the scents of India, with the fragrance of champa and its lily white flowers from the Jehlum Valley, with the pastoral beauty of Himalayan peaks, and the simple calmness of shepherds tending their sheep in quiet valleys. I invented myself and who I am. I am *India*. And who are you, my prince?"

Who am I? I wish I had known the answer to that simple inquiry.

"You look perplexed. Is it that difficult of a question?" she had asked, gray-white smoke lingering on pouty lips.

Who was I? Who am I? Was I now metamorphosing into something or someone as a result of my encounter with her, with India?

"Re-invent yourself, my prince. Be who you want to be. Forget the others. It is about you now and it is about us."

"How does one re-invent oneself?"

"Don't you feel it?" she had asked.

"Feel it?" I had sullenly responded.

Surely I had felt something. I was overwhelmed by her presence, enthralled by her simple, yet complex, nature, and her beauty that was born of sainthood. But her absence had debilitated me, wrecked me to the point of the deepest depression I had ever experienced. And, yet, now, she was seated across from me, as I was attempting to extricate myself from the incessant misery of the abyss into which I had sunk due to her desertion, and asking me if I *felt it*. But what had she meant? Should I risk a response that defined *it* as our future, as unremitting love? Should I venture that response, I had asked myself, as I looked into imploring eyes, serene, yet at the same time somewhat troubled. She was a cauldron of inconsistencies, and as Jung's concept of opposites washed across my mind, like water flowing from a fountain, I looked deeply into her eyes and said, *yes, I do feel it.*

She then shifted in her chair, her black velvet dress contoured to her hourglass form, as if painted there by Michelangelo. Its midnight-dark color contrasted severely with her alabaster skin, and her dress, the color of the nightmares of my deepest depression, was devoid of creases, perfect in every way, and was a stark comparison to my unkempt and erratic appearance. Was she really two persons, two images, two distinct personalities of varying degrees of intensity? Which India now sat across from me? Which India had I hopelessly fallen in love with, the purest of pure, or the intense, mysterious visage from the depths of darkness? *It*? Yes, I felt *it*, but I was not exactly conscious of whether my understanding of *it* equated with hers.

"Feel *it*, my prince. Slowly close your eyes, and re-invent yourself," she had said, as if the very heavens would change with her words.

I had stared deeply into those onyx-like eyes for some moments before my eyelids felt like lumber and slowly receded across tired eyes. I had begun to envision a whiteness of the whitest white I had ever seen, a white rivaled only by her alabaster skin, and this whiteness was now the whiteness of the purest white feather I had ever seen, and that floated above me as I lay prostrate on the ground. It descended slowly, and gently laid itself upon me as I marveled at its gleaming texture and innate religiosity. And as this feather, which symbolizes the wind, hypnotized me, I felt a calming breeze flowing across my face, and then the wind picked up, and this whitest of white feathers floated above me, gently rising and slowly disappearing into nothingness.

As I opened my eyes, Salvadore was strumming his guitar as he always had, and was approaching my table. It was a table occupied only by myself. India was gone.

"You were sleeping. Dreaming, perhaps?" Salvadore had asked.

"Dreaming? It wasn't a dream. It was real. It was . . . had you seen her leave, the young lady who was seated with me, here? Do you know where she went?" I had frantically asked, pointing to the empty chair opposite me.

"No, senor, maybe it was all just a dream. What were you dreaming about?"

Purity. Her. "I was dreaming about a feather, a white feather that was floating above me. Then it disappeared, like her," I had said, as I focused on the empty chair.

"Feathers can mean many things, my friend. In gypsy lore, my people believe that feathers mean lightness and height. I suppose that is a good meaning, eh, senor?"

"I don't know what any of it means," I said, slipping back into the abyss.

"Feathers can also mean dryness and emptiness. That could be unfortunate," Salavdore had said, as he began playing a sad gypsy ballad, and tears began welling into his aged eyes.

The last thing I remember of that enigma of an evening was soft gypsy music falling on me, comingled with the tears of Salvadore, and his acrid breath of cheap, red wine and the smell of crab shells.

CHAPTER 6

Hours melded with days, and days became of no consequence, as the months changed, with the seasons following. It was spring now and, with my small inheritance dwindling, I found myself in the deepest part of the abyss into which I had fallen. Suicide? Yes, dear reader, thoughts of suicide persisted like stale conversation from unwanted dinner guests. But somehow they had been pushed back to the inner confines of my mind, and out of nowhere, as I opened the drapes in my chambers, as the spring sun hit me full flush, thoughts of *invent yourself* floated above me.

Invent yourself. For the first time in a long time I realized that my problem was not with India but was with myself. India had only exposed the issue and provided a solution. *Invent yourself.* Yes, she was right, if she did, in fact, even exist, if I hadn't just imagined her and *invented* her myself just to keep from becoming a lunatic. India's words drifted across my face, a tired face, haggard with the depths of depression, but soon I was feeling *it*. And so I reconciled myself to re-inventing myself. Into whom or what I would become remained a mystery, and so I sought out assistance. And that assistance took the form of a maven of the workings of the inner psyche. Her name was Doctor Amelia Lane, and I soon became, at least according to her, her *most interesting patient*.

CHAPTER 7

There was a couch, and there was soft light. It filled the room and created an ambience of truthfulness. There would be no lying here, no false promises or inflated and exaggerated falsehoods. As I had entered that small room, which I had envisioned as a dungeon where my very thoughts would be painfully extricated from my inner soul, I felt at ease and then she spoke, as she swiveled her chair to face me, and her faithful docent who had escorted me into her inner chambers departed.

"Mr. Walton, I'm pleased to meet you," she had simply said, as if I were there to sell her life insurance.

Her name was Dr. Amelia Lane. She was a psychiatrist that had been referred to me by my personal physician. She sat with her legs tightly together and she was wearing a short, blue shirt that terminated just above her knees. She was in her mid-forties, about my age, and I assumed that we would have much in common, at least because of our ages.

She beckoned me to sit opposite of her on the couch, and as I squirmed into position, waiting for the inevitable plethora of questions to be fired at me machine-gun like, she flipped a switch on her desk, and the only thing left aglow in the room was my face.

"Shall we begin?" she had asked.

It was a voice that, in a strange way, reminded me of India's. There was no pretense in it, no dividing paths leading to subtle incongruences, just a straight-forward and simple use of words spoken in a feminine and somewhat sexy way. *Shall we begin?*

A vacuum filled the room like silence before a eulogy. I did not know whether to speak or to just wait as the sweat began to drip from the crevices of my forehead. Inexplicably it was I who broke the silence.

"Are you going to ask me questions?" I had inquired.

"Would you like me to ask you questions?" she had responded.

Weren't female psychiatrists all old maids who wore dresses terminating just above their ankles, and wearing dull, black shoes with buckles? But her shoes were stilettos and her tight, blue miniskirt was etched in my mind, as I searched for a response.

"Well, isn't that how it works?" I had managed to blurt out.

"How what works?"

"This."

"Well, Adam, what are your thoughts about *this*?"

I was caught off-guard. I was ready to answer specific questions like, *do you feel depressed, Adam?* Or, *do you have trouble sleeping, Adam?* But now I was tasked with defining *this*. What *this* was exactly, I wasn't sure. That's probably why I was there, sitting on a plush couch in a room with soft light, and a softer voice of an inquisitor of uncommon beauty falling upon me. And so I reached inward and pulled a rabbit out of hat and began talking about *this*.

"Well, I realize that I need help. I seem to be depressed most of the time," I had told her, indicating that *this* was my chance to emerge from my cocoon of defensive reactions and rejection and rejoin the human race.

It had sounded good to me. It sounded intelligent. But was it stale and pedantic? Would she think I was a mere academic reciting a word salad from a psychological handbook? Was I simply not addressing issues and wallowing in a maze of doubt that really didn't define much of anything, and certainly didn't define *this*?

"What makes you depressed, Adam?"

She had shifted in her chair. I couldn't see her but I felt her movements as soft air floated toward me. I smelled her perfume, which reminded me of plantain lilies in late August, and I detected the essence of her femininity, as I imagined her tight, blue skirt was climbing up her legs like creeping ivy, as she waited for my answer.

"Relationships," I had responded. "I simply have troubles with relationships."

"Relationships? What kind of relationships?"

"Women, of course."

I had assumed that was obvious, but then again, certainly there were a plethora of relationships that defined the human spirit. Unfortunately for me, my problems lay with the feminine gender, and that's what I had put on the table.

"Do you think I'm obsessed?" I had asked. "I mean, with my failures with women."

"Obsessed? Well, Adam, what do you mean by obsessed? After we cross that hurdle, then we will consider your concept of failures."

My notion of whom should be asking me about my depression and anxiety was exactly opposite of the woman who sat opposite me in the dark, and who was asking me questions with a sexy twang in her voice that reminded me of *Stella* in a *Street Car Named Desire.* Certainly, this was no mere school marm with buckled shoes and a chastity belt, who would get her feathers ruffled when an obscene word was muttered by one of her students.

"So, Adam, *obsessed*, would you like to tell me your feelings about obsessed?"

There it was again, that soft, sexy voice that secreted sexual innuendos, sublime, yet begging a response. It was a voice that could make a man's knees buckle and then straighten them out again while standing in the eye of a cyclone; a voice that was imploring, yet at the same time provocative, a voice that rose just slightly as it stressed the word *obsessed*, as I imagined her tight, short skirt rising above her knees and slightly exposing her inner thighs, offering an invitation to her secret desires.

"Well, I was obsessed with India. I'm sure about that."

"Tell me about India. Have you ever been there?" she had asked.

And so I told her about India. And she learned of my obsession.

CHAPTER 8

Epilogue

He spoke again as the dark smoke trickled toward her, as if ice were slowly melting.

"And so, signorina, what is your pleasure?"

Her pleasure? Well, that was an interesting thought. Her pleasure was now seated directly across from her. His male scent, feral yet refined, was the mixture of sexual wantonness and tamed aggression. The reluctance in his eyes cautioned her that to gain entry would be no simple task, and that to truly let her in would require the unremitting opening of her soul. As their eyes met like meteors on an unveering course, it was as if they were jousting, and the loser would be the one who blinked first and showed the first sign of submissiveness. So she held tight, her emotional hatches battened down, and met his stare with auburn eyes born of autumn colors, and that floated on a sea of doubt, wondering whether she should surrender and let passion take its course.

"My pleasures, signor, are quite simple," she said, as the waiter filled her glass with champagne. "I am not a complicated woman, if that's what you seek."

"I too seek the simple pleasures in life," he said, as he reached for her glass, and then sipped casually, his lips coming in contact with the remnants of her red lipstick, and her clandestine feminine scent that remained secreted inside.

Licking his lips, he exclaimed, "Magnifico."

He then pointed to the waiter to fill his glass with the very same champagne, and then offered it to her, after casually licking the rim seductively, as if to seal the bargain.

As she sipped slowly from his glass, she noticed that his legs were now uncrossed and that the bulge in his crotch was swelling like Krakatoa about to explode. She imagined him as a prince on a white steed, his armor shining in the sunlight as his legions followed behind him waiting for the simple wave of his hand. Her tight, red shirt was climbing up her legs like a serpent in heat on a hot rock, as Krakatoa throbbed, ready to expel its hot lava. And then he spoke.

"You need to re-invent yourself," he said.

"Isn't that what you have done? Re-invent yourself?"

He glanced down at his cigarette case, and his fingers deftly caressed the embossed name *Aden*. His name was Aden, but he wasn't from Aden. In fact, he wasn't from anywhere, to be exact. His dark skin was taut and sinewy, and his swarthy appearance exuded a stark masculinity that she considered inexorably tempting, and reminded her of Greek fishermen casting nets on sun-drenched seas. He wore a European cut suit, black in color, and that fit him as if it were glued on. His pants were pocketless and he wore no belt. He slowly opened his cigarette case, removed a slender, charcoal colored cigarette and politely asked, "Do you mind?"

She didn't mind. In fact, Aden's presence was what she had been unconsciously praying for. Sitting at the table where her most recent client had sat for months on end was her way of learning from the past. It was a habit of hers to visit the locations of her patients that played significant factors in their behavioral disorders and idiosyncratic misconceptions of life. So that is why she found herself in the small, outdoor café, with cobblestone flooring, and presently seated across from a god of extraordinary masculinity, as an old, gypsy guitarist strummed slowly on an ancient guitar as he watched from the corner.

"Re-invent myself? That's exactly what I have done, with your help, of course," said Adam. "Now it's your turn, Amelia."

SUDDEN OPPORTUNITY

By James L. Whitmer

CHAPTER 1

She had the figure of an hourglass. He had been riveted on her since she had entered the room and had sat directly across from him, seating herself as a princess would do at her first formal appearance. But she did not as much as notice him, and she had immediately begun to make small talk with two other attendees who sat next to her on either side, at the quaint dinner party sponsored, in part, by his former boss and now present managing partner in the boutique intellectual property law firm that they had recently formed. The other sponsor of the dinner party was his ex-wife, and now fiancée' of his *now* present partner. Quite messy, he had thought to himself, but that was only a minor inconvenience, as he remained riveted on the princess, imagining the possibilities, and seeking a sudden opportunity, but none was forthcoming.

CHAPTER 2

His attempts to engage the princess in conversation were futile. He was thwarted at every salvo, first by his ex-wife who seemed to monopolize the princess' attention throughout the evening and then, at the most opportune time, by his present managing partner who had escorted the princess onto the balcony overlooking the affluent part of the city for the remainder of the evening. The cards dealt to him were simply of no value, and he discarded them with the casualness of a beggar throwing away his plastic cup after being refused a penny on the street by a non-attentive pedestrian.

So that evening he lay flat on his back in his bed, staring at the ceiling, images of her hourglass form floating above him, and praying that he soon would fall asleep and live in a dream-world where she dominated his existence. How long it took to reach that dream-world he really couldn't remember, but when he awoke in a fit of spasms, the bed sheets tightly encircling his legs like ankle bracelets, and cold, damp sweat reeking its ugly stench from every pore in his body, he recalled the nightmare from which he had emerged. It certainly was not what he had intended when he let himself float into her hourglass form that had been hovering above him. Rather, it was the opposite, as images of a stark and weather-beaten hourglass projected itself into his mid-brain where he discerned an inversion of sorts, a mixing of good and evil as the salt crystals slowly migrated from top to bottom, and a relationship between the Upper and Lower Worlds was born, neither of which he had considered in his previous life. For now that previous and inconsequential life was gone, and what he had encountered in that very same nightmare impinged on his psyche and demanded clarification. And so he became fixated on her, on the princess, on her figure in the form of an hourglass, and on finding the true meaning of his life, which could only come to fruition by unraveling the existence of her, the princess from the inversion.

CHAPTER 3

It was now day three of his encounter with the princess, and he had settled on a thought that a diary would be *apropos* for his search for her. Attempting to recall every snippet of the events of their first encounter, he was unable to recall her name, as he had never formally been introduced to her. So with the weekend interval now passed, and with her hourglass figure lingering in his memory from that brief encounter on Friday evening, never to be erased, he sought out his managing partner on this rainy and cloudy Monday morning in hopes of unraveling her true identity, a small, black diary secreted in sweaty hands and a laundry list of questions seeking release from the prison of his mind.

Jonathan Barnett was no schoolboy when it came to making tough decisions. Tough decisions usually meant that someone was going to be hurt, either in the form of a putdown or in their pocketbook. In short, Mr. Barnett was not someone you would invite to your parlor on a Sunday afternoon with which to play bridge. Promptness was to be expected, and clarity a must when dealing with Mr. Barnett. So the young man with a princess of extraordinary proportions on his mind had developed a game plan, simple and straight-forward, just a few innocuous questions as to whom she was and then back to the misery of his work in the law firm that he detested.

"Good morning, Jonathan, that was quite a lovely party Friday evening," said the young man.

He found himself in Barnett's office, the only sounds being the ticking from the clock on Barnett's desk and the incessant pounding of his own heart that seemed to want to expel itself from his chest cavity. Barnett looked up from a tangle of papers on his desk, removed his glasses, and reached for a Styrofoam cup of coffee that served as a sentinel between the young man and his partner of demonic persuasion.

"Glad you liked it," Barnett said with a gruff, downing the coffee and then crushing the Styrofoam cup in gnarly hands.

Barnett was a big man with a big chest. Gray hair protruded from his collarbone region like snakes seeking a cold rock on a hot day. His suit was rumpled and his tie was knotted and loose, as if he had been an altar boy on a sweltering day in a church with no windows.

"Immensely," said the young man.

"Well, then, what is it? Something's on your mind. Spit it out, boy, and then let's get back to work," Barnett said, reaching for a pack of Camels that littered his desk along with a graveyard of ashtrays.

"Well, sir, I was just wondering about that young woman with whom you spent much of the evening at the party. Well, sir, I was just wondering, is she going to be a new client?"

"Hm, interested, huh? Well, to be exact, yes she is. And, frankly, William, I was thinking about referring her to you, you know, to work things out."

His heart stopped beating. The incessant *thump, thump, thump* was now flat-lined, as silence permeated the room. It was the type of silence experienced at Omaha Beach when the mortar shell burst in the sand in front of you, destroying your eardrums; it was the meticulous silence before the incision was made on the operating table; and it was the absence of laughter when a stale and unfunny joke was told. It remained and persisted for what seemed like eons, but, in actuality, was only a moment or two.

"Yes, sir, I would gladly welcome it," said William, his vice-like grip on the small, black diary increasing at the rate of an object approaching the speed of light.

"Well, then, here's her information. Now get on with it," said Barnett, beckoning William to approach, as the folder in his outstretched hand was thrust forward.

William held that folder in desperate hands, as if to lose it would result in a catastrophe of immeasurable dimensions. Yes, his mind began to release itself from the prison of her anonymity, as he looked down at the folder and repeated softly the name that Barnett had scribbled on it. *Anjana*, nothing more. And the young man realized that this was, in fact, a sudden opportunity.

CHAPTER 4

Anjana, quite an interesting name to say the least, thought William, as he seated himself in his office, which was quite smaller than Barnett's. Opening the folder, he found it completely empty, but written on the inside cover was an address, and nothing more. No telephone number, no e-mail address, no business card, just simply an address, 101 Astor Place, Apartment Number 2, Chicago, Illinois, stared back at him. And no last name was listed. *Anjana*, he repeated to himself, this time whispering it to hear what it sounded like in real time.

He glanced out of his window, as the November winds were kicking up leaves that soon would cover the ground like an autumnal blanket. It would be a twenty-minute or so walk to her apartment, he reasoned, and so he donned his overcoat, and clutching the empty folder he made his way outside, the name *Anjana* etched in his memory, never to be erased.

CHAPTER 5

What would he say to her when she opened her door? That, of course, was assuming that she would be there when he arrived. He held that thought tightly between clenched lips, as the name *Anjana* simply wanted to escape from within him, and then moved forward with logic that was born of the intellectual law practioner that he was. He would simply introduce himself, engage her in a meaningful businesslike conversation about whatever it was that had brought her to Barnett's dinner party in the first place, and then use every ounce of restraint in his very being not to portray himself as her would-be future lover, a fate to which he had been cast and from where there appeared to emerge no other option; a fate that beckoned him onward, releasing him to her beauty, and engulfing his very essence, as he whispered her name over and over again.

His hand was in mid-air as she opened the door. It was as if she had expected him. It was as if they were already one. He lowered his hand, dwelling on her presence within the doorway, searching for something meaningful to say. Her eyes met his, and he saw within them contentment that he had never experienced, nor envisioned before. They were soft eyes, the color of the autumnal blanket that now swirled around his feet. They spoke to him, whispering her name *Anjana*. He found himself repeating her name over and over. And then she spoke.

"Yes, I am Anjana. And I have been expecting you," she said, opening the door further, and disappearing inside.

He followed her, gently closing the door behind him, and soon found himself in a small sitting room, where the gloom from outside that casually seeped through the lone window contrasted with the ambient light cast by two lit candles near the table where she had seated herself on a chair that resembled a throne. He found himself staring at her throne, attempting to sort out her apparent mystic façade.

"Oh, that," she said lightly. "I'm a collector of sorts. Didn't Jonathan tell you?"

Jonathan had told him nothing. Maybe that was good. Maybe it wasn't, but at this juncture of their acquaintanceship, he was learning, and it appeared that there was quite a bit to learn, as he found himself again whispering her name under his breath.

"It's Hispanic. Can't you tell from my eyes? I'm from Andalusia," she said.

Her eyes were magnificent emblems of innocence. He imagined her as a virgin, his for the taking, to worship and to adore for eternity. They were eyes that were immune from deceit, impossible to manipulate, and above all else, portals to her soul, a soul that could only be won by a seeker of absolute truth. It was at that moment in time that he swore an oath to himself that he would be that seeker, her prince for all eternity, because, after all, he was in the presence of a celestial princess, who not only cast a cloak of unremitting love over him, but an aura of earthly desires and pleasures beyond his wildest imagination.

"What are you thinking about?" she asked, as if she recognized that he had been daydreaming.

"You. I'm thinking about you, and your name, Anjana. It is quite unique. I have never met a woman with the name Anjana."

"It is not so unique, as you say. You have certainly heard of the names Jana or Diana, haven't you," she said, her lips pouty and soft, as if to whisper those names gave her some sort of innate sexual pleasure.

"Yes, of course, but . . ."

"Well, William, those names are similar to mine. In fact, in Hispanic folklore they are the names of witches. Do you believe in witches, William?"

Witches? This celestial being with eyes that could not lie was now speaking of witches. Her hourglass form was tempting him to reach out and pull her toward him, as she shifted seductively in her throne. And then he remembered his nightmare about the hourglass and the inversion of worlds at opposite ends of morality. He looked again deeply into her eyes, and eyes that were moments ago portals to eternity were now pools of lust and carnal fantasies. He reached out and pulled her towards him. Her skirt was removed easily, and his pants followed accordingly. He was inside of her, thrusting like he had never thrusted before, as panting depicting every form of sexual perversity filled the small room, and the last thing that William heard before he passed out from exhaustive carnal bliss was, *you do believe in witches, don't you, William?*

CHAPTER 6

The medical examiner looked down at the body on the cold steel table.

"Interesting," he said. "Never seen one of these before."

Detective Wren looked over the medical examiner's shoulder.

"One of these?" Wren asked.

"Yes, his heart appears to have simply exploded within his chest cavity, as if an explosive went off."

"No explosives at the crime scene, Doc. Just him, half-naked, and bed sheets full of semen. And, yeah, a manila folder with the address and a name written on it," said Wren.

"A name? That should help you out."

"Maybe yes, maybe no. It is an interesting name, but it's only one word, you know, like Madonna or Prince or . . ."

"Maleficent?" asked the medical examiner.

"Good one, Doc, a witch from *Sleeping Beauty*."

"I imagine it's a female name, especially with what you found at the crime scene, and him being half-naked with an exploded heart," said the medical examiner, gently pulling the white death sheet over William's head.

"*Anjana*. The name scribbled on the folder was *Anjana*. Ever heard it before?" asked Wren.

"*Anjana*? Rings a bell. Something about witches in a college course I took light years ago. Check it out in your spare time," said the medical examiner. "Call me if you uncover anything interesting. In the meantime, I've got another customer on the next slab to attend to."

"Do you believe in witches, Doc?" asked Wren, cinching up his overcoat, readying himself for the cold November wind that was presently battering the windows of the medical examiner's office.

"Witches? Other than having married one, no," said the medical examiner, a sardonic grin masking his tired face.

CHAPTER 7

Detective Bartholomew Wren found himself in a place that he was unaccustomed to, a place of a foreign dimensions, a place that somehow sent shivers up his spine, and undulating spasms down his legs. He even began to produce a seeping sweat down the back of his neck that conjured up memories from long forgotten past events. Detective Wren found himself seated in a library.

The petite librarian with hair grayer than the foggiest day on the Isle of Mann held out a book to Wren in small hands devoid of ornamentation. The sour look on her face was reflected off of her shiny name badge that was clipped to her dour looking, and even grayer, sweater. Her name was Ms. Pence and her occupation defined her very being, strict, silent, and above all else, perfunctory in her duties.

"This is the one that will help you, detective," she said, placing the rather large and tattered book on the table directly in front of the detective.

With that Ms. Pence disappeared into the labyrinth of volumes in which she had dwelled for the past 40 years.

Anjana. There it was on page 240 of the immense volume. Wren adjusted his reading glasses, and began to read what he believed would be the key to the door that would open up the mystery of the corpse with the exploded heart.

The name Anjana originates in Hispanic folklore. Some researchers believe that the present day names of Diana and Jana are derivatives from the name Anjana. The name Anjana is rarely observed in present day occurrences, primarily because the name depicts images of witchery. Witches, according to folklore, were believed to have taken on the form of old women, in order to test the true nature and qualities of their human counterparts. But, in fact, these witches, in their true form, were beautiful young women, virgins, fair-haired and having delicate eyes, and clothed in tunics that flowed to their ankles and which were made of sequined flowers and silver stars.

These witches carry a gold staff adorned with sparkling jewels, and wear green stockings of Sylvan beauty. They are the guardians of animals and live beneath the earth in underground palaces of overflowing wealth, and treasures of unforeseen magnitude. The touch of their staff turns things of ordinary sameness into objects of beauty and wealth. This staff symbolizes a linkage of unrelated concepts, like wealth and poverty, beauty and ugliness, good and evil, and is the emblem of those relationships. Their green stockings are symbolic of their innate virginity and contrast with the primitive forces of lust and desire. Spiritual powers flow from them on an unconscious level and have the ability to sway the minds of lesser beings.

Wren stopped reading and closed the book. Quite a story, he thought, as he whispered the name *Anjana*, just to discover what it sounded like, pretending that the mysterious person who used this name, if at all, did in fact exist. *Anjana*, he repeated softly again, and then closed his mind to the thoughts of witches with green stockings.

CHAPTER 8

The case of the man with the exploding heart had been closed for some time now, and Detective Bartholomew Wren found himself buried with new and interesting cases of homicide, suicide and accidental death, but none as interesting as the case with the mysterious name *Anjana*. And so as he sat sipping his bourbon and water in the quaint bar located a stone's throw from his modest apartment, after a long day of looking at battered corpses, and blood filled crime scenes, his mind wandered again to that name of extraordinary curiousness, *Anjana*. He closed his eyes and whispered it, sipping slowly, as the bourbon massaged a tired and needy throat.

"Yes, that's my name," she said, standing above him at his table, appearing to be waiting for an invitation to sit.

Wren looked up dumbfounded, and observed a woman of startling beauty staring deeply into his eyes.

"May I?" she asked, indicating the chair directly across from Wren.

Wren stood up, and removed the chair so that the princess could sit. As she seated herself, Wren's heart was pounding with the vitality of man twenty years his junior, and the blood now pumping through his veins rivaled that of Jason and his Argonauts seeking the Golden Fleece.

"I am Anjana," she simply said. "I was seated over there," she indicated with a delicate hand that Wren imagined caressed violets softly and massaged innocent admirers. "And then I heard you whispering my name."

Their eyes met in a checkmate. The rook of the princess was soon to take his king. There was no way out, as he gave in to her presence, to the innate exactitude that flowed from eyes born of autumnal blankets, and skin the color of pearls that beckoned him to savor her ecstasy.

Her leg was now underneath the table. It was gently massaging his tired limbs. He was aroused beyond anything he had ever felt before, and his eyes melted like soft wax, as her stare intensified. She reached underneath the table and pulled up her tunic-like dress adorned with sequined flowers and silver stars, revealing forest green stockings. Wren was riveted on those stockings as her legs encircled his and the rapture in her eyes signaled a *sudden opportunity*.

"Do you believe in witches, Detective?"

THE
BLACK
LIMOUSINE

By James L. Whitmer

CHAPTER 1

It was a shiny black limousine that pulled up to the curb just outside of his apartment. He looked down at it from his second story window. It was as sleek as a seal and as a long as a country road. The windows were tinted a slightly darker shade than the limousine's exterior, and exactly who or what was inside remained a mystery; and yet, somehow, deep inside of his gut, he knew that he was destined to become a passenger.

Closing the blinds, he returned to the bathroom and finished dressing. It was Claudia's birthday. She would be 21 at the stroke of midnight. And by that time he expected to have her fully inebriated and sexually pliable. After all, isn't that what women were for anyway?

He returned to the window and looked out. The black limousine was gone. So much for riding in that behemoth of the night, he thought. Returning to the bathroom, he looked into the mirror one last time. Damn, he was a good-looking stud.

CHAPTER 2

The limousine was crowded as it usually was when a decision of heaven or hell was in the offing. Just who would enter the confines of this mobile coffin of the night remained to be seen; as the evening was young and the expected debauchery was not as of yet in full swing. So each of them sat, not knowing which of them would stay and which of them would casually exit when their unexpected guest arrived. Oh, yes, it was always an unexpected pleasure, because who really knew the exact time, place and manner of one's own death?

CHAPTER 3

Claudia looked uncommonly buxom as she sashayed across the dance floor towards him. He grabbed her by her ass with both hands, and pulling her toward him he whispered into her ear one of the thousand obscene lines he had memorized over the years. By midnight she would literally be drunk on her ass, and regardless of where that happened, he would have his way with her. That was his style and he certainly wasn't about to change.

As the band blared out some type of disco tune from the '70's, Donna Summer panting and sighing, he ordered a round of drinks for the small entourage that had accompanied Claudia to the table. No mind about the bill. Once Claudia was blitzed out of her mind, he would rifle though her purse and take whatever he needed to make up the difference, tip the waitress, and keep whatever was left for himself. Fair? Not quite. But the penultimate narcissist that he was had to live up to his own high expectations. Knowing that one was a true psychopath was something to be proud of anyway, wasn't it? Fuck the world! Damn he felt good about himself.

CHAPTER 4

The black limousine was parked with its engine running just outside of the nightclub where Claudia's birthday party was in full swing. The tinted windows remained up. There was no need for air conditioning or heat, because the occupants simply were immune to such measures. They sat stiffly, each ruminating as to whether dismissal was in the cards in their particular case, or whether they would accompany the soon-to-be guest on his or her next, and final, journey. Sometimes it was a long wait. Sometimes it was rather quickly accomplished. But each of the occupants sat quietly awaiting the fateful outcome, in the long and sleek black limousine.

CHAPTER 5

It happened in the alley just outside of the backdoor to the nightclub. He had her half-naked and she didn't even realize it. It was more fun that way anyway. A couple of vagrants who were dumpster diving turned to watch. That turned him on even more as he ejaculated inside of her, ripping her pants off as he did. Damn he was a wild man! Grabbing her by her hair he pulled her behind the dumpster, pushed her down, and kicked her in the face until she was unconscious. Glaring at the two bums as if he would disembowel them, they stumbled clumsily away, dropping what was in their hands, and running down the dimly lit alleyway.

Time to blow this joint and hit a few other dumps, he thought. He'd make something up about Claudia having to leave because she was drunk, and that he had to get up early and work the next morning. That usually worked. Just lie, lie and lie. That came easy. Pathological lying was simply a part of his repertoire. As far as the evidence, so what if his fingerprints were found on Claudia's clothes, wasn't he seen with her all night anyway? As far as DNA evidence, that was of no concern, as well. He'd make up something about having had consensual sex with her hours earlier. That would simply take care of that. Besides his criminal history was squeaky clean and his DNA wasn't in any of those silly databases maintained by the police. Sure he was a psychopath, but he was a smart psychopath and knew how to control his emotions. Low arousal and risk-taking seldom got the better of him. He knew they were there, deep inside of him, but he controlled them with the passion of the manipulative, self-effacing bastard that he was.

But as he re-entered the club, he remembered that he had forgotten to take the money out of Claudia's purse. So he returned to the dumpster, rolled Claudia over, and grabbed her blood-soaked purse that she still clutched in hands of broken fingers. Reaching down he felt a hand upon his shoulder. It was a heavy hand, and the pain became increasingly painful as the wrench-like grip tightened.

CHAPTER 6

He was pushed unceremoniously onto the floor of the limousine. The main protagonist stood above him, his face shrouded in a black hood. The figure did not speak, but his presence was oppressing and painful, as the batterer of women began to feel an aching of immeasurable proportions in his joints.

"Prepare yourself for your final accounting," the figure said, as the rapist attempted to stand.

"Not so fast. It is just beginning. Hold your ground," said a voice from the front of the limousine.

A whoosh of air slowly drifted past him as two occupants at the rear of the limousine stood and prepared to exit.

"I have no place here. I have tried time and time again to dwell within you. But you rejected me. You simply do not believe in my merits. It is all upon you now, and you must deal with the consequences," Guilt said.

"Behold your fate," said Remorse. "It lies within your unforgiving and petrifying body."

"Come, my friend. Our domain lies elsewhere," said Guilt, as Remorse slowly followed Guilt toward the back of the limousine.

Superficial Charm flashed a sardonic smile revealing snow-white teeth, as Remorse and Guilt exited the limousine and vaporized into the still and cool night.

Glibness and Callousness arose and helped the unconvicted felon to his feet. They sat him down between them and both began whispering to him, one in each ear.

"You are among friends, now. Be who you are. To hell with everyone else," said Callousness.

"They are simply peasants. You are the true king of your own empire. Let's get on with it. Stay with us and our other friends," said Glibness.

Before he could speak, there was a tussle at the front of the limousine. Places were being exchanged, and apparently realignment in seating was taking place. The seat where Mitigating Circumstances had been sitting was now empty, and was being eyed by Aggravating Factors. But before an exchange could take place, the limousine's engine revved up and the abrupt movement caused the rapist to fall flat on his back. The limousine was now moving at a slow but steady pace as Mitigating Circumstances hand-in-hand with High Self-Esteem leapt from the open backdoor and vaporized into oblivion. As the pace of the limousine's exit steadied, several voices were heard speaking in unison. It seemed as if a seat in the front of the limousine was being made ready for him.

CHAPTER 7

He looked down at his feet. The pain was agonizing as he attempted to untie his shoelaces. It was of no use. His feet were solid rock. His ankles were throbbing and turning to stone as a voice from the front of the limousine assailed him.

"Your place is up here," Hatred said. "You have earned it. Now come, and seat yourself between myself and my co-conspirator, Evil."

The front of the limousine was as dark as the abyss into which he was surely destined to occupy. He dragged himself along the floor, as his ankles solidified into petrified stone. Superficial Charm continued with his sardonic grinning, but remained seated in the back, apparently knowing his place in this vehicle of the gradation of horrors. Glibness and Callousness, likewise, remained in their respective places, simply urging the rapist to get on with it.

The rapist's eyes darted back and forth, seeking help from the accomplices who remained motionless, but none was forthcoming. As he inched slowly to the front of the limousine he eyed two new figures that mysteriously emerged from the vapid darkness. As his thighs began turning to rock, he beseeched them for help, but deep laughter from the front disrupted his train of thought.

"They will be of no help to you. They are of no help to anyone. You created them in others. You made them, and now you want *them* to help you. Crawl, coward, your place is waiting right here," said Cowardice, standing and patting the empty seat between Evil and Hatred.

He looked to the two sunken figures that had not spoken. They were now sitting apart and hugging themselves, apparently sulking, their faces covered with decaying cloth.

"Did you fail to hear my command? They will be of no help to you. Gloom and Rejection are simply along for the ride. The true game is up here. Now crawl and take your proper place," ordered Cowardice.

He was now made of stone from the waist down. He was propped up on his elbows when he finally caught a glimpse of the laughing figures seated in front of him. The three figures each had his very own face. He was simply looking at himself as he was lifted from the floor of the limousine and placed in the lone empty seat at the front of the black coffin of death.

CHAPTER 8

"What happened to the others?" the rapist gasped.

"What others?" responded the hooded figure that had initially thrown the rapist into the limousine.

"There were others, several of them. They sat here, next to me. They had my face. Where are they?"

"There are no others. You were simply looking at yourself and all that you were?"

"Were?"

"You are dead. You are turning to stone," said the hooded figure.

The rapist was completely turned to stone from the neck down. His limbs were simply pillars of rock. All that remained of his former self was his head, and that was throbbing as he felt his very veins being turned into stone.

"Where are you taking me?"

"I am taking you nowhere. You have taken yourself. I am a simple conduit to an inauspicious end. Enjoy the ride. It will be over shortly and you will be deposited with the other social miscreants who have occupied that very seat from time to time. I am a simple conveyor of filth and human degradation, of which you are a welcome and deserving guest. With that the shrouded figure turned away from the rapist and hastened to exit the coffin of death. As the rapist's cheeks turned gravelly and hardened, his tongue felt rough and stiff, yet he managed to scream.

"Who are you? Where I am I going?"

The shrouded figure turned toward the rapist.

"You are going where all the other heretics and nonbelievers dwell. You will meet my wife shortly and share her suffering, as she will share yours. As to who I am, I am Lot," said the shrouded figure, as the rapist became a pillar of hardened rock.

CHAPTER 9

"What do you make of it, Sarge?" asked Detective Starling.

"Sexual assault followed by a savage beating. Her face isn't much of a face anymore. It will take some time to I.D. her," said Sergeant Granley.

"What about the guy? No doubt the perpetrator, but there's not a scratch on him."

"Checked his underwear. It's got semen all over it. I'd bet my pension it matches what's inside of Victim Number 1."

"Yeah, but what did *he* die of?"

"Found some significant amounts of *meth* in his pockets. Judging from his bloodshot and dilated eyeballs, he's probably been smoking the shit all night. I'd say he overdosed on it right after he finished attacking the girl. You know, his adrenaline was pumping, testosterone up, and then all that meth . . . bingo, one dead disgusting piece of shit. It's just all my opinion. The medical examiner will have to work it all out. Now let's get the evidence tagged and bagged. The death investigator will be here shortly to take the body."

"Anybody see anything?"

"Yeah, just a black limo pulling away, that's about it. We'll have to check it out."

"Lots of black limos in the city, Sarge."

"Not with license plates H-E-L-L."

THE GIRL
ON THE RAFT

By James L. Whitmer

CHAPTER 1

It appeared as dot on the horizon. A dot the size of pea, yet my eyes focused on it as if it were my salvation, my way off of this desolate beach upon which I lay. I squinted, the sun deeply penetrating the crevices where once my eyes had dwelled in painless bliss. But now the pain was a never-ending stinging from undulating heat that floated like ocean waves above my face. But the real waves were out there, out there lapping up against that single, solitary dot, which seemed to be growing larger, as it became the object of my existence. And so I wiped away the biting, yet beautiful, white sand from my face, the very same sand upon which I lay, and upon which I had existed for what seemed like eternities. That crystalline sand of sparkling purity that had assaulted my eyes, and that had embedded itself in every pore of my tortured and sunburned body, and that had encrusted the portals to my very soul and the portals to that dot, that single, solitary dot with its hypnotic powers, and so I strained to make out whatever it was.

It was slowly moving inward, inward toward the foam covered beach upon which I had dragged myself, my legs swollen and sore-laden with blotches the color of dried prunes. Their weight was immeasurable. They were oaken dead limbs devoid of feeling; tree trunk appendages simply awaiting amputation, yet I pulled at them with desperate hands, as if to do so would ensure their survival. But that dot, that dot was my religion, my belief in hope, in rescue, and as it became larger the surcease of depression appeared a possibility. Something I had not experienced for endless months on this godforsaken beach of death that masqueraded as a beach of beauty.

But was it really only a dot? Or was it something more? Did I have the courage to believe in . . . or was I desperately imagining . . . or was it . . . a raft! Yes, a raft of sorts. No, it was a large wooden door, with a tarnished and seaweed encrusted brass handle that gleamed in the teasing sunlight. But that floating door, with its jagged wood-worn edges, spoke to me . . . told me that it had been ripped from its hinges by some violent force and had been thrown into the sea like a mere wooden splinter. But clinging to that brass handle and sprawled haphazardly across the door's circumference was an arm that disappeared into the blue-gray ocean that lapped against its sides. And then the arm was moving, and a torso was being pulled upward and onto the floating wooden door, and then she was visible. And then what was once only a dot on a rolling landscape of mysterious, watery depths was the form of a young girl, no more than seventeen, with the face of a saint and the emerald eyes of a sacred deity.

CHAPTER 2

She was kneeling on that floating door in a sea that was as placid as a frozen lake. She was lifting her arm and beckoning me forward. My legs were menacing enemies as they left deep ruts in the sand, a mosaic of futility neatly ensconced in white beauty. Somehow I made it to the water's edge, the frothy white foam from that sea of despair depositing itself along my beleaguered torso, lapping up against me, urging me on. On to her, and her raft and . . . but no . . . the raft was moving away, floating out again. Out to that desperate and wanton sea where the Gods of Neptune played with men's souls. Out . . . 50 yards now. Half a football field, but I could certainly make 50 yards . . . swim . . . no dog-paddle 50 yards, my legs being useless stumps that could neither kick, nor help keep me afloat. I was in the water now, the salt brine licking my lips as if I had invited it to do so. It was unwelcome, but it remained there as if painted on a canvas of deceit. But that raft   that door it was no longer a door or a raft. It was simply a dot, a single, solitary dot on the far-flung horizon that was no more than a line on a page. And soon the setting sun would engulf it like a seabird diving for its morning catch. I held my breath as the whitish-gray foam and salt brine attempted entry into a mouth swollen with festering blisters. I coughed out phlegm the color of lima beans and rolled onto my side, and then struggled backward to the beach that had been my home for endless eons. And looking up I saw nothing. Only a line painted with the tints of twilight and brushed with the deepening hues of a charcoal night remained. That dot which had been my salvation, that single, solitary dot, had simply disappeared.

CHAPTER 3

How I had reached the trunk of the palm tree under which I lay was an empty void in my mind. I awoke to the cawing of several large birds that were chewing on something dead that had washed ashore. In my hand was a frond from the palm that was shielding me from the relentless sun. I cupped it gently in swollen hands, remembering that its moisture had assuaged the merciless thirst that had rent itself upon me. I licked it fiercely, seeking its moisture, but none was there. It was dry now, and shriveled, and crumbled in my hands into an ugly gray dust, as I clutched it with the desperation of a dying inmate. And I was an inmate, an inmate unmercifully assigned to this beach of dread, to this stagnant realm of lost hope and despair that was now my prison. And as my thirst returned with a vengeance, I looked upward through the spaces of the palm fronds above me into the sunlight with the luminosity of a thousand candles; searching, searching for a meaning as to why I was imprisoned on this beach of ivory beauty, with rolling sea waves the color of watercolor masterpieces, and the sunlight of golden thrones. But no meaning was forthcoming, and no answer to the riddle of my existence played itself out like a simple game of cards.

My legs were pinions that would not flutter, parts to a human mechanism that were frozen in time. They existed in their own stagnation, forcing me to drag them with the fury of a tortured sinner, as I slowly moved over the hot-white sand to get a better view of the horizon. Ah, the horizon where a few hours before I had seen her. But had I seen her? Or was it simply my imagination playing a hideous game with my mind, urging me on to nothingness and a deep-seated depression that only those in limbo had experienced? But . . . as I focused on that line that was the horizon of my dreams, that perfectly straight and endless line with neither a beginning nor an end, it appeared again. That simple dot, that single, solitary dot floating on a seascape of the deepest purple and washed by pastels of golden hues born of chrysanthemums. And my heart lifted, as if a weight of immeasurable proportions had been flung aside, and the anvil of lost hope was replaced with thoughts of that dot, and of her, and of the essence of her beauty.

CHAPTER 4

The biting sting of the centipede on my arm caused me to lurch to one side, my lifeless legs of no help in rolling away from the squirming mess of endless tentacles, with their acid-like expulsions etching deep red welts into my sunburned arm. Its ugly brown color was all around me, each body segment composed of a set of writhing, slimy legs. It felt as if a hundred hypodermic needles were being plunged into my skin, as the acidic goo from the thousand-legger sought out every pore and crevice on the flesh of my arm, creating a highway of intersecting lines where my flesh had burned away, exposing white bone. I swiped at it, spit at it, wrenched my body into contorted shapes, but the monster did not budge, and the pain overwhelmed me, and all became black, as thoughts of that single, solitary dot fought to keep me conscious.

CHAPTER 5

A voice in the distance awoke me. Or was it a voice, or just the relentless, burning sun playing games with my mind again? I rolled over onto my side, my face encrusted with granules of crystalline, white sand, the beauty of which on any other day would be overwhelming; but on this day, in this unforgiving abyss of depression and lost hope, they were enemies to be vanquished, wiped away like so many pesky gnats. But that voice . . . there it was again, and so opening pinched eyes from the never-ending assault from the sand, I squinted, attempting to focus on the sounds, and . . . it was her! She was back, on that floating door, and kneeling and waving to me, as if I should swim to her and escape this hellhole of misery. I could not make out her words. It was more of a song, a song that mermaids would sing at twilight when soft breezes blew across gently undulating waves on sapphire seas. The melody was hypnotic, and she was close, close enough for me to make out an angelic face, and eyes of the deepest forest green.

I struggled to right myself, and then remembered that my legs were useless, tethered to invisible leg-irons and wrought with the weight of a sunken ship. I crawled in a zig-zag pattern, attempting to avoid the army of centipedes that swarmed around me, appearing to guard the beach, and preventing me from reaching her.

The tentacled sentinels were massing for an assault, defending their beachhead, and depriving me of her beauty. She, who was the personification of spring and new beginnings, of the depths of relief from the endless pain and suffering in which I dwelled, stared at me from a distance. She was Persephone, the goddess of light and beauty, and I was her betrothed. And yet I was denied her presence by these villains of savagery that were now approaching my struggling body in search of a noontime meal. The centipedes somehow sensed that my legs were useless, and that is where they attacked first. Paralysis was my savior, as the rotted flesh of my legs felt no pain, as the intruders feasted on decaying bone and fetid tissue. And so I mimicked their movements, as they continued their orgy of destruction, and slithered forward to the lapping waves of whitish-green that smelled of sea-salt and the alleviation of misery. But as I looked up, the sea had become turbulent, as if Neptune himself had risen from its watery depths and had blown his caustic breath across it, causing waves to appear where the glass-like surface had moments before held her presence on a tranquil vista envisioned by saints.

In her hands were flowers of the utmost beauty, roses, I believe, colored in shades of the deepest red. But the violent seas were upon her, and upon me, as I retreated backwards away from the incessant waves that washed away the tentacled monsters from half-eaten legs; legs that were not legs anymore, but simply stumps of rotted flesh and swollen red meat, waiting for the next dinner bell to summon the savage beasts.

Through sweltering winds and waves that covered me with seaweed and driftwood, I managed to see her clinging to that floating door upon which she lay. Hands that once held roses now held splintered wood and slippery flotsam that had encrusted itself on her solitary home. And like Persephone, who had been gathering flowers when the earth opened up, and who had been sucked into the depths of the underworld by Pluto, the god of the dead, she was now being sucked into a whirlpool, a watery abyss swelling with ravaging winds and the wailing of desperate souls. And into that abyss she plummeted down into oblivion, as Neptune, in the guise of Pluto, carried her away from me to be his queen in hell.

CHAPTER 6

The sea was calm, as calm as I had ever seen it since I had been imprisoned on this landscape of hell. As I shook off the cobwebs of unconsciousness, I realized that I was floating on my back several yards off of the shore, which was littered with the carcasses of a thousand dead centipedes, their tattered appendages disengaged from their bodies and wriggling in the morning sun. The salt water was warm, and therapeutically massaged my ravaged stumps of legs like a nurse attending to me on her daily rounds.

I had survived! I was floating in the sea I had so desperately attempted to reach, but which I had failed to do so. And now the sea, my newborn friend, would take me to her. But would she return? Thoughts of her being swallowed up, and sucked into that vortex of death impinged upon my brain like a hot branding iron. The last glimpse of her beauty was singed in the deepest recesses of my mind, as the whirlpool to limbo reappeared in my memory, dismissing the possibility of seeing her again. But I *was* one step closer to finding her and leaving this place of dread. I *was*! And so I searched the horizon with desperate eyes from slits tethered to raw skin, slits that barely opened, and eyes that were encrusted with sea sand and the intensity of Judas and the patience of Job. And I searched the horizon for that dot, that single solitary dot, for her, and for my salvation.

CHAPTER 7

I didn't feel it at first. It started with a simple tugging, and no pain. But then as the flesh at the top of my rotted legs was being ripped apart, the pain shot through me like white-hot lightening. And then I saw them. I attempted to kick with the stumps of my legs that remained, but paralysis had taken its toll, and my rotted appendages remained motionless, simply food for the next attacker. I grabbed for something that was floating in the sea next to me. It was piece of a broken oar; its jagged edges were sharp, and a metal oar-lock to which it was attached had somehow embedded itself into the petrified wood. I seized my new weapon and swung with the fury of a madman. I imagined myself a whaler wielding a makeshift harpoon and being exhorted by Ahab to kill the beast that was attacking me.

The sea snake was an ugly green color, the color of slime on the underside of rotted wood. It was as long as me and wrapped its tail, coil-like, around me, and slithered its tongue along my loins. Black and decaying flesh, my flesh, was spewed from its mouth as I wielded the *ersatz* harpoon and landed it flush on its hideous head. The blow knocked it off of me and it was wriggling in the sea as the second blow reached its mark. It was now as motionless as the sea around me, and it floated belly-up in a whitish-gray mush that clung to its scaly body. Then I realized that my fingers were embedded with splinters from the broken oar that I clutched in my right hand, and that the metal row-lock was covered with the whitish-gray mush that had emanated from the serpent's head. I released my grip, the blood flowing back into dead white fingers, and the sensation of normalcy returned to a hand that once delicately had played the cello.

My relief was short-lived, as my dead adversary's companions were now upon me. They encircled me, their hideous pointed snouts protruding from the top of the water like sentinels to hell. But seeing their brother dead and floating in a pool of its own stagnant and discolored blood, they appeared to sense the futility of continuing the assault upon me. Like the Ouroboros related to Saturn, the god who symbolizes time, they turned their once ravenous heads away from me, and began biting their tails. The last I saw of them was when they submerged into the sea, and blood the color of rusted copper floated to the surface, pooling around the form of the first attacker.

But I continued to clutch my weapon in wary hands. And as I turned and breathed heavily, I found that during the foray with the serpent from hell, I had floated back to the beach, back to where I had started time and time ago. Time? Was there really such an entity? But time was surely the only true companion that I had in this desolate environment where neither human shape, nor human emotion existed, other than my own. And certainly in time, desolation was my everlasting fate. But time? How long before *she* would return, if return at all were in the offing? Was time really my enemy, as the serpents from the netherworld that had been summoned by Pluto surely were? Or was time my companion, to nurture and to coddle, until *she* returned? But she would return! It was all I had. It was all that dwelled within me. It was the essence of my very being.

And so I looked out across that placid seascape where instants before a battle for life-and-death had played itself out in my favor; and I searched for her, for that dot, for that single, solitary dot that I knew would return. But instead I saw the figure of Saturn rise above the waves that were now being forced ashore, as if a typhoon were gaining its momentum. And Saturn, who symbolizes time and devours all creations, including living beings, things, sentiments and thoughts, was now sucking deep into his mouth the serpents who had encircled me, and was biting off their heads and swallowing them whole. Saturn, who was holding an hourglass in one hand and a scythe in the other, continued to suck until the sea serpents that had bitten off their own tails were now deep down inside of his entrails. And then the waves subsided, the gray frothing of their swells simply pooling beside my distorted form, lying again on the beach of dread. But as Saturn descended to the depths below, the last thing visible was his scythe. And from that scythe the vestiges of hope evolved, and I remembered that the scythe *can* have a double meaning. Cutting and devouring were certainly present, as evidenced by the timely dispatch of the serpents from hell to their ignominious graves; but also present was the scythe's curved shape, which corresponds to femininity. Thoughts of femininity then implanted themselves in the cortex of my memory. And thoughts of her returned. And so I stretched my tired body to see over the receding waves, and looked out again at the forlorn horizon. And it was there! That dot, that single solitary dot! It was floating toward me and getting larger, as the sun reached its apex in a blue-gray sky above me. But looking out again, the form of Saturn was nowhere to be found.

CHAPTER 8

"How long?" asked Doctor Strayer.

"It started about an hour ago. But I'm not exactly sure," said the nurse.

She was Nurse Natalie Eliot, and had been on rounds since early in the morning. That was almost twelve hours ago, and fatigue was slowly taking its toll. But in this small town, in this small hospital where nurses were scarce, she was destined to remain on duty for another eight hours. And though she looked young for her age, many of the patients mistaking her for a mere high-school student doing volunteer work, she, nonetheless, was skilled in her craft and surely understood the meanings of a flat-lined EEG and an occasional blip on a heart monitor.

"Well it is important, Natalie. I mean, if it's really more than just a simple anomaly," said Doctor Strayer, checking the heart monitor again for the third time in a matter of several minutes.

"But he's brain dead, at least that's the indication from the EEG, isn't it?" asked Natalie.

"Hmm, yes. He's been brain dead for the past hour. When was he admitted?" asked Doctor Strayer.

"Last night, shortly after I started. Both legs were half-severed in the accident, and well . . ." said Natalie, as she lifted the bed-sheets, exposing recently amputated limbs.

"Hmmm, yes," said Doctor Strayer. "And he flat-lined on the EEG about an hour ago," he continued, perusing the patient chart.

"He's not coming back is he?" asked Natalie, as Doctor Strayer reviewed the *Do-Not-Resuscitate* order clipped to the patient chart, and then retrieved a small light source from his coat pocket and shone it directly into my open but dilated eyes.

I wanted to scream at the top of my lungs. I wanted them to hear me. *I am alive! I am!* But I just couldn't see straight as the light was menacing my eyes, and the form of the nurse who called herself Natalie approached me and leaned forward, a small cup of water in her hand, saying something, almost singing to me, almost, almost . . . .

CHAPTER 9

She was kneeling in front of me. Her raft . . . her door was floating out to sea. Was she real, or was she simply the specter of a Nicean princess? She held in her hand a conch shell of cool water that soon I was slowly sipping from. I was lost in her presence, in her translucent eyes that were riveted on mine, as if to tell me that I was saved. That it was over.

As I drank, the conch shell cupped tightly in wind-worn hands, I closed my eyes and thought only of her and the relief of sorrow and pain. My savage thirst was my demise, because as I opened my eyes, she was gone. As I searched the shore frantically, I thought I had caught a glimpse of the slender torso of a mermaid, half-submerged in a gentle sea, only its sleek and feline fins waving above the blue-green waves. Her sweet singing remained in my mind, as I closed my eyes, knowing full-well that this was the end.

CHAPTER 10

Natalie surveilled the hospital room for the last time, as the unfortunate professor of medieval history and part-time cellist was wheeled out of the room, the *Do-Not-Resuscitate* order neatly clipped to the gurney. Dead tired from the ordeal that had started hours ago: the train accident, the delirious professor who kept screaming that he had seen a raft and a beautiful girl, and then mythic gods and sea serpents who devoured their own tails, and then the horrific double amputation, followed by brain death and an occasional anomalous blip on a heart monitor, Natalie slumped into an empty chair, delirious in her own right.

It was hours before she awoke, but when she did, she found that she was clutching a book, and it was opened to a passage written by her great-great grandfather, Thomas Stearns Eliot, from *Morning at the Window*: *"I have heard the mermaids singing, each to each; I do not think that they will sing to me."*

Deep down inside where only self can meet self, she envisioned herself kneeling on a floating wooden door, with a seaweed encrusted brass handle, in a placid green-blue sea, and softly singing to a dot, a single solitary dot, on a distant beach of the whitest and purest sand that she had ever seen.

THE LUCENT HARP

By James L. Whitmer

CHAPTER 1

When he had moved into the small apartment without a particularly poignant view of the city, he hadn't really noticed it. But as the days passed, the soft melody that emanated from the apartment above him became increasingly familiar, as he searched for his keys, unlocked his door, and made his way into what he now called home. It was usually just past midnight when he finished the night shift at the precinct, and a short walk and only a few minutes later when he was struggling up the flight of stairs to the second floor and Apartment #2A—Front, that he detected the sweetness of the musical cacophony that floated downward, assuaging his entire being in soft waves of contentment. The stench of the city and the dregs of human carnage floated away, and the seemingly senseless evil that permeated his every waking hour in the Detective Bureau passed into oblivion, as he concentrated on the musical notes that lingered above him in wafts of gentle air.

Sleep, a welcome friend, was nurturing and almost immediate, as the melody of the harp hypnotized him into self-bliss. He was a slave to its wanderings and he slept like a newborn infant cradled in its mother's arms after a mid-day feeding. And when he awoke, he was refreshed and absorbed in anticipation of what the new day would bring. As he exited his apartment to begin the day with his morning run, the hallways were empty and devoid of any sound. The harp was silent, but on this occasion the footfalls above him were heavy and inconsistent with such delicate musings born from the strings of such an exquisite instrument. As the floorboards creaked with an eerie foreboding, as if whomever was treading above

91

him was not the true purveyor of ecstasy that he imagined sat at the stool gently plucking the harp strings, he reasoned that he must endeavor to meet the lovely creature who played such tender notes. For surely such a creature must be angelic in nature, and surely infinitely beautiful. Who else could elicit such sensual affectations from such a lucent harp?

CHAPTER 2

It had been almost a week before he ascended the stairs to the 3rd floor and knocked on the door of the only apartment that occupied that level. It was morning and he had just finished his daily mile-and-a-half run. The sweat dripped erratically from his forehead onto his soaked tee shirt, as the dank hallway exacerbated the flow of salt-soaked liquid from open pores. He wiped away the nuisance with a taut and sinewy forearm that had accosted many an offender, and waited for a response. Light footsteps, distant at first, and then fading into soft nothingness, permeated the silence that soon was broken by a voice that only seraphim could birth.

"Who is there?"

"I'm James. I live below you, on the second floor. Could I . . ."

"James?"

"Yes, James. I'm your neighbor. I . . ."

"The police detective?"

"Why, yes. I . . . how did you know? I mean, I . . ."

Soft footsteps deftly approached him and the door was gently unlatched but remained chained. Spain could not see much, as the interior of her apartment remained dark, even though the sun was shinning brightly outside and illuminating Spain's face through the lone hallway window.

"I'm Sarah," the voice said.

"I'm glad to finally meet you, Sarah. I have heard you playing almost every night and I just wanted to . . ."

"Did you enjoy it? The harp is such a finicky instrument, don't you think?"

Spain was used to talking through half-open doors and vented windows. That was simply part of police work. But this wasn't police work, and she somehow knew that he was a detective, so why the bolt-and-chain act?

"Because I really don't know you," she said.

"What?"

"Before I let you in, I need to know more about you. Don't you think that's fair?"

"Well, I . . . yes, surely I understand. But how did you . . ."

"Know your thoughts?"

"Well, yes. It seems . . ."

"Detective Spain, there are many things I know about you, and many things I don't. Be patient and enjoy the music. After all, I am playing for *you*."

With that the door slowly closed, and the padding of soft slippers disappeared into the silence that surrounded the confused detective.

CHAPTER 3

It was a distinctly different style of homicide this time. And Spain simply could not get it out of his mind as the day wore on. Reaching down deep into the crevices of his mind to resurrect the black humor of the police subculture was of little help, and so he struggled to concentrate on other things, and not on the decapitated and swollen body of the victim of extended torture that had lain in the bathtub soaking in a pool of days' old bodily fluids only hours before.

"Pretty nasty, huh, Sarge?" asked Detective Williams.

She was Natalie Williams, Spain's partner in Homicide for the past two years. Natalie was lean and mean, and carried herself with the aplomb of a student of English literature and the fierceness of an alligator wrestler. She was unmarried, never married, and never-to-be-married. Her girlfriend's name was Susan, a clinical psychologist in private practice from the Gold Coast area of the city. And like Susan, she simply hated men, except for Spain. Somehow Spain was different in Natalie's eyes, and so the partnership of the misandrist and the womanizer blossomed slowly at first, but gathered momentum as their mutual foray into the evilness of the city melded them into a common thought process.

"Nasty about sums it up. The only thing missing is evidence of a sexual assault and a broad axe as the murder weapon," said Spain, holding the bloody knife in his evidence-gloved hands.

Williams' lips upturned slightly, revealing her acknowledgement of Spain's attempt to play the police subculture card.

"Got to get this over to the lab," said Spain, placing the murder weapon back into its brown paper evidence bag receptacle that was simply marked, *bloody scuba knife.*

"Then what? How about a drink with Susan and me? Looks like you need one."

"Thanks but no thanks. Susan hates me, you know that. And I certainly don't want to be psychoanalyzed again by her at this juncture. And besides, it's been a long day. It's well after midnight and you know I'm a creature of habits."

"I know you're a creature and I know *some* of your habits."

"Running every morning, you know that. It keeps me sane."

"You've never been sane and never will be. Call me if you change your mind," she said, gathering up her things from on top of Spain's desk.

Spain wasn't listening and as Natalie sauntered out of the squad area, apparently fantasizing about doing the horizontal mambo with Susan, Spain was dwelling on the soon-to-be soothing notes of the harpist above him. And this time he would make entrance, one way or another, into her apartment and hopefully into her life. The need was etching at his heart, causing it to pump in anticipation, for surely she must be an exquisite creature of the night.

CHAPTER 4

Unlike every other early morning when Spain ascended the stairs to his apartment, there simply was no music to be heard. Spain strained, remained still, and waited. Seconds passed into minutes, and minutes lingered, being sucked into an inescapable vacuum that when Spain finally glanced at his watch, he realized he'd been standing in the same spot for almost an hour. And yet, still, only silence surrounded him. But then he heard it, slowly at first, but then more rhythmic, more refined, until it blossomed into a menagerie of soothing, yet vibrant, chords of contentment. He hesitated at first, lingering to fully absorb the sheer magnitude of the absence of misery and human malevolence that had thus far filled his day. Then inexplicably he found himself at her door, knocking frantically, as if his very life depended upon the music flowing from her harp. The fierceness of the knocking caused his hands to bleed, and the sweat to pool on his face, as if someone had poured hot liquid onto it from a boiling cauldron.

He was breathing heavily as the door slowly opened, the chain remaining in its usual spot. Through the slight opening her voice effused into the now silent hallway like melting snow from the tips of Spruce trees in a sunlit afternoon; but except for Spain's heavy breathing, and the heaving of his chest, silence ruled their worlds. And then she spoke.

"I knew you would come. But you are late and I had fallen asleep. I feared for your safety," the angelic voice said.

"I was afraid that . . . I didn't hear you playing and I . . ."

Spain's panting was cut short by her soothing voice, a voice from the heavens, and rivaled only by the music from her celestial harp. The door closed slightly and Spain heard the clinking of the metal chain being released from its mooring and then the door opened, and she stood before him.

CHAPTER 5

It was a small room in which they stood facing each other. Spain's panting, which had momentarily subsided, began in earnest again, as the light from the hallway slowly crept into the pitch-black room and illuminated her face. She wore a mask of gold that covered her eyes and forehead, leaving only her cheeks and mouth fully exposed. Her hair, the exact color of the mask, cascaded onto bare shoulders that resembled the color of ivory, and which appeared to have never experienced the light of day. Her lips were pursed and violet, and her high cheekbones indicated to Spain that she was of American Indian descent. But her eyes were hidden beneath the mask of gold, which revealed no openings from which she could gaze upon him. Yet she grasped his sleeve in her delicate hand and deftly guided him to the cushioned stool that was intricately placed in the center of the room.

"I didn't know. I'm sorry. I . . ."

"That I am blind?"

"Well, yes. I guess that explains the darkened room and your . . ."

"Musical talent?"

"Yes, I guess that's what I was trying to say."

"I live in darkness, as being blind there is no need for light. My other senses, my acute awareness to sound and to touch, have compensated for my lack of sight. As such, I have developed my musical abilities. And I have chosen the harp as my instrumentality of choice."

"You mean instrument, don't you?"

"Instrumentality, my dear Detective Spain. Now behind you on the far wall is a light switch. Turn it on for your own convenience. You will learn better if there is light."

"Learn?"

"You are here to learn how to play the harp, aren't you?"

"Well, I . . ."

"The switch is behind you. If you are to play, you will need to see the strings."

Spain stumbled to the wall, and desperate hands searched the chipped surface for the switch. Finding it, he flipped it upward, and the room was illuminated in a soft yellowish glow that mimicked her hair and the golden mask that concealed her countenance.

"Are you more comfortable now?" she asked.

Spain was breathing shallowly as he focused on her. She sat upright on the cushioned stool like a sentry at parade rest, waiting for the signal to call her to attention. She wore a black robe, the color of the deepest, darkest night, which covered her from above her chin to the tops of her velvet slippers, which matched the color of her lips. Her alabaster hands were the only other parts of her body that were exposed. At the ends of her long and slender fingers were nails of average length and polished with a velvet hue; and with them she appeared to sensually caress the strings of an invisible harp.

"You, no doubt, have many questions. Do not feel ill at ease. It is normal," she said.

She patted the cushion next to her, and nodded for Spain to sit.

Spain's mind was racing, as the Circadian rhythm of his body had been turned upside down. His thoughts were like the grains of sand in an hourglass, slowly slipping away from him. Why he had come to this place, he couldn't remember. He only vaguely recalled the innate need to do so.

"To learn," she said.

"What? I'm not sure I . . ."

"You have come to learn, my dear Detective Spain."

"To learn to play the harp?"

"The harp is only a means to an end, a mere instrumentality. You have come to learn something much more important."

"And what is that?"

Sarah removed her long fingers from the apparent strings of the harp, and placed them surgically underneath the lower part of her golden mask. Carefully removing her mask, she exposed the true meaning of what Detective Spain had been searching for.

"You are here, in this place, at this time, to learn whether man is essentially good or evil."

CHAPTER 6

Susan casually sipped her Long Island Iced Tea. She was a smallish woman in her mid-forties who enjoyed the more than occasional cocktail at the end of the day. She was a night person anyway, usually seeing her clients later in the evening hours. So Natalie's shift in the Homicide Division neatly melded into Susan's hectic schedule of counseling the insecure and troubled castoffs of society that she called her clientele.

"Long day?" Susan asked, as Natalie slowly stirred her double bourbon on the rocks, not that it needed stirring.

"How can you tell?" asked Natalie.

"You have that victim-offender look impressed on your face. So which is it, victim or offender?"

"Well, we wrapped up the shift with a particularly disturbing days' old homicide. Lots of bodily fluids all over the crime scene; you know, just another senseless foray into the world of Neanderthals."

"Speaking of Neanderthals, how's Spain doing these days? He hasn't been tagging along with you much after hours lately?"

"He sends his regards. Exactly what those regards are, I'll leave to your imagination."

They both laughed and then assaulted their respective beverages with a vengeance wrought from being overworked and undersexed.

"But anyway, now that you've asked, he's been acting a bit peculiar lately. I think he's interested in someone, but he hasn't exactly confided in me as to whom she is. But I'm sure she has nothing at all to do with police work."

"It's about time he settled down anyway. He's going on forty-five, isn't he?"

"Sounds right. Yeah, maybe this is it. Maybe it'll work out this time. But his sullenness lately is odd. We were on surveillance the other night and he nodded off and began mumbling about a harp and harp music. When he woke up, I asked him about it but he was tight-lipped, so I didn't press him."

"Harp music? He's in love with a harpist?" asked Susan.

"Odd, isn't it. Where in the hell would he meet a harpist?"

"Now, that's an interesting question. Let's save that one for next time," Susan said, draining her Long Island.

"Here's to next time," said Natalie, clinking glasses with Susan and then ordering another drink for each of them.

Now what would a harpist look like, thought Natalie.

CHAPTER 7

She had the most beautiful face that Spain had ever looked upon. Her immaculate smile was countenanced in purity and contoured in humbleness. The essence of perfection dwelled within her; and Spain was transfixed by her very presence, ensconced by her beatified aura. Her eyes, however, remained closed as she spoke. And then Spain realized it. There was no harp. They simply sat next to each other on a cushioned stool in front of *nothingness*.

"The music . . . where does it come from?" stuttered out Spain.

"The music is within us. It is within me and certainly, Detective, it is within you, as well. But to answer your question about my harp, you are sitting right in front of it. Just reach out and feel for it. It is there as clear as the nose is on your face."

Stone extended a hand into thin air, and then slowly he reached a little further. But nothing happened.

"You must believe, Detective. If you don't believe it's there, you will never find it."

Sarah reached forward and, with open hands, began plucking the strings of her invisible harp. The music was as before, soothing and uplifting, and it enlightened Spain's mind to the point where, he too, reached forward with the intent to grasp the invisible strings of the lucent harp. But what he found was not ecstasy in the embodiment of plucking pliant and cooperative harp strings, nor did he experience the pedagogy of the musical discipline characteristic of Sarah's genius. Spain found only tension and resistance, as he attempted to create beauty and elegance from sheer nothingness.

"It is of no use," said Spain, removing his hands from mid-air and placing them back upon his lap.

"It is of no use because you dwell in a world of confusion. Detective, you must take the next step if you are to realize the beauty of the lucent harp, and the inherent beauty of mankind. You must not dwell on what is evil. You must attack evil and forever reside in the pure manifestation of the vibrancy of life."

"But my job is filled with evil. It is what I am."

"It is if you so choose. Now, Detective, you must choose, or you will forever be condemned to the *Garden of Delights.*"

With that, Sarah gazed upon Spain's taut-lined face and opened her eyes. They were hollow shells devoid of substance and filled with barren promises. Spain looked deep into those desolate spheres, seeking relief from the stress and destruction of life's forces, but finding just the opposite.

"Look deeply, Detective, and you will see who you really are and from where you have come. But most importantly, you will see what you are destined to become. Look deeply and realize your fate."

The mutilated body of an infant, the victim of child abuse, that Spain had investigated three weeks prior emerged in full intensity. Its blood-covered torso twitched in the cavities of the hollow spheres as Sarah plucked from the harp. But it was not pleasant music that resulted, only dark mysterious chords that foreshadowed death and demise. The cavities of despair now held images of wife beatings and rapes, of suicides by hanging and suffocation, of gunshot wounds to the head and decapitations. The spheres grew larger and images of truncated victims from drunken traffic investigations, and burns and bruises of toddlers caused by drunken parents, emerged. Spain was pressing on both sides of his head to keep it from exploding. And then it was on him in full force, the death of his father by a self-inflicted shotgun blast to the face.

The Lucent Harp
James L. Whitmer

The sounds from the harp reached a crescendo, reeking havoc upon Spain's mind. Love was nowhere to be found. Evil ruled the day, and Spain sprung from his cushioned prison and ran toward the lone window, as the hideous sounds from the harp pursued him.

The crashing of glass was heard by several neighbors on the street below, as Spain's mangled body dripped blood onto the black wrought iron fence upon which he had impaled himself. The witnesses looked upward, as if questioning how something like this could have happened on such a lovely and quiet evening.

CHAPTER 8

Susan sipped her Long Island Iced Tea. The more than occasional cocktail at the end of the day was a constant reminder of the world in which she lived. She stirred her drink with a long straw, removed it slowly, and then deftly licked the dregs of lemon and rum from it, as she carefully eyed Natalie, waiting for her to speak.

"I should have seen it coming. I should have done something," whispered Natalie into her drink, not making eye contact with Susan.

"We're speaking as friends now," cautioned Susan.

"Friends? Sure, but that's what I should have been to Spain; his friend, and I should have . . ."

Natalie's thoughts were sucked into her drink, along with the tears that were slowly dripping down her cheeks.

"Suicides are curious beasts. Sometimes they just come out of nowhere," counseled Susan.

"But I thought he was okay. He had indicated that he had met someone. I finally had got it out him that she lived above him and played the harp. And . . . really that's about all I really knew."

"But no one really lived above him. The apartment was empty, wasn't it?"

"It hadn't been lived in for over a year and a half. When the investigators went in, it was caked in dust and barren; not a tick of furniture was present."

"No harp, either, right?"

"Completely empty, except for the broken glass from the window that Spain apparently jumped from."

"Apparently? What other possibility is there? There was no sign of a struggle, was there?"

"The front door was forced open. That's about it."

"Any suicide note or anything like that? Voice message? E-mail? Anything?" asked Susan.

Just the voice message he left me, that he had met someone who lived above him, that she was a harpist and that he was going to take a few days off. That was just yesterday. That's it."

"But no one did live above him and there is certainly no evidence of a harp or harpist, am I right?"

"You are right. So what do you make of it?" asked Natalie, motioning toward the waitress and ordering another round.

"Well, somehow or other he became obsessed with the image of a harp and a female harpist. That much seems clear. The harp is well known in symbolism and dreams to be a bridge between heaven and earth. A simple explanation is that Spain was tired of his time on earth, tired of the drudgery and filth of his job, and simply was seeking eternal salvation. That's simplifying it quite a bit, but that about sums it up from a psychological point of view."

"So he just jumped out of a third floor window and killed himself."

"Things like that do happen in life," said Susan.

"But why a harp of all things? That just seems quite odd."

There is tension in harp strings. There obviously was quite a bit of undetected tension in Spain's life. His striving for the attainment of supernatural life in the hereafter could be equated to the tension inherent in the strings of the harp that he had heard, and that he imagined he could play. Maybe he just finally realized, in his own mind, that he couldn't quite play those strings, and thus all else was futile folly. Maybe? But it's a big stretch."

"So the strings of the harp, if played to perfection, symbolize the essence of love, and the failure to play them properly leads to tension? So the tension is in the strings themselves and ultimately leads to dejection and, in Spain's case, suicide?"

"Better hang up your Homicide shield, and start working with me in my practice," said Susan.

They both forced out a laugh, and clinked glasses to Spain.

CHAPTER 9

"Have you ever heard of Bosch's *Garden of Delights*?" asked Sarah.

"No, I can't say that I have," said Detective Weston.

He was Detective Ben Weston and he worked in the Crimes Against Children Section with the State's Attorney's Office. He'd been on the job for over twenty years and had seen about enough of what had to be seen.

"Well, Detective, it is a triptych, a three-paneled painting, in which Bosch has depicted a human figure crucified on the strings of a harp."

"Is that what you are going to do to me, Sarah? Crucify me to your harp?"

"Well, Detective, harps and harpists over millennia have been linked to the fascination with death. Some scholars say that it is akin to Freud's *death-wish*."

"I have no *death-wish*. Ever since I first heard you playing above me, I wanted to meet you. Because I knew you would be beautiful, and you are. That certainly is not a *death wish*. Now where is your harp?"

"It is right in front of you, Detective. Just reach out and touch the strings."

Detective Weston looked at thin air, and then back at Sarah, and then back at the lucent harp.

THE
INTERROGATION
OF BILLY RIVERS

By James L. Whitmer

CHAPTER 1

Squad 6—Chicago FBI Office

The gray metallic box stared at him. It was 11:00 p.m. and the Squad area was deserted. Stone remained alone, slumped at his desk in his rumpled suit. His white evidence gloves were clumped in the corner of his top desk drawer near some fingerprint cards from earlier in the day. He needed them now. Somehow they were on his hands, imploring him to get on with it. Removing the plastic evidence bag, his thoughts were lost in a wilderness of mirrors, as he probed the lock with a small penknife. It held fast. Something bigger he thought. Removing his boot knife from his duffel bag, which lay on the floor, he jammed the knife under the lock. Hitting the butt end of the knife hard with the palm of his hand . . . once . . . twice . . . it gave. The lock fell to the floor like a tired vagrant in search of a resting place.

Lifting the metal cover, time slowed, as if someone had unplugged the clock on the wall. He glanced over his shoulder at the clock, the minute hand and second hand pointing downward in a *V*, like the face of a sad clown. Ticks became minutes and gravity weighed in, as Stone's hands reached for the contents of the gray coffin. Fearing the inevitable, he lifted a small, discolored, white envelope from within. His body felt awkward and out of place, as if he were an intruder. He set the envelope in front of him, the lone contents of the metal box, and prayed that he was wrong.

"Hey, Stone, it's after eleven. What the hell are you still doing here?" asked the night clerk making her rounds.

"Ah, just some loose ends," said Stone, looking down at the envelope.

The night clerk nodded an, *oh, well*, and continued on her way, disappearing at the far end of the hallway that connected the radio room to the Squad 6 area.

Just some loose ends. Stone took a deep breath, preparing himself for an entrance into hell. It was real time now as he flicked open the envelope with the tip of his boot knife, and spilled the contents onto his desk calendar. Photographs. Four . . . no five. He counted them, face down, nudging them gently with the tip of the knife.

"Make sure you turn off that computer before you go, huh, Stone?" said the night clerk, a small-faced, African American girl who walked with the precision of a cat and wanted to be an Agent. She was attending law school during the day and carried *Torts I* under her arm along with her security checklist.

"Yeah, sure. I'll be out of here shortly," said Stone, as the girl's heels clicked in a tick-tock fashion, fading in the distance.

Stone flipped over the first photograph, the one closest to him. Time stopped dead cold, and then reversed itself. He stared at the photograph, first realizing and then believing. Knowing now that Rivers was right. The other photographs were turned over in sequence . . . all confirming the first. Pieces to a puzzle that fit like a well-tailored suit, the tailor, the person Stone must find.

Picking up the phone, he dialed Padino's home number.

"Yeah," said Padino groggily, as if roused from sleep.

"Yeah, Dave. It's me."

"Hang on."

Padino righted himself. Phone noises. Said something in the background.

"Yeah. You got it then?"

"Just where he said it would be. We didn't need a warrant. We got consent. His mother signed the forms."

"You opened it yet?"

Stone was lost in his thoughts.

"You opened it yet, Stone?"

"It's her," Stone said, his eyes riveted on the photographs like spit on a referee's whistle.

Silence. Dead silence. The kind of silence that follows bad news and is accompanied by heavy breathing.

"Son-of-a-bitch."

Stone's listless eyes glanced at his watch, and then at his hands, the white evidence gloves clenched in his fists like smothered doves.

"You'll leave tomorrow then, right?"

"First flight I can get. Hell, I'm tired."

Stone's eyes watered. His stomach felt like etched glass, his voice scratchy, as it trailed off to a faint echo.

Padino was saying something but Stone didn't hear. He was being sucked into the vacuum of the photographs, becoming part of the crime scene. Like foam in a whirlpool being sucked down . . . down . . . down.

"Sorry, Dave. What were you saying?"

Stone realized that he had dropped the receiver, the photograph of the headless corpse imprisoned in his ivory hands.

"I said, I think it's better if I call the Judge in the morning."

"The morning . . . yeah, the morning would be better," said Stone, as he arranged the other photographs in sequence, one through five. *Five* remained in his hand.

"You'll call Kolb then?"

"Kolb? Right. Yeah, I almost forgot. Yeah, I'll call right now."

Stone paused, placing *five* back in position.

"Dave, I'll leave all this stuff in your safe. It's got to be sent to the lab first thing. There's gotta' be prints all over these . . . pictures. The box too."

Stone glanced down at the gray coffin, a swastika scratched irregularly in the left corner of the lid. A swastika, like the ones carved on Billy Rivers' palms. Nothing else.

"Have Gina photograph everything and make copies. I'll need them when I interview Rivers. FEDEX, okay?"

"Sure Stone. Sure. Go home and get some sleep. Okay?"

The line went dead as Padino's voice faded away like a train whistle in a tunnel. The ruined mess of Billy Rivers lay before him begging for closure.

Stone scratched his initials and the date on the cover of the box in the corner opposite the swastika. He then initialed, dated and numbered the photographs. Laying them back in sequence, face down in front of him like a poker hand, he dialed Kolb's number. *Five* was somehow in his hand again, taunting him to look.

"Yeah, Kolb."

Kolb's voice sounded strained, as if he had been interrupted from something enjoyable.

"John, it's Stone."

"Hey, man, Christ, it's almost midnight. This better be good."

Stone heard a woman sensually panting in the background for Kolb to come back to bed.

"Sorry I interrupted you."

On other occasions Stone would have said something funny and made Kolb laugh. A laugh that ended with a jibe aimed at Stone. But the timing was off now, the sense of urgency overwhelming, like a black crow battering itself against Stone's window of despair. Nothing funny came out. Nothing at all.

"Stone? Stone? You still there?"

"Yeah, John. Yeah."

Kolb pressed on, seeming anxious to return to his nocturnal activities.

"What is it? You got something or not?"

"Get your things together. We're leaving tomorrow morning."

"Yeah. Where to? The armpit of the Midwest, Indianapolis?" asked Kolb.

Kolb seemed to be sitting up, his voice clearer. The feminine panting in the background seemed to have stopped.

"El Reno," said Stone.

"El Reno? That's not the Midwest. That's in Texas, ain't it?"

"Oklahoma. Just be ready. Meet me at O'Hare, the United Terminal. Be there at 6:30 sharp. And bring a suit. Okay? Padino will call your commander in the morning."

"The Judge's daughter?"

"Yeah," said Stone, as he hung up the receiver and placed *five* back in place.

As he left the Squad area, he glanced at the sad clown's face. After midnight, but he saw only *five*.

Somehow he made it home. He pulled into his driveway, exhausted. The wrinkles in his crumpled suit rose up like contours on a map. *Five* was in his mind, indelibly, like black ink on a white blotter. His theory of small successes had somehow gone down the drain. There would be no small successes with Rivers, only winner and loser, and winner take all. *Five* confirmed that.

Stone's legs were heavy like dumbbells. His eyes were scratchy and felt like used cat litter. The nervous sweat under his arms had hardened hours ago, leaving salty, rust-colored stains on his shirt. His socks clung to his feet like masking tape. But *five* was still there. He slumped over the wheel, mental exhaustion making a coward of him.

As sleep overtook him, the image of the violator remained. The violator holding the severed head of Rita Suarez by her long, jet-black hair like a yo-yo. The middle finger of the offender's hand, blood-covered, thrust forward toward the camera in defiance. The expression on his face only conjecture, as *five* ended at the violator's neck.

Five. Five. Five.

Stone was unconscious at the wheel.

CHAPTER 2

O'Hare International Airport—Chicago, Illinois

It was hot. Already in the high 80's, it was only 6:30 in the morning.

"Hey, Stone, what'd ya' do, sleep in your clothes?" laughed Kolb, his s's catching on his teeth like feathers in chicken wire. Kolb had a slight lisp, but only when he laughed, which was often.

Stone had dozed off on the airport bench, but now Kolb was inches from his face, seated next to him. Kolb was a space violator.

"You look like shit," Kolb laughed.

Regaining his personal space, the arbitrary distance from one person to the next where comfort in discourse lies, Stone sat upright, stretched, and then shot back.

"Shit's your middle name," he said, as he grasped Kolb's hand with the grip of a blacksmith. "Good to see you."

Kolb's grip was just as crushing, one of the few things they had in common.

"How the hell are you, partner? You look strung out. Worked late last night?" asked Kolb.

Kolb's face had that curious look, somewhere between . bewildered and Missouri.

Removing the photocopies from the pocket of his crumpled suit, Stone handed them to Kolb. Kolb was not a big man, rather slender, but wiry. Sinewy, not muscular like Stone, and short, compared to Stone's 6'4. Kolb's mustache was the color of Georgia clay and did not match the color of his hair, which he combed over his receding hairline, giving him the look of a rooster.

Stone remembered meeting Kolb almost three years ago. His rooster appearance struck a chord in Stone causing him to laugh, *You're a Democrat, aren't you?* Kolb, caught off-guard, had responded, *Yeah, so what?* Stone chuckled to himself as he remembered Kolb's response because the rooster was the emblem of the Democratic Party from 1842-1872, and Kolb looked like a damn rooster.

That was three years ago when the disappearance of Rita Suarez, the daughter of Federal District Judge Antonio Suarez, had drawn them into the same investigation. Kolb, a Chicago Police Department homicide dick investigating a missing person, and Stone, an FBI Agent, ostensibly investigating a possible kidnapping, which eventually turned into a civil rights matter. They had been married to the *Suarez* case for three years now, and, at times, seemed married to each other.

"You *still* look like a damn rooster," said Stone.

Kolb, grim-faced, was studying the photocopies. His face was as gaunt as his wardrobe. He was wearing tired cowboy boots and faded blue jeans. A Hawaiian shirt, a mixture of mustard yellow and ocean blue, frayed and tattered, hung outside of his jeans. It barely covered his weapon, a 9 mm, semi-automatic Sig-Sauer pistol, coal black in color.

Stone stood and stretched, the salty crust in his armpits crackling like old dice being tossed on concrete. Stone shifted his weight and readjusted his *Jack-Ass* shoulder holster. Stone was a *wheel-gun* guy and favored a Smith & Wesson, Model 66, .357 Magnum revolver with night sites. The double speed loaders, which hung on his belt, weighed down his left side.

"Jesus Christ," said Kolb, handing the photocopies back to Stone, and adjusting his glasses. "Remind me to smash this sick fuck's head into the nearest wall when we find his sorry ass."

"You'll have to get in line," said Stone.

In certain respects they thought alike. And if Kolb had worked for the Bureau they certainly could have been partners. But as Stone scratched the stubble on his chin, he knew that he and Kolb were cut from a different pattern. Stone was single, never married, with an occasional girlfriend. Kolb was married, with an occasional wife, and many girlfriends. Stone's favorite movie was *Gettsyburg*. Kolb favored *Weekend at Bernie's*. Stone's idea of a relaxing evening was sitting in his favorite armchair, sipping red Georgian wine, and listening to Chopin's *Sonata in G Minor*. Kolb preferred poker with the boys and half-dressed, large breasted wenches serving drinks, with ass-kicking hillbilly music playing in the background.

Despite these differences, they enjoyed each other's company and fit well together when it came to police work. If anything, Kolb was a hard worker. Not the brightest crayon in the box, Kolb was somebody you'd go through a door with. Stone graduated from Yale. Kolb matriculated at the University of Viet Nam, 3 tours. Stone was the strategist and tactician, Kolb the gambler and *gumshoe*. That's how it was at the beginning. That's how it was now.

"Let's go, rooster-face. We've got a flight to catch. And I hope you brought a suit."

"Sure thing, asshole," Kolb said, lifting his carry on gym bag to Stone's eye level.

The departure board read United Airlines, Flight #445, to Oklahoma City, departure time 7:05 a.m.

As the jumbo jet leveled off, Stone plugged in the headset and dialed up Wagner's *Ride of the Valkyries*. Kolb tuned into re-runs of *The Mary Tyler Moore Show*.

A tall, slender stewardess in her mid-twenties was speaking over the intercom at the front of the plane. Her jet-black hair was the length of Rita's. *Five* was back in Stone's mind, a malignant reminder of the task ahead. Stone closed his eyes, willing the music to consume his thoughts. But *five* was still there. Ever-present. Haunting.

Five. Five. Five.

CHAPTER 3

Federal Correctional
Institution—El Reno, Oklahoma

Billy Rivers, Inmate # 24567, was in the room when they arrived. His orange prison jumpsuit was two sizes too big, and hung on him like a small tent. Rivers said nothing as the guard unshackled one cuff and then reshackled it to the metal pole, which extended from ceiling to floor where Rivers sat. Rivers' feet remained secured with heavy chains.

"He's all yours, boys," said the guard, a gruff-looking, overweight, Hispanic male, his face pockmarked like a bad road.

As the guard exited the windowless interview room, Rivers looked up at Stone, and then pointed at Kolb. Rivers' cuffed hand extended only so far. His bloodless eyes swam in a stagnant yellow mist. He spoke with a bark, like a hungry dog. His syllables were truncated, making the sound of a *whoosh*, like a meat cleaver hitting its mark.

"Who's the asshole? I said I wanted to talk to you. Just you. Not some other asshole . . . like him," Rivers said, nodding toward Kolb.

"Billy, you know we work in pairs. Remember Agent Rice?"

"Yeah, that fat asshole. Couldn't even see his shoelaces because of his belly."

"Well, he got transferred. This is my new partner. Detective Kolb."

"Okay, so *who* is he?"

Rivers paused, blinking, his slits for eyes secreted in a canyon of scar tissue on his dog face.

Kolb remained silent, standing in the far corner of the room, arms folded. Stone was seated directly across from Rivers, who fidgeted uncomfortably, as if he needed a *fix*.

"That's Detective John Kolb, Chicago Police Department, Homicide. He's been working the *Suarez* case with me from the start."

"You mean almost from the start. How come I never met his lazy ass?"

Stone was churning inside with contempt for this piece of shit. But Stone *knew* Rivers. Knew Rivers better than anyone. Knew his tics, his foibles, his games, and, most of all his bullshit, inside and out. Learned to read him over the years. Knew the buttons he pushed. The people he conned. First it was stolen trailer-loads, then armed hijackings, which led to his numerous arrests and convictions. Lompoc, Oxford, Terre Haute, the prison farm in Indiana, and now here, El Reno. All federal joints. Cases made by Stone against Rivers. Stone was biting an invisible bullet, and he sensed that Rivers knew it. Sensed that Rivers enjoyed it, from the hard-ass smirk that squirmed among the quagmire of scar tissue on Rivers' face.

"That's right. Agent Rice and I interviewed you initially and then you got sent away. Terre Haute, wasn't it? The farm?"

"Yeah, they had me pickin' fuckin' tomatoes."

Stone plodded ahead.

"The *Suarez* case. That's why we're here, Billy."

"Good looking bitch. Too bad. Would've loved to get some of that," Rivers said, licking his pencil lips. His eyes riveted on Kolb.

"Got any cigarettes?" Rivers asked Stone.

Rivers' stare was back on Kolb again. Trying to get a rise. The sick yellow mist had cleared. His eyes were now red pinpoints set in a sea of dull gray, waiting for a reaction from

Kolb. None came. Kolb remained nonplused, looking down at his boots.

Stone removed a pack *Camels* from his shirt pocket and slid them sharply across the table to Rivers. Props. Little successes. Get him at ease. Get him talking. About anything. Just get him talking. Stone leaned back, waiting for an opportunity.

"Am I gonna' eat 'em or you got a match?"

His bullshit grin stretched from ear to ear, ending at the tip of a scar that ran the length of his left ear lobe and terminated at mid-ear, resembling a cursive *C*.

Stone struck a match and lit the cigarette, which dangled from Rivers' mouth like a worm on a hook. Inhaling deeply, Rivers leaned back and scratched his nose with his free hand exposing his palm on which a blue swastika was tattooed. He laid his hand flat on the table, thumping his fingers in a staccato rhythm still staring at Kolb.

"Are those new ones?" Stone said, indicating the tattoos on Rivers' knuckles. Looking for common ground. A possible opening.

Rivers exhaled yellowish-gray smoke in Kolb's direction and looked down at his knuckles. A blue swastika was crudely etched above each knuckle. Five in all . . . Stone reflected bitterly.

"Yeah, did it myself. Last month. One for every joint I been in. Federal joints, that is," he laughed, now displaying both palms to Kolb.

"Matches these," Rivers continued, attempting to push Kolb's buttons.

The blue swastikas on Rivers' palms screamed out, harbingers of havoc yet to be unleashed on humanity.

"Wanted to get *Born to Raise Hell*, but that shithead Speck beat me too it," Rivers laughed, inhaling, holding it in.

Pointing to the swastikas on Rivers' hands, Kolb chimed in, grinning a cop's grin at Rivers.

"Get one of those right in the middle of your fucking head and you'll look like Charles *fucking* Manson . . . . shithead!"

Too early. Way too early for that. The ground gained by Stone had just been fumbled away by Kolb. Stone glanced at Kolb, who appeared to understand, as he inched back to his corner.

"Fuck off, four eyes. This interview's over," said Rivers, exhaling messy smoke that enshrouded his head, forming a funnel cloud.

Kolb gently removed his glasses, placing them in his coat pocket. Rivers had a way of getting to people. Especially cops.

"Billy, let's talk about those photographs," said Stone, father-like.

"Been here two months now. It sucks. Lompoc was better. Tennis courts there. Got to play fuckin' tennis everyday."

Stone nauseated inside at the thought of this pathetic sociopath hitting a little yellow ball for hours, while the headless torso of Rita Suarez rotted in a coffin fashioned by Rivers.

Rivers gulped some of the spent smoke and laughed, making Stone's stomach turn even more. Stone mentally regrouped. Focused.

"What *exactly* do you want, Billy?"

"Now we're getting' somewhere."

Rivers leaned back, stretching his shackled legs as best he could. He put his arms behind his head like a director of a corporation at a board meeting, restrained slightly by his cuffed wrist held tightly by the metal pole.

"One . . . I want out of the fuckin' *hole*. Two . . . I want general population. Sucks being locked down for twenty-three fuckin' hours a day. Three . . . I want a deal on the Lompoc thing. No death penalty. And that's just for starters."

Stone stared at Rivers whose tobacco-stained teeth failed to reflect light. A black hole protruding from his gaping, smiling mouth, sucked in dead air, while thin gray smoke encompassed his dog-like face. The lines on his cheeks intersected at odd angles with a plethora of scars on his chin, forming a mosaic of spider webs. Rivers was short, 5'6" maybe, and skinny, about 150. Burned out from dope and booze, Rivers was the definition of a man who had spent the majority of his adult life behind bars. Tattoos of all kinds adorned his body like cheap evening wear, most of which were concealed by his prison jumpsuit. Stone had seen them all at one time or another. Strip searches and the like. The head of a black panther on his left forearm; spider webs on his elbows; a skull and crossbones on the top of each shoulder; a coiled serpent spitting fire nestled in the small of his back. There were others, but too many for Stone to remember. Now he needed Rivers to talk. And Rivers was dictating terms.

"Billy, you're here because you killed a guard at Lompoc. That's also why you're in solitary."

"No shit," said Rivers, thumping his fingers on the table.

"Let me work on one thing at a time. Okay?"

"Yeah, you do that, Mister FBI man. Then we'll talk about that . . . *bitch*. I ain't sayin' nothin' 'til I'm outta' the fuckin' hole."

Rivers turned toward Kolb. His cold stare met Kolb square on.

"You got that Mister CPD man?"

"John, go get the guard. Tell him we're ready."

As Kolb exited the room, Stone sensed an opportunity.

"I have the box and the photographs. That shows you're cooperating."

"I been cooperatin', man. I just want a deal. I didn't have nothin' to do with that *bitch's* murder. I just had the pictures, man. Got 'em from the dude who *offed* her. Real sick dude, man. Real sick."

Rivers paused, inhaled, and held the smoke in, waiting for Stone to speak.

"Who is he? The man in the photographs?"

Stone's cold stare could have frozen hot cat piss.

"You wanna' know, Mister FBI man?"

Rivers exhaled, the smoke attacking Stone's face.

"Get me the fuck outta' the *hole* and we'll talk."

Kolb was back with the guard. As Rivers, shackled, shuffled toward the door, the guard removed the pack of Camels from Rivers' hand.

"Won't be needin' these in the *hole*," he said, as he stuffed them in his pants pocket with greedy fingers.

Halfway through the door Rivers peered back.

"Hey, Stone, how's my old lady? She give you any money for me?"

Stone only shook his head.

"Fuck that *bitch*," Rivers said, as he limped pathetically through the door.

The interview room was a vacuum of silence as Rivers made his way back to the *hole*. The clinking of leg irons against rust-stained linoleum hung in the air like shards of glass falling on ice.

CHAPTER 4

Office of the Special Agent in Charge (SAC)—Chicago FBI

Blair Crenshaw was the typical SAC. Lots of Bureau time. Little *street* time. New to the office, having been transferred, reluctantly, from Salt Lake City, this was his first full week. Padino wasn't looking forward to breaking in another SAC on the *Suarez* case, opening old wounds and rehashing frustrations. Crenshaw would make three. Wilson was first. On his way out at the time of the disappearance, he proved to be a non-factor. Owens was next. Tried too hard and too often. Got in trouble with the press. Too many sound bites and too few results. Managed to *fumble-fuck* his way into early retirement, leaving Padino with the reins. Now it was Crenshaw's turn.

Entering Crenshaw's outer office, Padino glanced at his watch. 4:30 p.m. Late in the day, but time could work in their favor with the judge.

"He just got in. He was inspecting the firearms range all day. SWAT exercises, you know," said Doris, Crenshaw's secretary.

A little mouse of a woman with an inordinately large rear end, Doris had seen them come and go. SAC's that is. Fifteen in all, in her thirty odd years in the Chicago office. She was known affectionately by the agents as *Dimples*, as in *ass of a thousand*. A nickname fondly bestowed upon her by Stone.

"Thanks, Doris," said Padino, knowing full well never to refer to her as *Dimples* to her face.

The last agent to do that wound up with ten days on the *beach* and a transfer to Clovis, New Mexico.

Padino pointed to the inner door with a quizzical look on his face, as if asking if it was safe to enter. *Dimples* nodded and returned to her desk. Her derriere, packed tightly into a pair of lime green stretch pants of the K-Mart variety, swished up and down as she walked, half-hypnotizing Padino. Padino knocked once on the door to the inner sanctum, pushed it gently, and stuck his head through.

"You ready, boss?" he asked.

Without looking up from a stack of communications lying in front of him on his oversized desk, Crenshaw nodded and motioned Padino to a chair opposite him. Padino limped through the door. An *Ace* elastic bandage that covered his recent knee surgery slithered down his leg like an adder in need of a mate. It trailed along under his pants cuffs as he moved.

Noticing the snake bandage, Crenshaw said, "How's the leg coming? I understand you had surgery recently."

"Yes, sir. Just the scope. Old football injury. Tore the meniscus right here. That's all," Padino said, pointing toward his left knee, as he eased himself down into the chair opposite Crenshaw.

Padino's pedestrian appearance was in stark contrast to Crenshaw's natty look. Padino's suit clung to him as if it was frightened it might be discarded. Dull brown seersucker. Generic. Too many washings or too few, Padino didn't know and, quite frankly, didn't care. Small lint balls, resembling miniature snowmen, were everywhere, especially near the pants cuffs. The cuffs hung over his shoes, the obligatory wingtips, black not brown. Brown would have been better but they were missing in action, one of his six boys the culprit. Probably Bobby, the youngest, using them as pontoon boats for his toy soldiers. Padino's socks did not match either. One was blue and ankle-length, the other black and ending at mid-calf, but unnoticeable in a dark room. His tie was plain, a tired red color of some sort, and knotted in such a manner that allowed several gray chest hairs to protrude from underneath, like thistles. His dull white shirt was unbuttoned at the collar.

"I know you wanted to meet earlier, Dave, but that SWAT exercise just took too damn long. You know what I mean?" said Crenshaw.

Padino didn't know. Didn't have much use for exercises. Was more concerned with *doing*, with real things. Like putting shitheads in jail.

"Yeah, boss, those things tend to drag on, especially with Bennett in charge."

Flipping aside several drug taskforce forms in front of him, Crenshaw righted himself in his chair.

"These damn forms are confusing. I hope your problem is less . . . confusing, that is."

Crenshaw leaned back in his chair, sequestering his thumbs under his suspenders, which resembled a jigsaw pattern.

"So Dave, what's the problem?"

"It's not really a problem, sir. More of a . . . situation," Padino said, as he reached for the photographs neatly tucked in his coat pocket.

Crenshaw leaned forward as Padino placed the photographs on Crenshaw's desk.

"It's the *Suarez* case, sir. New developments."

Picking up the photographs, copies made earlier in the day by the photo-lab technician, Crenshaw's face turned eggshell white.

"My God! Jesus! Oh, my God!"

Then silence as Crenshaw placed the photographs delicately on his desk, face down, as if they were infected. Staring blankly at the photographs for several moments, Crenshaw looked up, meeting Padino's gaze.

"You'd better start from the beginning, Dave."

"She's the daughter of Judge Antonio Suarez. His chambers are on the 26th floor of this building."

"Does he know . . . about this?" asked Crenshaw, who appeared visibly shaken.

Padino glanced at his watch. Almost time.

"No, sir."

"Well, you're going to have to tell him then, aren't you?"

"No, sir. *You* are. The Judge is expecting us."

"When?"

"Now."

CHAPTER 5

Chambers of Judge Antonio Suarez, Northern District of Illinois

He was standing by the window when they entered. Judge Antonio Suarez was a small man with petite, manicured hands. His black robe was draped delicately over the back of his chair like a funeral shroud. He stood before them, expressionless, as if knowing that news about his daughter was about to be dispensed like bad medicine.

Padino had been in the Judge's chambers many times. Mostly with Stone. The Judge liked Stone. Respected him. Knew Stone was working his ass off to find his daughter. Or at least her body. But Crenshaw, this was new territory. First impressions were important, especially to Crenshaw.

"Good to see you again, David," said the Judge, approaching them.

"Good afternoon, Judge. I'd like to introduce our new SAC to you, Blair Crenshaw."

Crenshaw appeared a bit nervous and stammered something as he shook the Judge's hand. Padino stepped in quickly.

"Judge, if we could . . . I'd . . . we'd like to inform you of some new developments in the case."

"Please, sit down," he said, circling his desk in a deliberate pattern. Preparing himself.

"AUSA Binder is unavailable. She's out of town. But I did talk to her by phone and I apprised her of the new developments. She'll be back tomorrow," said Padino.

"Go on, David," said the Judge, cradling his head in his hands.

"Just to keep things simple, SAC Crenshaw has only been *on board* one week and is not fully knowledgeable of the entire case."

"Understandable," whispered the Judge.

"So, if I rehash old issues, please, bear with me."

Padino noticed Crenshaw fidgeting with the evidence envelope he held in his hands and that contained the crime scene photographs.

"Judge, we received a communication . . . a letter, actually. Yesterday. From Billy Rivers, an inmate at the Federal Correctional Center located in El Reno, Oklahoma."

"Yes, Rivers. But didn't you rule him out early on?"

"Well, not exactly *ruled him out*. Kind of put him in the inconclusive pool of possible subjects."

Waiting for Crenshaw's response, which was not forthcoming, Padino continued.

"Sir, Rivers was identified by several witnesses as having made contact with Rita on the night of her disappearance. He was also recorded on a surveillance camera conversing with Rita at a liquor store near the University of Chicago where she was enrolled. Subsequent interviews with Rivers were negative, and no other contacts between Rivers and Rita have been identified."

"As I recall, our concerns with Mr. Rivers stemmed from the fact that, at the time, he had just been released from federal custody and was on probation. Being a convicted felon, we felt justified in pursuing him as a subject," said the Judge.

"Exactly," said Padino. "But . . ."

"What was he convicted of?" interrupted Crenshaw, his hands clutching the photographs in a mass of white knuckles.

"Property crimes mostly. Truck thefts. Interstate shipments. Stuff like that. His overall criminal history shows the usual. Assault and battery and the like, but no sexual assaults. No arrests for rape," said Padino.

"Yes, I remember now. So we wrote it off as a mere coincidence," said the Judge, pausing, standing upright.

His small, fragile frame appeared pencil-like as he approached the window and looked out.

"Should we have?" he asked.

Silence. The kind of silence that permeated the pilot house before the captain of the Titanic made the announcement that the ship was sinking.

Crenshaw looked at Padino, appearing to ask with his eyes if the time was right to reveal the contents of the envelope. The envelope he held vigilantly in his hands.

"Turning from the window, the Judge said, "She's dead, isn't she?"

"It appears that she is," said Crenshaw in a low monotonic response.

Crenshaw began to lift the envelope. Grabbing his hand securely, like a lead pipe in a vise, Padino interjected.

"Judge, we're still evaluating the letter from Rivers . . . and the evidence Rivers directed us to. The original evidence is on its way to our lab at Quantico. Fingerprints. Hairs and Fibers. DNA analysis. It's still too early to jump to conclusions."

"And the evidence you found conclusively proves death?"

"Yes. Photographs. But we still have a lot to do. Please, bear with us," said Crenshaw.

Padino sensed a helplessness surrounding the Judge.

"What can I do? Besides wait? Damn it all. It's been almost three years and I can't put it behind me."

His back was facing the agents now. His voice quavered. Padino sensed the Judge was crying. Expected it, but didn't know if it would help. If it was *his* daughter, he'd cry too. Men should be able to cry. Especially if your daughter was brutalized by some animal. Someone like Billy Rivers.

Turning to the agents, the Judge's eyes were beet red and swollen.

"Where's Agent Stone?" he asked.

"He went with Detective Kolb to El Reno this morning to interview Rivers," said Padino.

"Any news yet?" asked the Judge.

"Just that Rivers wants certain *things* and that he has more information," said Padino.

"What *things?*" asked the Judge, now taking the offensive. "What *things* does he want?"

Telling the Judge of Rivers' demands, Padino recommended that Rivers be brought to Chicago and that the Grand Jury be reconvened.

"I'll write the order now. You'll have it in twenty minutes. How long will it take to get him here?" asked the Judge.

"Depends on the circuit. Two to three weeks tops," said Padino.

"Agnes," called the Judge.

A female law clerk with bright brown eyes and an overabundance of enthusiasm quickly entered the Judge's chambers.

"Handle this immediately, please, and hand-deliver it to the FBI when it's ready," said the Judge, as he handed the hastily written court order to Agnes.

"Yes, Judge," she said, bowing and disappearing as quickly as she had entered.

"Gentlemen, I thank you for your sincere efforts. Your professionalism is beyond reproach. And, David, when Agent Stone returns, please, have him see me."

It was more of a plea than a request, thought Padino, as he rose from his chair, feeling that he had stemmed the tide of depression that was engulfing Judge Suarez. But only for a while. At some point the Judge would see the photograph of the headless corpse of his daughter. And the rest of the photographs . . . the worst. The severed head of his daughter in the hands of a psychopathic killer. Photograph number five. Stone's *five*. But now the judge would be able to sleep. Somewhat. After seeing *five* he would never sleep. *Never.*

CHAPTER 6

Metropolitan Correctional Center (MCC),
Chicago, Illinois

A thousand-legger skimmied across the table in front of them. Rivers' fist came down hard with a thud, embedding the insect in the crevices of the wood-worn table like a mosaic. Its legs still squirming, the insect formed a spiral pattern right out of *chaos theory.*

"I hate them fuckin' things. Had 'em all over me when I was in the *hole* in El Reno. Fuck that place. This is more like it," Rivers said, as he glanced around at his surroundings. "Except them fuckin' things is still around. My cell's full of 'em. Must be somethin' about joints they like."

Rivers continued his soliloquy, as he wiped his fist on his sleeve.

"Shit's sticky. Killed a big one last night."

Rivers liked to kill things. Stone knew that early on.

Rivers glanced over at Kolb who was standing in his obligatory corner in the interview room. Arms akimbo, glassessless, Kolb stared back, as if Rivers didn't exist.

"You done good, Stone. Got me outta' that piss-hole El Reno."

Stone slid the pack of *Camels* across to Rivers. Then the matches.

Breathing in deeply, enjoying one of the few pleasures while incarcerated, Rivers leaned his head back, and exhaled toward the ceiling. The faint red glow from the tip of the cigarette sputtered as Rivers spoke.

"*Camels* . . . good shit. *Chesterfields* was what my old man smoked. Used to buy 'em for him at the gas station near our house. Got the wrong kind once. *Old Golds,* filtered. Beat the shit outta' me for it. Said filters were for pussies. Never smoked filters myself after that," he said, rolling the unfiltered *Camel* between his urine-colored fingers. Placing his elbows on the table, the rolled up sleeve of his prison jumpsuit, this one blue, revealed a menagerie of scars, burns and tattoos.

"Another new one? The sun?" Stone offered, looking for an opening.

"You're good, *G-Man.* Yeah, got it at Sandstone. That's in Minnesota, shithead." Rivers was looking cross-eyed at Kolb, who returned a tired salute indicating that he knew that fact.

"Leavenworth, Terre Haute, Sandstone, Oxford and now here. Three fuckin' weeks on the circuit."

Rivers half-exhaled, then sucked up the blue haze with both nostrils like a vacuum cleaner. He held up his left forearm, which sported a tattoo of a red sun about the size of a quarter. It was on the inner portion of his arm and disappeared when he flexed his bicep muscle. Several small, reddish-brown scars circumvented the sun.

"Got it smack dab in the fuckin' middle," he said, pointing to the sun.

Rivers held up his arm so Kolb could see.

"I can thank my old man for all those little ones," he said, massaging the area around the sun tattoo.

Stone waited patiently, letting Rivers ramble on.

"Cigarette burns. I was only seven when he did it. Beat the shit outta' me all the time, too."

Rivers held up his other arm, revealing a blue lion's head colored with a red mane. It was located just above his wrist on his inner forearm. It half-covered an ugly, raised welt.

"Did that too. Scalded me with boilin' water, then locked me up in the basement. Hell of a decent guy," said Rivers, pointing to the welt.

Rivers inhaled and held it in while Kolb appeared to be digesting this new information. But to Stone it was *old hat*. Stone knew of the child abuse. Knew of Rivers' lengthy juvenile record. The animal killings. The arsons, small at first. Bigger later. The psychiatric reports. Sociopathic personality with mood swings. Possible catatonia. Symptoms of withdrawal. The bedwetting that persisted into adulthood. The numerous incarcerations as a minor, the last being for involuntary manslaughter of his father when Rivers was thirteen.

Squishing the butt of the cigarette onto the table where the bug was smashed, the butt stood erect in the middle of the now dormant appendages, forming an umbrella with spokes, but no cloth. Rivers admired his artwork, an eerie gleam in his yellow pits for eyes.

"Finally had to *do* the son-of-a-bitch. Used a mallet. Made pink oatmeal outta' his fuckin' head. Fuck him."

Stone waited for Rivers eyes to meet his. Looking up from the bug umbrella, Rivers spoke first as their eyes met.

"What about my fuckin' deal?"

"We've talked to Judge Suarez," said Stone, knowing full well that no deal had been struck.

"And?"

Stone needed to know where the body was. Needed Rivers to come full circle before any deal could be cut. Rivers must tell them where to find Rita and the identity of the violator in the photographs. And then what kind of deal was possible for a sadistic sociopath like Rivers? A murderer too, maybe, or an accessory after the fact. No, there would be no deal for Rivers. Not just yet anyway.

"Billy, there are a lot of loose ends we need to address before we start talking about a deal."

"Hey, man, I gave you the pictures. The bitch is dead and *he* did it, not me. Just find *him*, man. That's gotta' be worth somethin'," he said.

The cigarette dangled from his mouth, bobbing up and down with each barked word. It held fast, as if it was glued to his lower lip.

"Yes, it's worth something. It shows she's dead and we've got a murder to solve. That's it," said Stone, playing hardball on Rivers' court.

Rivers drummed his tattooed fingers on the table, the blue swastikas rhythmically floating in air. His face was severe, the deep-cut scars pulsing and beckoning like *Ahab* on the back of *Moby Dick*. Rivers waited. Out of aces. No more cards to play.

"The lab results came back on the photos. You want to tell me about them?" Stone asked, hands folded on the table in front of Rivers, as if they were in a confessional.

Priest and penitent, Stone thought. Now it was the penitent's turn to talk.

"Told ya' already, man. *He* was fucked up on angel dust or some other shit when I stole 'em. The pictures. Thought they'd come in handy if I got *pinched.*"

Inhaling. The blue haze was sucked into the crevice Rivers used for a mouth. He barked out a laugh.

"And they did, fuckin' *A*. Got me outta' the fuckin' hole."

Rivers' laugh was disgusting. Guttural. Feral. Spastic. Stone had heard it before, many times. It foreshadowed apprehension on Rivers' part. New information forthcoming. Not a full confession, but a weakness. A weakness that could be probed and coddled. Stone was winning. Rising, Stone brushed the invisible dirt off of his pants with both hands and looked at Kolb.

"Let's get out of here, John. We've got work to do."

Kolb was halfway to the door, about to call for the guard, when Rivers pounded his fist on the table.

"I ain't lyin'. You got what I got. That's it. Don't fuck with me. It's the guy, man. You owe me."

"Your prints are all over the photos and the metal box. No one else's," said Stone.

"So what, maybe he wore those faggot white gloves like you use. Big deal."

"And maybe he didn't," said Kolb.

"Maybe you took the photos . . . *Billy*. Huh?" Stone again.

The air was smoke-filled, heavy and stale. Silence lingered like an unwanted houseguest. The perfect atmosphere for the truth. An interrogator's *Nirvana*.

"Yeah, what if I did? I didn't kill her. It ain't no crime to take pictures, is it? It's not like I raped her or nothin'. I didn't do shit. Taking pictures, yeah, maybe, if I did. Last I heard it was a free world. First Amendment. Right, Stone?"

"Then why is your semen on some of the photos?" asked Stone, staring into Rivers' eyes, which were now narrow slits.

"What?"

"You heard right, shithead. *D-N-A*." Kolb from his corner.

"DNA analysis. Some of the photos contained semen stains. Yours. If you've forgotten, the Bureau of Prisons is quite accurate in keeping medical records for inmates," said Stone.

"Inmate . . . that's you, shithead." Kolb again, feeling frisky.

"Your records were quite voluminous. And they matched," said Stone.

Rivers, stoop-shouldered, leaned backward, extinguishing the remnant of the *Camel* in the palm of his hand. His face was expressionless. He said nothing. His eyes were tightly closed, as if he was mustering up courage or more lies. Which would it be? Roll the dice, Stone thought.

"John, get the guard," said Stone, forcing Rivers' hand.

"I didn't kill her," blurted out Rivers, eyes sealed.

"What'd ya' do with the photos, jack-off on 'em?" Kolb said, approaching, getting into the game.

"You dig that kinda' shit, don't ya, shithead?" Kolb again, even closer, *slicing the pie*, violating Rivers' personal space.

Nothing. Ear-ringing silence.

"I'm outta' here," said an exasperated Kolb.

Stone turned as Kolb opened the door and called for the guard.

"Wolf Lake."

The words were barely audible. Stone's eyes met the sociopath's.

"*He* did her at Wolf Lake," Rivers said.

Kolb closed the door.

"Back in the woods. Shit, man, *he* threw the bitch in a old well by some rundown shack. Fishin' shack or somethin'. I ain't never been there but that's what *he* told me, man. Now what about my fuckin' deal?"

Stone walked toward Kolb, opened the door and yelled for the guard.

"We'll talk about a deal after we find the body."

"And after you I.D. *his* ass," said Kolb.

"Told you already, man. Don't know the dude."

Rivers was smiling his sick smile, as if he had bested his interrogators. But Stone was keeping score. Rivers still led, but the good guys held all the face cards.

CHAPTER 7

Wolf Lake Area, Hegewisch, Southeast Side of Chicago

It didn't take long to find. Two local fishermen directed them. The old shack stood alone, like a monolith from *Stonehenge.* Heaving to one side, it appeared on the verge of toppling over. The State Police got there first and then the County with their dogs. The crime scene tape was up, its eerie yellow glow a reminder of man's inhumanity toward man. A lazy fog was making its way across the open field, which led to the shack when Stone spotted him. He was a large-faced officer restraining a yelping bloodhound.

"I'm Sergeant Hickman with the County. Lonnie Hickman. You must be the *G,*" he said, looking at Stone and Kolb.

Hickman was built like a fullback for the Green Bay Packers. His squarish frame was accentuated by wide shoulders you could place a level on and come up *plumb.* His arms were short, his hands thick. He smelled like a man who was good with dogs. The bloodhound that was dragging him was the color of concentrated bile. The hound anxiously strained at the leash. Frothing spittle oozed from both sides of its panting, elongated mouth.

"Sit, yeller," Hickman commanded.

Yeller sat abruptly at Hickman's feet, then shook his snout vigorously, making room for fresh spittle to flow.

"He's the *G.* I'm with the City," said Kolb, surveying the area.

Hickman pointed to the shack with a short stubby finger.

"We secured it just like you ordered, sir. Can't find anything that looks like a well, though. We looked all over. Out back. Over there. Nothin'. Been at it since sunrise. Old yeller here's plum pooped out. You sure it was a well? Damned if I'd put a well way out here."

"Thanks, Sergeant. Our evidence techs will be arriving shortly. If you could just secure the area until they arrive and . . ."

"No problem," Hickman interrupted. "Always love working with the *G*. Went to the National Academy in '95. Great Place. Hey do you know an Agent Wilkins?"

Stone wasn't listening. Hickman's voice trailed off as Stone pondered the present circumstances. Thinking. Reflecting on the *shitty* grin on Rivers' face; the narrow scar tissue forming slits where eyes should have been; eyes that were hidden, floating in a yellow cesspool of hatred. Did Rivers best him again? A wild goose-chase looking for some non-existent well in some godforsaken backwoods? Rita's body, Rivers knew its resting place. But where? There must be a well here. Rivers knows. Exactly. But he's playing games again. Just to make it difficult or . . . to show he's in charge? Bargaining power . . . the true sociopath. The well is here. But where?

"Stone, nothing out back. Just like they said. Your thoughts, partner?" Kolb asked.

"It's here. We just have to find it."

Yeller stirred as the FBI Evidence Recovery Team (ERT) arrived on foot, having positioned their two vans at the base of the small hill where Kolb's squad car was parked.

Eight hours of searching produced nothing further. Kolb sat on an overturned tire picking the burrs off of his pants as the evidence team packed up.

"Just some used condoms, candy wrappers, old beer cans, shit like that. No sign of a well," said Agent Bill Evans, head of ERT.

Stone looked back at the shed. What secrets did it hold?

"You want it bagged?" asked Evans.

"Yeah, bag it all," said Stone.

Maybe we'll get lucky, Stone thought. Stone knew that serial murderers, especially lust murderers, were ritualistic in nature, often returning to the crime scene for sexual gratification to act out their perverted fantasies. Remembering them. Reliving them. Maybe that bit of candy wrapper held a fingerprint. Maybe that used condom contained semen that could be DNA matched to Rivers or the violator. Maybe? Lots of maybes.

"Yeah, better be sure," added Kolb.

Kolb knew too, Stone thought. He'd been through this before. Many times. Different victims. Different subjects. But the same result . . . unsolved homicides. Yes, better be sure.

"Yes, just to be sure," said Stone.

Kolb rose, kicked the tire with his tired boot, and flicked the last burr off of his pants with his index finger. He looked at the shack, then back at Stone.

"I know," Kolb said.

"Get his ass out here and show us."

"And that's what he wants . . . wanted all the time. That's how he played it all along. Just like every damned one of 'em. Ace in the hole. Damn, and we ain't got a choice," Kolb said, watching the sun begin to fall.

CHAPTER 8

Metropolitan Correctional Center (MCC), Chicago, Illinois

Stone was standing, leaning over the table, pointing at Rivers. His finger almost touched Rivers' dog face. Stone restrained himself, as the adrenaline rush gave him a pulsating headache, like drinking a glass of ice-water too fast. Stone's tone was acidic, but Rivers didn't flinch. Just leaned back with that sick smile on his face. Stone sensed he was losing.

"Stone, should I get the guard?" asked Kolb, sequestered in his favorite corner.

"Hey, man, there's lots of lawyers in this piss-hole. I been talking to one. Not dealin' with those fairy-assed Federal Defenders anymore. Naw . . . fuck them."

Stone halted in his tracks. Looked down at Rivers who was squirming like a sprayed bug. Halting Kolb with his free hand, Stone removed his other hand from in front of Rivers' face. Listened. Rivers' voice was shrill and could have shattered glass.

"Yeah, the pencil-dick said cop out to assaulting a federal officer. That's it. No murder *beef*. No manslaughter. Just do some federal time and stay out of the state joints. A federal felony, man. No state time. Okay? No state charges. A year and a day, right?"

Confused, Stone felt Rivers was about to give something up. Knew he had to keep the conversation going. The off-white, drab white walls of the interrogation room reminded Stone of the color of dirty elephant tusks. The walls were closing in on them, like an EL train being filled to capacity.

"That's correct, Billy. All federal felonies carry a sentence of over a year."

"Okay, give me a year and a fuckin' day. That's what ya' do in plea deals, don't ya'? Year and a day? I'll do your fuckin' year and a day. That's it. That's the deal, man."

"No . . . you'll do *your* fucking year and a day," Stone said.

Stone was burning excess calories just keeping up with Rivers' fragmented thought processes, like *Adagio* dancers doing the *Fandango* in Rivers' birdcage of a mind.

"You're running out of time, partner," said Kolb, approaching, violating Rivers' space.

Stone backed off. Sensed that Kolb was going in for the kill.

"Listen you little puke-face, you pull that shit again and you'll rot in a *hole* worse than El Reno for the rest of your pathetic, meaningless little life. We'll make that guard murder in Lompoc stick and send your worthless ass up to San Quentin for some fun and games with the big boys. San Quentin . . . that's in California, dickhead. Lots of fairies out that way. Bet they'd like to get shacked up with a sorry, little fuck like you on *Queer Street.*

Rivers was caught off-guard. He tried to regain the offensive, but Kolb was right there. In his dog-face. Breathing heavy, spraying a mist of aggression on River's flushed, rag of a face. Kolb's mustache was touching Rivers' scar tissue.

"We don't need you, asshole. We'll make the Lompoc murder, then we'll hammer you with the *Suarez* thing. Circumstantial evidence is gonna' fry your ass like greasy bacon. Have a nice fucking day, puke-face."

Kolb eased back as Rivers attempted to rise. Kolb stuffed him back down, like a longshoreman throwing a duffel bag under his bunk.

"Guard," yelled Stone, sensing Kolb was done.

Kolb turned and faced Stone. Kolb's face resembled a spent cartridge. Looking down at Rivers' face, Stone was reminded of dregs at the bottom of a wine vat. Hard to say who got the better of it.

The fat, Hispanic guard, with a face resembling a road map appeared at the door to the interview room. "You guys done for the day?" he asked, cinching up his belt.

Stone nodded as Kolb gathered up his notes.

"Man, that was quick. It's usually a marathon session with you guys. Coming back later?" he asked.

"Never," Stone said, his back to Rivers.

"Yeah, we're busy guys. Got a date with a real honey. Big tits. Great legs. How about you, Stone?"

Stone smiled and said, "Yeah, same thing."

"How about you, shithead? Got a date with your left hand?" laughed Kolb.

Stone realized it was *high-risk / high-gain*. Had played these same cards before. But not with Rivers. Fifty percent success rate. Roll the dice. Do what Napoleon did . . . engage the enemy and see what happens.

"I'll take you to hell!" Rivers shouted, his voice piercing, like notes from a bad trumpet.

"I'll take you. Get me my deal, man, and I'll take you."

"Fuck you, asshole. You'll take us and then we'll talk about your fucking deal," said Kolb.

Rivers was back in cuffs now as the heavy, Hispanic guard roughly led him from the room. As he passed Stone and Kolb, he yelped like a stray dog.

"I'll take you, man. Do it. Get me outta' here. I know where she is, man. Don't fuck with me."

Rivers' head was on a swivel, staring back at Kolb. As Kolb's stare followed Rivers down the corridor Kolb mouthed the words, *Fuck you, asshole.* Stone turned his back on it all and pondered his next move.

CHAPTER 9

Office of Assistant United States
Attorney (AUSA) Madeline Binder, NDI

Her office was as neat as a pin. Hats from several federal agencies were displayed like trophies on the top of her file cabinets. Battles fought . . . cases won. DEA was there. So was ATF. A lone FBI hat hung over the bust of Shakespeare on her desk. A special place, and a gift from Stone, signifying their first case together, a truck hijacking, and the defendant was Billy Rivers. Madeline liked Shakespeare, but she liked Stone more. Much more. And Stone knew it.

"He keeps calling. Collect. Seven times yesterday alone," said Stone.

"And a couple times already this morning," said Kolb.

Kolb looked at his watch. It was almost noon.

Madeline had a runner's body. Slender. Her attire was strict, and lawyerish in every sense of the word. If you pinched her, you'd come up empty. All muscle, no fat. Hair like Rita's, jet-black and shoulder-length. Green eyes like a gypsy queen. As tall as Kolb, but just right for Stone's 6'4". She was wound tight like a Swiss clock, and sharp as a tack. Her voice had the flavor of cinnamon when she spoke. Her laughter was sophisticated, yet girlish, and her *mean* look she used in court faded gently in social settings, where her demeanor appeared almost pedestrian. Stone understood it as boredom. Her adversaries interpreted it as aloofness with a tincture of arrogance.

"Well, Stone, it's *your* call," she said.

She stood and stretched, faced the window and looked out toward the approaching evening. Turning abruptly, she focused on Stone's eyes.

"Do you think he did it?"

"Fifty-fifty. If he didn't, the creep in the photos did," said Stone.

"Are we sure the *creep* isn't Rivers?"

"We ruled him out. His body size doesn't fit. Quantico did a work-up for us. No, the *creep's* a singular offender, as Quantico put it."

"Okay, then. Just take it slowly with *Billy Boy*. You know how much I detest sitting in the same room with him. Just find Rita's body and get a confession," she said, as she winked at Stone.

"Do *you* think he did it?" asked Stone.

"Flip a coin," she said, not looking up.

Her hair fell snowflake like on her shoulders. She crossed her legs like a leopardess, revealing just enough thigh to distract Stone.

Stone loved her thighs. But there was not time for that now. Later, when this was all over, Stone would address that issue. But he must stay focused and get this *thing* behind him. And what about *her*? Rivers had brought them together. They were a team now. One way or another, Rivers would seal their fate. Fate . . . Stone believed in fate. Luck . . . well, that was another matter. But luck always played a part. What was Rivers' fate? Would he be lucky? What did the cards hold for him? Life in prison, lethal injection or a free pass?

"Call me immediately when you know something," she said.

Stone nodded. Kolb rose from his chair.

"Even if it's late, call me at home. Don't hesitate, okay?"

Their eyes met and Stone understood. He would call her regardless.

CHAPTER 10

Wolf Lake Area, Hegewisch,
Southeast Side of Chicago

The two fisherman were there again. Their Ford station wagon had that tired look. It lazily tilted forward toward the lake on a slight decline. It's rear tires were chocked with old bricks. Wood logs were placed under the front tires. It wasn't going anywhere. The back hatch was open and the tailgate was pulled out. Buckets of worms and other slimy creatures, Stone couldn't tell, rested on the tailgate along with several reels of old fishing line. A catfish, a twelve-pounder at least, lay on a newspaper next to the fishing line. Ready for cleaning, its glazed, sallow eyes stared up at Stone, as if asking, *Back again?*

Stone approached the taller of the two men, but before he could speak, the man held up a ruddy, work-worn hand, silencing Stone.

"Shh," he whispered.

He held his fingers in the shape of a *V* over his mouth. Spit oozed through the *V* as he whispered.

"Big buck over yonder. Seen 'im twice this mornin'."

He spoke with a Georgia twang, as he pointed to the thickest part of the woods, and located directly behind the old fishing shack.

"Ain't seen one that big in years. Least ways, not round these parts. Back home, got lots of 'em."

The tall fisherman's complexion was ruddy like his hands. His face had the look of someone who spent most of the time sleeping outdoors. He was tall, not as tall as Stone, but his feet were bigger. Size fifteens maybe, and wide as breadboxes. He wore an old, tattered, red ballcap. The insignia was obliterated by the same mess that was found in the bottom of his worm-bucket. St. Louis Cardinals, Stone guessed. Maybe Boston Red Sox. Hard to tell with all that muck on it. Khaki overalls, one strap mended with duct tape, hung on him like a tired curtain. His shirt was white in spots, but mostly mud-covered, as if he had been digging for worms.

"Orville's my name," he whispered.

Kolb, approaching, tipped his cap to Orville.

"Remember? Told ya' all about that old shack yonder. Couple days ago weren't it?"

"Sure, Orville, I remember. How ya' doin'? Catch anything besides that big carp?" Stone asked, pointing to the catfish.

"Catfish, bottom-dweller, scavenger, hell, they all taste 'bout the same. Still good eatin'," Orville chuckled.

Orville licked his lips, as if he hadn't eaten in days.

"Fixin' to do 'im up real good right now."

Orville paused and put down the big knife he was holding, a ten-incher with a serrated blade and a knobbed wooden handle.

"Whatcha' all doin' back here? Lookin' for somethin'?"

"That's right, Orville. We are looking for something. Maybe you can help us . . . or your friend."

Stone pointed to the second fisherman who was seated on an old, bent, lawn chair facing the lake. The ebb and flow of the lake water massaged his bare feet as he hummed. His fishing pole rested in his hands like a buggy whip.

"Naw, don't think so. Old Seth, he's blind. Goin' on now ten years. If ya' all need any help around these here parts, it'd be me. Been comin' and goin' roundbouts last twenty years. Ever since I retired from the mill . . . steel mill way over yonder."

Orville's grin was as broad as a four-lane highway, as he pointed with a long, bony finger in the direction opposite to where the fishing shack stood.

"We couldn't find the well last time," Stone said.

"Told ya' 'fore, ain't no well 'round here. Remember? Just that sorry excuse for a shack up yonder." Orville pointed in the direction of Kolb and Rivers, who was seated on a stump, handcuffed.

Rivers looked up at Orville and mouthed *fuckin' hillbilly.*

"What'd *he* do? Kill somebody?" asked Orville, pointing to Rivers, still seated, his orange prison jumpsuit blending in with the large orange ball rising in the east.

"Something like that. And this is my partner," said Stone, indicating Kolb.

"Anything?" asked Kolb approaching.

"Just talking to Orville. Getting some basics."

"It's here. Somewhere. I ain't lyin' to ya'," panted Rivers from the stump.

Out of breath and out of shape, Rivers coughed up phlegm as he spoke. Too much walking and too many cigarettes.

"Hey, Stone, got any more cigs? Damn, we been trapsin' all over this place for the past hour. I need a smoke."

"We got nothing, Stone. This little prick's full of shit," said Kolb, eyeing Rivers like a baker eyes bad bread.

"What about the other guy? Ask him yet?" Kolb pointed towards Seth, who was fiddling with a worm and a hook.

"Orville here says he's blind."

"Big fuckin' deal. He still might know something. Hell, my grandmother's blind and she still paints pictures. You watch shithead. I'm going down to talk to . . . what's his name?"

"Seth," said Orville and Stone in unison.

"Fuck this shit. It's here," mouthed Rivers, as he slumped into a crouch.

Rivers tried to reposition his wrists, which were being eaten alive by the metal restraints.

"Do somethin' about these damn cuffs, man. Look at my fuckin' wrists. They're raw meat."

Rivers' wrists had the color of a rusty faucet and the texture of old hamburger.

"When we find the well I'll loosen them," said Stone, his face a blank page.

Kolb and Seth appeared to be playing *monkey-see-monkey-do*. Their arms flailed in the air like box-kites floating in a March wind. Pointing and gesticulating in circles and other geometric shapes, the windmiling abruptly stopped, with Kolb patting old Seth heartily on the back. Approaching Stone, Kolb had that quizzical look on his face that signaled *new developments*.

"He says there's another shack. That way. About a mile off. Said there's something behind it, like a hole in the ground. Maybe a well, but he doesn't know for sure."

Kolb pointed due west of where they were standing.

Stone looked at Rivers.

"Ring any bells?" Stone asked.

Rivers strained. His feral eyes squinted, as the yellow ball in the east shone directly on his dog face, illuminating a mess of intersecting welts and scars. The marks twitched in a spasmic death march on his face, which was taut, leather-like, as if he was about to be *drawn and quartered*. Rivers tried to remember.

"Maybe. It was fall then. Maybe September. Lots of leaves all over. Not like now. Things looked different then. Not like now."

Rivers looked at the thicket of trees and tall grass in the west.

As they prepared to move out, old Seth was smiling. His pole was bending, forming a perfect *U*.

"It's a big 'un. See ya', boys, and good luck," said Orville, his breadboxes making deep imprints in the soft mud as he lurched along toward old Seth.

It was getting hotter when it should have been getting cooler. It was almost twilight now and they all were perspiring heavily. Rivers especially. Jumpsuits breathe irregularly, especially the prison variety, thought Stone, as Rivers huffed and puffed his way up the small incline which led to the second shack.

"That's it, man. I'm sure. Yeah, I remember now. Yeah, pulled her up this little fuckin' hill. See, man, I told ya'. Gimme' a fuckin' cigarette."

Rivers crouched on his haunches, breathed heavily, his sick grin barely visible in the dwindling light.

"*You* pulled her up that little hill?"

Stone's stare melted the elation on Rivers' face into a sweaty mess.

"*You* and who else?"

Rivers, still crouching, breathed in heaves. He appeared to be searching for more lies. His tongue was tied in a *Gordian knot*; his mind twisted and bent, was pulled tight, and secured to his fractured thoughts with a chimney hitch. He panted like a stray dog but nothing came out. His eyes, nomadic, fought the landscape, searching for a way out.

Stone sensed a breakthrough. A small victory. Not Waterloo . . . more like Borodino.

"Where's the well, asshole?" demanded Kolb.

Trickles of hot, salty sweat glistened in Kolb's eyes as the orange globe disappeared from sight, swallowed by the tops of the tall pines. As the mosquitoes buzzed around Rivers' dog face, he pointed.

CHAPTER 11

Squad 6, Chicago FBI

"If she's down there, we got his ass," said Kolb.

Stone nodded.

"He gave it up and didn't even realize it. That's the way it usually goes. Try to get a confession and . . . nothing. The next thing you know the guy pukes all over himself."

"Bottom-line, Rivers was there. Helped pull the body up the hill and then stuffed it down the well," said Kolb.

"Right."

"Yeah, but who was he with?"

"The *creep* in the photos?"

"Yeah, the *creep* in the photos. Who is he?"

It was almost midnight. The calls had been made. All but one. Padino was notified and ERT alerted. The search for Rita would begin at first light. Stone looked at the clock on the wall. He wanted to call her but Kolb wouldn't leave.

"Hey, John, we're starting real early tomorrow. Go home and get some sleep."

About to take a sip of coffee, the mug to his mouth, Kolb glanced at the clock.

"You're right. I'm outta' here."

Just then the night clerk passed by, Contracts I neatly tucked under her arm.

"You guys staying all night?" she asked.

"My partner's leaving right now. And I've got just one call to make," Stone said, as he prodded Kolb to leave with the raising of his eyebrows.

"C'mon, I'll take you down the prisoner elevator. I've got to check something in the parking garage," she said.

"Same spot? 5:30?" Kolb asked.

"Yeah, just you and me. No shithead tomorrow."

"You got it."

Stone fished for her phone number in his rolodex, as the sound from Kolb's and the night clerk's footsteps disappeared down the corridor. He had called it only once. She was married then and it was difficult. Scribbled on the back of her business card, the number had a large *X* drawn through it. Drawn by Stone. It was after midnight now. Damn Kolb for lingering. Maybe she was sleeping. He dialed the number.

"Hello?" The voice was crisp, like fresh lettuce.

"Madeline, it's me Stone. Sorry for . . ."

"Thank God, you called. I've been waiting all night. Just tell me the good news." Her voice was anxious, inviting.

Stone reached under his blotter and pulled out a worn photograph. She was wearing a white bikini. Her skin, the color of ochre, made her look *Scheherazade-like*. Erotic. Her gypsy eyes were dark green, like rough-cut emeralds. Stone was standing next to her, his arm around her waist. The white sand beach contrasted sharply against the deep blue, cloudless sky. Some out-island in the Bahamas near Bimini. But that was then. Before her divorce and the ugliness that followed.

"Stone, are you still there?"

"Sorry, ah, just flipping through some notes here."

"You okay?"

"Just . . . tired."

Stone placed the photograph back under the blotter.

"We found the well but it was too late. To dark to start. After three years, another day won't matter. We'll start first thing in the morning."

"Great. That *is* good news. You'll call me right away then, first thing?"

"Of course. You're still the prosecutor."

Too formal, Stone thought. What happened to the two of them, he asked himself. Stone reached for the photograph then stopped himself. He wanted to say something. *Something* unrelated to this Rivers' business, but couldn't find the words. Couldn't think straight.

"Anything else? Did Rivers say anything?"

"Rivers was there. The son-of-a-bitch was there for sure. He told us but didn't realize it. He helped drag her up the small hill in front of the shack. Dead already. Him and somebody else. But he didn't say. Wouldn't give it up."

"The other guy in the photos?"

"Don't know. Not for sure, anyway. Could be but Rivers is tight-lipped on that one."

"You'll have to drag it out of him, I suppose," she said.

Talking like a prosecutor now, there was no hint of the gentle feminine quality in her voice that Stone enjoyed, and desperately wanted to hear.

"What we do know is that Rivers was there. Dragged Rita's dead body up that hill and was there when she was thrown down the well. That is, if we find her tomorrow."

"A dumpsite?"

"Yes, definitely. The background of the photographs has ruled out this place as the murder scene. She was killed somewhere else. Once we get the computer-enhanced work-up back from the lab, the enlargements of the photographs should reveal a better image of the background. You know, walls, furniture, things like that. Hopefully, we should be able to make something out and narrow our search."

"When?" she asked, sounding as if she was reclining to a resting position.

"Getting comfortable?"

"Yes, I am. Now when do you expect those lab results?"

"Should be soon," said Stone, reaching under his blotter, retrieving the photograph, staring at it.

"We've got to I.D. that other subject. He's the key to everything. Rivers surely knows him," she said.

Stone detected a raspiness in her voice, as if she was inhaling on a cigarette.

"Are you smoking again?"

"You know I smoke only after sex. Remember?"

Stone remembered. Something he'd never forget. Nor did he want to.

"Back to your question, *counselor*. Of course Rivers knows him. But he may only know him by a first name, a nickname or a *street* name. You know how these mutts are. We just don't know."

"If he didn't kill her, Rivers still has a problem. Accessory after the fact, concealing a felony. I imagine he'll play the drug card, claiming to be stoned out of his mind at the time. It won't do him any good though. Voluntary intoxication is not a defense to criminal liability. At least not in Illinois, and surely not in the federal system."

"Yeah, old Billy-boy is a definite *hop-head*. And there could be a drug angle here somewhere. Rivers the user, the other mutt the seller. Just a theory," Stone said.

"But we need more."

"*I* need more," Stone said.

It came out all wrong. It wasn't supposed to.

"I'm sorry. It's late," said Stone, placing the photograph back under the blotter.

"It's never too late," she said softly.

Silence on both ends.

She spoke first.

"I was hoping you'd call. Maybe even stop by to fill me up. I mean fill me in."

They both laughed. The kind of laughter that relieves tension, builds relationships. Brings ex-lovers back together. Back to their beginnings. Unrestrained and impromptu. Real, not feigned. Relinquishing, followed by deeps sighs and the catching of breath, culminating in shallow breathing on both ends.

"I need to see you, James. Away from the office. Seeing you there just makes it difficult. I'm . . ."

"I know," he said.

The photograph was in his hand again. He held it at eye-level. Imagining her as she was, as they were, when they were both happy.

"Tomorrow night, after everything's done. I'll come by and fill you in."

"Up?"

They both laughed.

Madeline's image persisted after the phone was returned to its resting place. The photograph still in his hand would not return to *its* resting place. It would stay with Stone.

CHAPTER 12

Wolf Lake Area, Chicago, Illinois—The Second Shack

A stream lazily meandered into the lake, its waters almost stagnant. Dark and wide in spots, but narrow where a felled timber bridged the gap, beavers' work, it formed a wooden tightrope to the other side. The well was not far away. Timpkins, a new Agent, found it behind a huge rock in the shape of a gladiator's helmet. About a hundred feet from the streambed, only small pieces of stone were visible above ground.

"Over here," yelled Timpkins.

A large, flat rock jutted diagonally toward the stream opposite to where Timpkins was waiting. The rock was slick, covered with a blanket of thick moss the color of malachite. Fallen leaves littered the area and several trees, scrawny willows, grew along the bank. Their exposed roots entwined around each other helically, like DNA strands. The gladiator's face was obscured by the virescent mess of crawling vines. Toadstools, reddish-brown, thrived at the base of the rock. A crevice existed where the gladiator's eyes should be. Timpkins was pointing at it.

"Behind there, a hundred feet or so. I marked it with orange tape."

"Good job," said Stone. "Go get the others."

As Timpkins negotiated his way across the downed timber, Stone moved on alone, anticipating a breakthrough.

It was deep, as far as he could tell. Kneeling over the old well as if in church, the sunlight glimmered through the canopy above. More willows in a tangled dance hung over the well, devouring the sunlight that attempted to penetrate the coffin, sucking it in like a black hole. Remnants of light spiraled down the abyss of death. About twenty feet from the surface, it vanished, reaching a dead zone.

When they arrived Stone realized that he had been there a while and somehow had lost track of time. Stone attempted to navigate himself up from the depths of the vortice of despair into which he had descended.

"Stone, ERT's here. You want photos first?" asked Padino.

"Yeah, Dave, good to see you. Shoot the shit out of it."

Stone stood up. His knees felt like he'd been shot with double-ought buck. Little rock chips were embedded in the crevices around his knees.

Padino directed ERT as Kolb caught up.

"Deep?" Kolb asked, panting.

"Deep enough, partner. Can't see a damn thing after about twenty feet," said Stone.

"Hmm . . . Henkel?"

"Naw, his shoulder's are too big. Better use the SWAT rat."

Turning, Kolb eyed the SWAT rat fiddling with his gear. The SWAT rat loved gear, especially gear with Velcro.

"Dorger, you got it," Kolb yelled to the SWAT rat.

Agent Ron Dorger was busy adjusting his rappelling ropes.

"Need another carabineer," Dorger said to Henckel.

"Kolb wants your skinny ass over there," Henkel said, pointing toward Kolb, as he flipped some safety line with a carabineer attached to Dorger.

"What?" yelled Dorger.

"You're *it*, man. Get your skinny ass over here," said Kolb, pointing to the well.

"Ten minutes," Dorger said, returning to his gear.

Stone watched as Dorger fastened and unfastened the Velcro straps on his jumpsuit. The sound of Velcro coming undone appeared to fascinate Dorger. It usually meant somebody was about to be killed. Dorger, an ex-marine, had often hinted that he could kill a man in thirteen seconds. Some thought it was bullshit. Stone knew differently, and had seen the SWAT rat in action first hand.

"All done," said Padino. "Checked all around, too. Nothing back there. *Nada*. Who you gonna' use?"

Stone nodded in the direction of Dorger.

"SWAT rat, good choice. He's small enough anyway. Henkel for sure would get his fat ass stuck halfway down. Let's do it."

Stone glanced down at his feet. A small wood beetle was slowly crawling across his boot. He snapped his toe and it went flying. The beetle landed near the RAT who squished it. Smiling.

As Dorger descended into the chasm of death, Timpkins and Henkel backed him up on the safety lines. Kolb and Stone manned the lights. A safety light was attached to the Rats's helmet. Padino watched, fingers crossed tightly, as the luminosity of Dorger's light faded into nothingness.

"Stinks down here," yelled up the Rat. "Walls are slimy as pus. Shit's growing all over the place."

Even with the lighting, the odd angles projected by the well walls and the increasing depth made it difficult to see the Rat. Stone strained and could only make out the orange life-line and the top of Dorger's protective, yellow helmet.

"It's getting narrower," Dorger said, transmitting over his handheld radio clipped to his shoulder.

"Copy," responded Padino. "Don't be a hero and get your ass stuck down there."

"Gotcha', boss. I'm gonna' do some probing with the pike."

The sounds of the pike-pole hitting the stone walls caromed up from the emptiness below.

"Do you think it's long enough?" asked Padino.

"Got it off Engine 5. It's a closet pick, three-footer. Anything else would be too awkward," said Henkel.

Henkel's brother was an engineer with Engine Company 5 in the City.

"Got something. Yeah, definitely got *something*. It's wedged tight as Henkel's ass during inspection. Hard, too. Drop me the line with the hook."

Dorger's transmission was intermittent and faint, but Stone got the gist of it and the line was dropped. It was attached to a winch on a small truck, County's, and was slowly engaged. The winch squealed, sounding like rusty nails being shaken in a tin can.

"Just tell me when to kick it," said the truck driver.

Thickset with arms the shape of large bowling pins, the truck driver squinched his eyes narrowly, as he tried in vain to hear Dorger's transmission. He wore a Cook County Sheriff's jumpsuit with the name *Ernie* emblazoned just under the breast pocket. An American flag was on the left sleeve, just below the shoulder. On the opposite sleeve in the same spot was the lettering, *Cold Hard Steel Meets Hot Sweaty Muscle*.

"I'm coming up," transmitted Dorger. "The walls are slippery as hell. Lotsa' gunk down there. But I got the grappling hook in *something*. Whatever it is, it's wedged tight. Wouldn't budge with the pike."

It took Dorger only about fifteen minutes to descend and plant the hook. Stone looked at him as he emerged from the mouth of the well. Slime covered Dorger's face, which was the color of burned toast.

"Shit," he said, as he shook the muck off.

The winch strained and the truck wobbled as Ernie *gunned* it. Dorger began unfastening his harness as Ernie cut the motor.

"Chock them back tires," he barked. "Or we're gonna' lose whatever the hell we got."

Timpkins grabbed a chock off the back of the truck and wedged it securely behind a rear tire. Then another.

"That oughta' do it. Start her up again," said Padino, fingers still crossed.

The winch hissed but the truck remained in place, the back tires spinning, spitting up dirt. Ernie was sweating profusely, his neck soaked with salty steam. Stone was reminded of the slogan on Ernie's sleeve.

"It ain't movin'!" Ernie yelled over the screeching of the winch cables.

Padino's face dissolved into a pool of apprehension as the winch was disengaged.

"Timpkins, saddle up laddy-buck. See if you can loosen it," said Padino.

Timpkins, the new kid on the block, jumped to attention. His box-seat grin engulfed his smallish, fishlike face.

"About twenty-five feet down. It's all bunched up. Poked it with the pike but couldn't budge it. Felt mushy in parts, but mostly hard. Here . . ."

Dorger handed Timpkins the closet pike.

A few minutes later Timpkins was twenty feet down. Maneuvering. He then yelled up that the line was caught on the wall. Henkel and Dorger adjusted the ropes, tugged hard, and then splayed out more line.

"Okay," transmitted Timpkins. "I think it's in. Can't see shit. Comin' up."

A clone of the Rat, Timpkins was covered with whatever lived at the bottom of the well. His fishface resembled a crushed can, but he still wore a grin.

"Try it," he said, removing his helmet that slid from his hands like a wet bar of soap.

Padino gave the thumbs up sign to Ernie.

The squealing of the winch, then a jolt, and the line moved freely.

"Got it. Musta' been wedged on the wall," said Ernie, salty goo dripping from his forehead, a steamy film forming in his eyes.

It was a burlap bag, the size that would contain a hundred pounds or so. It was midnight black and caked with well-bottom. Stone had seen this kind of thing before, mostly on drug cases; typically drug shipments coming up from Mexico, brown heroin, cocaine and hash, concealed in bags like these and camouflaged as chili peppers or some other inane commodity. Yes, hundred pound bags, just the right size for an average woman's body. Cut up and discarded like garbage, could it possibly be the body of Rita Suarez?

"Be careful, boys. Treat everything as critical," said Padino.

All five members of the ERT simultaneously turned and flashed a *fuck-off* grin in Padino's direction.

"Okay, boys. Sorry. I'll just wait over here," said Padino, moving to where Dorger and Timpkins were cleaning up.

The top of the bag, knotted, was tested first with Henkel's buck knife. It gave easily. The stench could have scattered a herd of wildebeests. Mud and slime from the bottom of the well clung to the burlap bag, which appeared pretty much intact.

"Looks like we got it. Looks like a body all right. Bones anyway. Lots of bones," said Agent Mitch Reynolds, the ERT team leader.

Reynolds was the *bone man* on the team, having been trained in forensic anthropology. He was a tall man, Stone's height, but skinny as a rail. When he turned sideways he could be easily mistaken for a fence post. He had that professorial look about him and wore hippie glasses out of the '70's.

"Let's get it over to County and the Medical Examiner," said Reynolds.

"Stone, take off. I'll meet you there. John, stick around . . . just in case," said Padino.

Reynolds continued to probe the bag gently.

"Hard to say, but it looks like a corpse. But . . ."

"Yeah, and . . . ," said Padino approaching.

"See for yourself," said Reynolds, holding up the end of the bag like a tent with Henkel's buck knife.

"Hmmm . . . yeah," said Padino.

"What?" asked Kolb, as he and Stone approached.

"Missing a vital part," said Reynolds.

"Huh?" said Kolb.

"There's no head. Gonna' make the I.D. tough," said the boneman.

"Maybe it's down in the bottom of the sack," offered Padino.

"Maybe its down in the bottom of the well," said Dorger, peering over Padino's shoulder.

"Maybe it's with *him*," Stone whispered under his breath.

Stopping himself, Stone didn't need to see. He knew enough. Knew the boys would be out here for a long while yet, dragging up whatever else was still down there. Down there on the bottom, maybe that's where Rita's skull was. Maybe not, but they had to give it a shot. Thorough crime scenes often result in overkill, but that's the Bureau way.

As Stone passed the truck, he turned to Ernie who was slumped over the wheel.

"Sometimes when it's hot we get a real mess come out. Whatcha' all got there?"

"A dead girl," said Stone, not looking up.

"Oh."

CHAPTER 13

Office of the Cook County Medical Examiner, Chicago, Illinois

He didn't call her. He'd let Kolb do that later. It just didn't seem right, not with Rita's remains fresh in his mind. Madeline would understand. After all this time she would understand. Stone was alone this time. Kolb remained at the scene baby-sitting Padino. Padino always needed company.

"He's on his way," said a female intern, crisply dressed in all white.

A young girl, and way too young to be looking at dead people all day, thought Stone.

It was approaching noon and probably getting hotter out there, Ernie working up a major league sweat by now, the Rat aching for another chance to descend into the pit, and proving his manhood, again. And then there was Kolb watching it all, talking with Padino, holding his hand while assuring him that the case would be made one way or another. Padino, crossing his fingers at critical moments in the search, a nervous tic he had developed over the years, would it work its magic? It had worked before . . . sometimes.

"Stone, hey stranger. You never stop by any more," he said, hand outstretched.

He was Dr. Benjamin Grimes, Assistant Medical Examiner for Cook County.

Grimes liked Stone and, hell, it was hard not to like Grimes. Grimes had been around a long time, almost twenty years, and all at the same facility. Good with cops, good with the Bureau, good with his staff, Grimes was a "go-to" guy, and Grimes was especially good in the morgue.

"How long do you think you can keep it quiet?" asked Grimes.

"About this long," said Stone, holding up his middle finger. "This kind of stuff gets around real fast. The press, they're always calling, looking for an angle. Somebody's bound to give it up. Hell, we had County out there with us, no offense."

Grimes shrugged his shoulders like an eighth grade boy who farted in class during a spelling bee.

"None taken. And the City was out there too. Kolb, right?"

"Yeah, but Kolb is tight-lipped. Always has been. But even our SWAT guys like to talk. ERT's not much better. Not intentionally . . . just banter, you know what I mean?"

"I do exactly, just like the Larson murders," said Grimes.

Grimes was a toothpick of a man, sixtyish with eyes like steel marbles. As tall as Stone, but the absence of musculature made him look like someone from the *Titanic* who didn't make it to the lifeboats. His voice was soft and somewhat feminine, in contrast to his hard, steely eyes. He spoke with a fatherly demeanor, deliberate yet reassuring. He wore soft-soled shoes, *hush-puppies*, gray in color. The collar of his spackled shirt, lime green, was visible from underneath his white lab coat. He always wore a bow tie. This one was the color of burned lima beans, a gift from Stone from a long-forgotten case. His plain gray pants, a bit too long, massaging his shoes, dusted the floor. Grimes was surely not a *dresser*, but give him a circular bone saw, and watch out.

"Right. But I think we've got some time yet. Anyway, correct me if I'm wrong, but a positive I.D.'s a ways off. No head, no dental comparisons," said Stone.

Grimes eyes worked methodically, like a dentist neatly picking at the gums.

"Right, but we're gearing up right now to do the DNA aspect as soon as we get the remains. But as you know, Stone, those results take time. Anyway, how soon before the rest of the gang gets here?"

"Well, hopefully, not too much longer. They're still dragging the bottom of the well for *God knows what*. I'm hoping the skull's there but . . ."

"You don't think it's there?" asked Grimes, mounting a lab stool cowboy-style.

"No. I think *he* kept it."

"Trophy? Memento? That type of thing . . . like Dahmer? Keeping it in his refrigerator somewhere?"

"No, Dahmer was nuts. This guy's evil. There's a difference. I don't care how the shrinks categorized Dahmer. Dahmer was screwy in the head, eating body parts, drilling holes in skulls to make zombies. Mentally . . . you know what I mean?"

Grimes nodded, his steely eyes tightly closed.

"Well," said Grimes, slapping his knees with his small hands. "As soon as we find out anything, I'll get you on the horn."

Stone nodded while Grimes' steel marbles danced rhythmically, as if he was in REM sleep.

"And the Judge, who's going to inform him?" Grimes asked.

Before Stone could answer the intern was back.

"Doctor Grimes," she said, her face contorted, as if she had just tasted bad wine. "They're here. Lots of them. You better come."

"The police?" asked Grimes.

"No, sir. I think it's the Tribune and the Sun-Times. WGN too."

"Damn," whispered Stone under his breath.

There was commotion at the front entrance to the morgue, reporters, stringers and cameramen all pushing their faces against the windows. Flattened noses against steamed glass, rumpled suits, ripped nylons, equated to a real mess.

"Well, if they're here, they're at the scene too," said Grimes.

"Better turn on the TV," said Stone.

Just then Kolb came through the rear entrance where the ambulances dropped off the dead. He was alone.

"It's a fucking disaster out there. Somebody leaked something to somebody," he said, as he wiped the sweat off his brow. "Damn, it's gotta' be 90."

"Find anything else out there, John?" asked Stone.

"Not yet."

"The remains? Are they on the way?" asked Grimes.

"Yeah, about twenty minutes behind me," said Kolb.

"You gonna' stick around here, Stone? Or you want me to?"

"I'll stick. But I want you to do a couple of things."

"Shoot, partner," Kolb said, as he saddled up next to Grimes on an adjacent stool.

"First, call Madeline and explain . . . explain . . ."

Kolb interjected, "Explain that you can't make love when your mind's on dead body parts."

Kolb's expression was factual, as if he had just called holding in a football game.

"Yeah, something like that. But a little more finesse, please.

Kolb smiled. Grimes smiled too.

"And what else?" Kolb asked.

"See the *Tinman*. Find out who's selling around the U of C."

"Crack?"

"Dust. The shit Rivers was arrested for when they revoked him."

"Yeah, *Tinman* should know. Hey, Doc, got anything to drink?" said Kolb.

CHAPTER 14

Meeting with Code Name Tinman,
Hyde Park, Chicago, Illinois

Tinman was always on time, especially when money was involved. Kolb felt for the crisp hundreds in his pockets. Two, given to him by Stone from Stone's personal funds because Stone didn't have time to put through an informant payment request. Technically a Bureau source on paper, *Tinman* had been initially recruited by Kolb. A smalltime dope bust, crystal meth, and *Tinman* had rolled over and was providing good dope intelligence ever since. But the CPD couldn't come up with enough money to keep the *Tinman* happy, and so *Tinman* was passed off to Stone, and the Bureau's deep-pocket.

Besides, Stone was good with informants and worked well with cops too. And Stone spent most of his time on the street, like Kolb, not behind a desk counting paperclips. So Kolb was okay with the *switchero*, as he termed it. But Kolb hadn't seen *Tinman* in some time, being too busy with other cases, mostly undercover work and other odds-and-ends. Insurance fraud, fixed automobile accidents, shakedowns and ice-pick in the back stuff had kept Kolb busy. But now Kolb was back.

So, technically opened as a Bureau source and paid with funds from the *G*, the *Tinman* had been working the streets around the University of Chicago and Hyde Park for the past two years with good results.

Tinman pushed his crippled shopping cart, formerly the property of Jewel Food Stores, up against the window where Kolb sat. The shopping cart was loaded with a conglomeration of orphaned items. Vacuum cleaner parts, hubcaps, pieces of cyclone fencing comprised *Tinman's* haul for the day thus far. He waved his pathetic junkie wave and made his way into the restaurant, and the booth occupied by Kolb.

"Where's Stone," he panted, his tongue exposed, hanging from his mouth like a victim from a window of a burning building.

The *Tinman's* ragged sweatshirt covered the tracks on his arms. Heroin, ancient history, or so Kolb thought. *Tinman* had kicked the habit a few years back. Methamphetamine was the drug of choice now. Meth freak, that's what Kolb called him. *Tinman* wore Calvin Kleins, pre-worn, not purchased from the rack, but purloined from some sleeping tramp. Chuck Converse All-Stars, white, low-cuts with untied red shoelaces, hung on his feet like bedroom slippers. He was in his early 40's, give or take a decade, *Tinman* wouldn't say. But with pillbox slits for eyes pushed into a weathered face of soft wax, he wore his age on his face. When he smiled a tongue the size of a flyswatter licked and massaged jaundice-colored teeth, bad teeth, what was left of them. Short, thin and anemic-looking, *Tinman* needed a good meal and, above all, a good bath.

"Hold your water, *Tinman*. I've got it right here," Kolb said, patting his coat pocket.

Tinman grinned, more yellow teeth, *Maginot's Line* after the Battle of the Bulge. Seating himself in a slumped position opposite Kolb, he breathed heavily. Kolb could see the dollars signs forming in his eyes.

"Still using?"

"Just to take the edge off."

"The edge is never off."

Kolb placed the two bills under his menu, exposing the faces of the inventor.

"Yeah, yeah . . . not much. I just need it now and then. You know how it is, Sarge. Just when I'm sick. It's . . . medicine."

To the *Tinman*, Stone was Stone but Kolb was always Sarge. In fact, Kolb made sure that *Tinman* didn't know his true name. That was good. No desperate phone calls in the middle of the night like Stone complained about.

"You gonna' gimme' that or do I gotta' do headstands?" pleaded *Tinman*, exposing more of *Maginot's Line*, the part after the barrage.

Two college students, the boyfriend-girlfriend type, sat down at the both next to them. *Tinman's* slits for eyes stole furtive glances in their direction. He began to mumble incoherently.

"Let's move to the back," said Kolb, redepositing the hundreds in his pocket.

"Naw, gotta' keep an eye on my merchandise."

Tinman blew snot from his left nostril, one hand covering the right. The gooey, green scum landed on the sleeve of his sweatshirt, Gold's Gym, *No Pain—No Gain*. Loud enough to draw their attention, he sucked up the mess, his bat ears peaking out from under his Cubs hat. The pair scampered to another table in the rear of the restaurant before the phlegm was ingested.

"Works every time," he grinned. "Learned it in college."

"You never went to college. Remember? Told Stone you dropped out after a week."

"Fuck you! A week's a week. So what if I didn't *gra-DEE-ate*? I still went. Now what about my money?"

His eyes, bloodshot and listless, shadowed the two bills in Kolb's hands, as Kolb massaged them tenderly.

"Oh, these?" Kolb said, holding up the hundreds to eye-level.

Tinman edged forward.

"Here, get some etiquette lessons and burn that sweatshirt," said Kolb, handing *Tinman* one of the *Ben Franklins*.

It was scooped up and in Tinman's grimy pocket quicker that a cat in heat could piss.

In his glassy, charmless voice he said, "Whatcha' want me to do for the other one, Sarge? Sing?"

"Dust, powder, designer drugs, that kinda' shit, find out who's selling it around here. Around the University . . . Hyde Park."

"Gonna' take time, Sarge. Gonna' need some expense money," he said, reaching for the other bill.

Kolb pounded down hard on *Tinman's* frail excuse for a hand, pinning it against the table before it got to the inventor. Control, control, control, that was the name of the game with informants. That's all they really understood, that and pain.

"Information first, or did you forget?"

"Okay, okay," he panted, as he slithered back into his slumped position.

His eyes, pouch-like, curled up, half-closing.

Kolb waited, fingering the hundred.

"Yeah, there *is* one guy, come to think of it. Over by the College . . . Chem Department, I think. Makes the shit over there. Angel-dust for sure. Never copped from him though. Don't really use that psychedelic bullshit."

"Yeah, you're just a sophisticated speed freak. Meth, right? An amphetamine connoisseur?"

Kolb's eyebrows were raised, prompting a reply from *Tinman*, pushing his buttons.

"Damn straight. Stay away from that *Cali-FOR-nia* shit," he laughed, a sorry little laugh from a sorry little asswipe.

"Okay, put on your thinking cap," said Kolb.

A pathetic grin formed on *Tinman's* leathered face. Miming pulling his Cubs hat over his bat ears, he darted furtive glances at the buried treasure in his shopping cart. He edged closer to Kolb.

"Find the prick . . . or pricks, who are selling this shit and you'll get more than this. I'm counting on you. Okay?"

Kolb slid the other hundred across the table. *Tinman* snatched it up.

"Yeah, *no problemo*, Sarge. Gimme' a couple days. I'll call."

"Call Stone, please," emphasis on the please.

"Right," he said.

As he rose to leave, remnants of his snot dripped in a stringy mess from his sleeve.

"And burn that damn sweatshirt," said Kolb.

Tinman was out the door and Kolb was on his cell phone when the yelling started.

"Hey, shiiiiit! Hey, asshoooole!"

An unknown beggar of the night was last seen running down 53rd Street with one of the *Tinman's* hubcaps under his arms.

"Yep, you're only as good as your informants," mumbled Kolb.

"Pardon me," the waitress said.

"Oh, just the Danish. Raspberry, please."

CHAPTER 15

Metropolitan Correctional Center (MCC),
Chicago, Illinois

Stone hadn't slept all night. His mouth tasted like a mixture of nail-polish remover and sour vermouth. His breath could have arced metal. He rubbed his eyes, scratchy and listless, as the unkind light tauntingly welcomed him back. He knew it was time for hardball with Rivers. Stone had lost all patience, but Kolb had helped keep Stone in check. *Good cop / bad cop* stuff, but Kolb wasn't here now, running down some leads the *Tinman* had provided. So Stone waited alone for Rivers.

It was a different room this time, smaller, and it would favor Stone, but Stone was still somewhat apprehensive. *How to break through and get to the next level?* Stone was thinking, thinking about Rivers and his chaotic histrionics, his flippant moods, his *button-pushing. Five* pounded in and out of his mind like cannon fire from the *1812 Overture.* The door suddenly swung open and Rivers, his hands cuffed behind his back, was prodded forward by the guard.

"He's all yours, boss. How long you think you gonna' be this time?" asked the guard.

Stone looked at his watch, then back at Rivers.

"It could be just a matter of minutes, but if our friend here sees fit, it could be longer."

"He ain't no friend of mine," hissed the guard.

The guard was thin and ill-postured. His face was acne-scarred, hiding a small mouth with bad teeth. His chalky complexion complained that he was from Southern Illinois, probably near Cairo. He had that *hillbilly look* in his eyes.

"Just open the door and yell when ya' need me. I'll be waitin' 'round 'bout the corner," said the guard, his keys clipped to his belt jingling like sleigh bells.

Rivers turned his back to Stone. Not saying anything, he lifted his cuffed hands.

Fuck you, thought Stone. It's hardball time.

"You know, *Billy*, sometimes you have to step up to the plate and hit the curveball."

"Huh?"

"We'll get to that later. Sit your ass down," ordered Stone.

"Bullshit. Take these off or I'm outta' here."

Stone turned toward the door, took two steps and was interrupted by Rivers.

"Okay, okay. You made your fuckin' point. Now just put 'em on in front of me. Huh? C'mon . . ."

Stone stared hard at the sociopath, his glare melting the veneer of self-conceit surrounding Rivers' stagnant grin. And Stone knew Rivers understood this time. No more games. Stone wouldn't hesitate to kick his pathetic ass all the way to the hole at the first opportunity. Reaching for his handcuff key, which looked like something a kid would find in a box of *Cracker Jacks*, Stone lifted it to eye-level. Rivers responded, assuming the previous position. Stone removed one cuff slowly, refastened it in front and then spun Rivers around. They were face-to-face now and Stone could feel the anger inside of him being reflected off of the bile-yellow glow from Rivers' irises. Pushing Rivers down into a ragged excuse for a chair, a Bureau of Prisons Special, Stone maintained pressure on the chain that connected the two cuffs.

"Shit, let go, man!" cried Rivers.

Stone pushed harder, feeling Rivers' pain, and gleaning his first true enjoyment since this nightmare had begun.

"Hey, man. Shit . . ."

Stone's free hand was over Rivers' dog face faster than a New York cop could pistol-whip a creep in Central Park. Rivers' mouth hung open, dry as the Gobi Desert in mid-winter. Stone felt the fear, saw it in his whinny little eyes. Stone pressed harder, puckering River's pencil-thin lips. Then Stone's boxer hands encompassed the dog face. Hard. It felt like wrought iron, rough and taut. Rivers attempted to bring his cuffed hands upward but Stone applied more pressure. Yellow gunk streamed from Rivers' eyes, not tears, just debris from years of incarceration and sitting in the hole. Stone released the pressure and sat down across from Rivers. Neither spoke, Rivers massaging his bent wrists and his dog face. River's bile-yellow appearance was replaced with a ghost-white sheet.

"Do we understand each other now?" asked Stone, hands folded.

No answer. More massaging. Rivers' ghost face had the expression of a wayward tramp that had missed the last boxcar.

"Look, man . . . okay. One of my kids is sick. I need to get outta' the joint to see her. Shit, she's only six. Kidney problems. We ain't got no insurance and I need help, man. I'll tell ya' everything . . . whatever ya' wanta' know. Just help me, man."

The pathetic look on Rivers' face was that of a small child learning to read.

"It's not what *I* want to know. It's what *you* know. About *that* night. The night in the liquor store. The night she disappeared."

Rivers sat motionless. His eyes danced spastically, as if he was getting ready to lie.

"Now or never. We've got enough to put you away for the rest of your life. We're gonna' nail you with *Murder One*," said Stone, knowing that *Murder One* was a Hollywood ploy that Rivers would bite on.

"I didn't kill nobody," he gasped.

Rivers scratched his ears with cuffed hands. Both ears. He was contorted like a male gymnast warming up for the rings.

"I'm not saying you killed her. But you were there. You took the pictures. You followed her to the liquor store and brought her back, to *him*" said Stone, rolling the dice.

"Yeah," said Rivers. "He said she was his girlfriend and they had a fight or somethin'. Told me to go get her, you know. So they could make up and shit. That's it, man."

The smile on Rivers' dog face held its edge.

"Got any smokes?"

Stone flipped him a pack of Salems and some matches.

"Menthol homo-shit. I would've expected that crap from four-eyes. Where's little snot-nosed Johnny anyways? Got'm hidden in a cookie jar?"

Rivers, lit up, inhaled stiffly, and removed the cigarette from his mouth. He twirled it under his nose, his tongue slithering out of the corner of his mouth like a cobra from a basket.

"Gathering evidence to keep you locked up," said Stone, smiling.

"Yeah, fuck him," said Rivers, inhaling more tar.

"The liquor store?" Stone prodded.

The cigarette rotated elliptically in Rivers' mouth as the smoke left in spurts.

"Yeah, sent me there. Said she was going for some wine or shit for some party. All girl party . . . sorority shit. Somethin' like that. The guy wasn't invited."

"Who?"

"The boyfriend. Lenny, Louie, Larry . . . can't remember the dude's name. Larry or somethin', I forget."

"Describe him."

"Worked there, man."

A blue-gray haze surrounded Rivers' dog face. His mouth, now a thin line, was clenched tight on the cigarette. The air was becoming stale and thick, but Rivers' eyes projected pinpoints of light from the mist. An interrogator's wet dream, Stone pressed on into this realm of the truth about to make its entry.

"Worked *where?*"

"The college, man. C'mon, a moron coulda' figured that out."

"So her boyfriend, Larry or something, worked at the college? Doing what?"

Rivers laughed, his deep guttural growling permeating the stench hanging in the stale air of the room.

"Sellin' dope. Makin' it, sellin' it. What else, shit."

"What kind of dope?"

"You gonna' help me out or not?"

Rivers' eyes, dimly visible now through the smoke, dictated a lost confidence. Regaining ground, his masterminding ego began to protrude from a milieu of hatred and evil.

"I have a friend at Cook County Hospital. He's in the Dialysis Unit. I'll look into it," Stone lied.

"Good. You do that soon, man."

"The dope, what kind?"

"Different stuff, man. Mostly *dust*. That shit's big in California, ain't it? You know, the shit they violated me for," Rivers said, his insipid glare Satanic.

"Ecstasy?" said Stone, remembering that Rivers had been arrested for possession of Ecstasy, and some other synthetic drugs that mimicked the effects of opiates, a few days after Rita had disappeared.

"Yeah, man, that's it. The guy made the shit in his lab."

"Where exactly is the lab? What department?"

"Department . . . huh? How the fuck should I know, man. Some lab . . . saw it only once. Never even went in."

Rivers grabbed the pack of *Salems*, spun it on the table, and finally removed a new cancer stick. He whispered under his breath as he lit up.

"Fuckin' homo-shit."

The new waft of expelled smoke rose and settled above his head forming a fake halo.

"Yeah, shit, been there only once, man."

"Would you be able to recognize the building where the lab was located?"

"Nah, man, told ya', been there *O-N-L-Y* once," said Rivers, spelling it out for Stone. "It was dark, man."

"How about the apartment? Where the guy lived?"

"Man, I was wasted. Totally, you know. Shit, everything was a *blurrrr*," he said, his r's caboosing onto the exhaled puffs of smoke that left his mouth in a depraved rhythm.

"Okay, we're getting nowhere. What went on? What did Lenny or Larry say?" asked Stone. "What did he look like?"

"White guy. Big dude. Like you, man. Hair . . . yeah, dark, real dark. Ugly face, too, you know. Real tough to look at, scars and shit all over it. That's it, man. Just one big, ugly white guy."

Stone stared through Rivers.

"Oh, yeah. Liked to wear leather and shit. You know, belts, whips, chains. Sorry dude, man. Shit, like that."

Rivers extinguished the spent *Salem* on the table, reached for the pack, then pulled back.

"Homo-shit," he whispered.

"Bondage asked?" Stone.

"Huh?"

"Liked to tie people up? Restrain them?"

"Yeah, that kinda' shit. Dude was fucked-up. Couldn't get it up unless the bitch was tied and shit. Told me that when he was stoned. Man, the dude was always snortin' somethin'. Got *real* mean, too. Nasty motherfucker. Not from around here, though. Out East maybe. You know, had one of those fucked-up accents. Said *soda* instead of *pop*. Shit like that. Hell, didn't even know what *jag-off* meant."

Stone was scribbling on a yellow legal pad the color of Rivers' eyes.

"How'd he kill her?" Stone asked, not looking up.

Twisting in his seat like a squished bug, Rivers said, "Take these off, man."

When the cuffs were removed, Rivers leaned back and breathed deeply. The stale air surrounded him, as if they were intimate friends. Rivers' eyes were closed, his breathing shallow. His arms were propped behind his head, as if he was about to do sit-ups for a fit-test. Silence, attempting to remember . . . or getting ready to lie, Stone waited.

"It's important, Billy. Don't leave anything out. You're doing the right thing. For yourself . . . and for your family."

Stone knew Rivers didn't give a damn about his family . . . really. Rivers gave a damn only about Rivers. That stuff about his kid being sick, that was all bullshit, some angle being played by Rivers. Stone had learned that from the many years of their ill-fated acquaintance. Rivers would sell his first-born for a packet of *crank*. But Stone was on a roll and felt that Rivers, with a little positive reinforcement, was about to *give it up*.

"Yeah, I was in the bathroom, man. Snortin' some white shit. Don't even know what it was, man. Mighta' been coke, don't remember. Came out and the bitch was tied up . . . to a chair, man. Tape on her mouth. Naked. So was he. Except the dude was wearin' cowboy boots. Liked cowboy boots, man. Always wore 'em. Mighta' lived out West, come to think of it."

Rivers spoke matter-of-factly, as if he was reciting a lesson in civics.

"Anyways, I said, *Hey, fuckhead, whatcha' doin*?"

"What did he say?"

Rivers disgustedly grabbed another Salem.

"Said I'm gonna' fuck her hard. Then she's history."

"Those were his exact words?"

"Yeah, didn't know what he meant by history. Thought maybe he was gonna' kick her out on her ass. You know, break up and shit. Didn't know. Just didn't know."

Another *Salem* was in his mouth. Unlit, it bobbed up and down like a worm on a hook, as the words spewed forth.

"Yeah, fucked her, man. Real hard. Couple times at least. Maybe three, four, wasn't keepin' track. Don't remember exactly. Always on her face. Laughed like a damn hyena. Whacked her good a couple times, too. Dude was an animal, man."

"And you, Billy? Did you just watch?"

"You mean did I get her too?"

"Did you?"

"Tried, man. Couldn't get it up. He wanted me too but I just couldn't do it. Too much of that shit in my system. My head felt like a squashed pumpkin best I can remember. Know what I mean?"

Stone didn't know, could only imagine. He felt nauseated as he tried. He was losing momentum, he thought. Had to get back on point.

"How did he kill her, Billy?"

Rivers put another butt to rest, jamming it onto the table. Looked at it, and then he flicked it away.

"Man, I had nothin' to do with that. Just watched, man. It was fast. Just came outta' nowhere."

Rivers leaned forward, his elbows with the spider web tattoos propped on the table. The wolf's head tattoo on his arm appeared to be alive and ready to spring. Rivers focused on it, and then rubbed it. Appearing hypnotized by the tattoo, Rivers spoke softly.

"Pounced on her, man. Had a butterfly knife. Took it outta' his boot. His fuckin' cowboy boots, man. Shit, slashed the hell outta' her face. Ripped her ears off. Hell, I thought I was on acid or somethin'. Real *Charlie Manson* shit, man. Slashin', gruntin', you know. Yellin', die, bitch, die. Shit like that. Blood . . . all over, man. I couldn't move. Slumped in a corner. Just watched, you know . . . and then, shit . . ."

Rivers paused and cupped his hands, then brought them to his mouth and blew into them. Beads of sweat formed on his bent brow as he relived the event. Droplets of wet goo spilled onto the table. First one, then several, pooling in front of him, then spreading out like spokes on a wheel.

"Then what?" asked Stone.

Stone's hands were under the table, trembling. His pen dropped to the floor, clinking, and sounding to Stone like a hammer hitting glass.

"Dude walked away, man. Covered in blood. Went in the bedroom, then came out dressed in leather. Just like in the pictures, man. Had a toolbox with him. Red, I think. Yeah, red tool box. Handle was busted. Wire, electrical wire held it closed at the latch. Shit, I still remember that. Took out a hacksaw, man. Started working on her. Took it off. Shit."

"Took what off?" asked Stone, summoning up what courage he had left to keep his voice steady.

"Her fuckin' head, man! The bitch's head! Shit, grabbed it by the hair and wrapped the hair around his wrist. It was ugly, man."

"And you took the pictures."

"Man, he told me to. Dude was dangerous. Made me do it. Told me to leave *his* head out. No head shots. That's why the picture's cut off. Dude's a violent motherfucker, man."

Rivers drew his arms into himself and settled back in his seat. The worst telling was over.

"I passed out. Shit, when I woke up the place was all spic-and-span like, except for the shitter. Dude cleaned the place up real good. Wrapped her body in some bags. Burlap bags. Saw 'em layin' in the corner by the door when I first got there."

"What did he do with the . . . head?"

Stone's fists were clenched. He felt as if he had just given a gallon of blood to the Red Cross.

"Shit," Rivers laughed, gulping stale air. "I went in the bathroom and saw it in the sink. Kept it, I guess. Man, the sun was comin' up. Been there all night. Had to get outta' there. It stunk so bad. Couldn't breathe. The bathtub was full of blood and stuff. Skin, hair, shit like that. Couldn't breathe, man. Came out chokin'. Dude was laughin' at me. Said he poured acid all over her and for me to stay outta' there. Shit, I pissed my pants right there."

"And the body? Where did you take it?"

"Shit, man. Told ya' already. You's found it in that old well, didn't ya'?"

Rivers had a petulant look on his face, as if he had already said enough. He withdrew inward, back into that sadistically, insane abyss, the world of Billy Rivers.

"The well . . . that's *your* old neighborhood, isn't it?"

"Yeah, so what. The dude killed her, not me. I just helped him get rid of the body like I told ya'. Anyways, I was stoned. Incompetent, right? Had all that shit in my system. Innocent because of insanity, right?"

Rivers attempted to show off his disjointed theory of criminal law that he had learned from various jailhouse lawyers, but he looked anything but lawyer-like.

"Who suggested that place? You did, didn't you?"

"I might've. Yeah . . . so what?"

Stone thought it curious that Rivers' old stomping grounds turned out to be the dumpsite. Why there? Maybe nothing. Maybe everything. Drop it. Don't alienate him. Keep on track.

"Was it daylight when you dumped the body in the well?"

"Yeah. It was easy. It was rainin' a little. Not much. Nobody was around. Boom. Slash. Cut her loose. Just dumped it. Just like that."

Rivers motioned like a diver on a 20-meter board.

"Then what happened?"

"Went back to his place. Drove in his car. Some beat-up piece of shit, a Bronco I think. Somethin' like that. Yeah, red Bronco. Anyways, went back. Did some more shit with the dude. Got really fucked-up. Him worse than me. So I bugged out and took the pictures with me. They were in that red tool-box he had. Took some of his dope, too. Shit, that's what fucked me up. That's how I got violated when the cops stopped me a couple days later. Damn, shouldn't 've taken that damn shit. Damn!"

"But you did take it and the photos, right?"

"Yeah, right."

Rivers leaned back. Relaxed, the blood flowed back into his forehead, which was the color of notebook paper.

"When did you see him again?"

"The dude? Fuck, never, man. And I don't want to."

"When we find him, you'll have to identify him. You understand that, don't you?"

"If it'll save my ass, damn straight. Fuckin' *A*."

Stone gathered up his notes. His stomach felt as if he had swallowed bad vinegar.

"That's all for now, Billy. I'll check with my friend at Cook County for you," Stone lied a second time.

His eyes meet Rivers.

"You do that Mr. *G*-Man and, hey, what about my plea? Tomorrow, right?"

"Yes, tomorrow, in front of Judge Mendelson. Whose your Federal Defender?"

"Some fairy-ass, fuck him. Just get me my year and a day. Tomorrow, okay? I gave you lots of good shit today. You owe me."

Rivers sat manacled, hands behind his back, as Stone called for the guard.

"Just one more thing, Billy."

"Yeah, what?"

"When you were arrested with the drugs, why didn't you use the photos to work a deal?"

"Who woulda' believed me?"

The guard with the hillbilly grin returned, grabbed Rivers roughly, and jerked him forward.

"Hey, next time, bring some real smokes. None of that homo-shit," said Rivers.

Halfway down the corridor Rivers looked back over his shoulder at Stone who was standing by the door. Rivers dog face glowed a sickly green under the dim light above. His eyes danced a liar's dance.

CHAPTER 16

Gi-Gi's Adult Bookstore,
Hyde Park, Illinois

"Over there," said *Tinman*, pointing to the building on the corner.

It was a one-story structure painted an ugly green. Above the front entrance an electric sign read, *Gi-Gi's Adult Books and Video*. The lights in *Video* were not working.

Kolb opened the passenger side of his squad, hitting *Tinman's* shopping cart. Aluminum cans and other assorted metallic junk clanged off tune.

"Hey, watch it, Sarge. That's my livelihood."

Tinman picked up a few stray cans, 7-Ups, and tossed them back onto the pile of junk.

"Get your sorry ass in here," said Kolb, eyeing *Gi-Gi's*.

"Yeah, Sarge, got some good shit for ya' They know him in there. You got my money?"

Tinman was wearing a long-sleeved cardigan sweater even though the temperature was almost 90 and as humid as Tahiti before the cyclone hit.

"You don't sweat, do you?" asked Kolb, whose armpits pooled in salty goo.

Perspiration from his brow dripped soot and ozone accumulated from the dank air into his eyes, causing him to blink. New contact lenses. That four-eyed crap from Rivers had pushed some buttons.

"Hell, no, man. Cold blooded as a rattler. Hey, Sarge, you got some scratch for me? Stone said you did. Promised me. C'mon, *Saaaarge,* I'm not feelin' too good today."

Tinman, half in the car, leaned awkwardly toward Kolb. His legs dangled like spaghetti onto the curb. Kolb pulled out an envelope from under his seat, showed it to *Tinman*, and returned it to its resting place.

"First tell me what ya' got. Then we'll settle up. *Comprende?*"

"Okay, sure, Sarge. The guy's name is Larry. Big guy. White. Used to teach over at the college. You know 'bout the time the girl went missing. Worked in some lab over there. Don't know which one, but he was makin' stuff and sellin' it. Not a lot, just enough to get by. Used a lot too. A real *hop-head*," said *Tinman*, clicking his fingers, getting ready for the scratch.

Kolb felt *Tinman's* nervous energy. The rhythmic clicking of his fingers on the dashboard, *Tinman* needed a fix. Street medicine.

Kolb pulled out the envelope. Tossed it to *Tinman* who caught it like a wide receiver with *stick-um* on his hands. Greedily opening it, he pulled out five one-hundred dollar bills, smelled them, and then tucked them safely in his pants pockets.

"New. Love the smell of new money. Makes me itchy all over. Tell Stone thanks. Okay, Sarge?"

"What else?" pressed Kolb, glancing at the sporadic foot-traffic entering *Gi-Gi's.*

"Liked leather. Wore the shit all the time. Cowboy boots too. Into bondage and shit like that. Shelly over there will tell you about him. Rented lots of videos from them. Kinky shit, you know what I mean, Sarge? Ropes, chains, whips. That kinda' shit. They sell all that crap over there, too."

Tinman was squirming, as if he had just taken a bath in formaldehyde. Ready to bolt. Ready to get his street medicine.

"Where is he now . . . Larry? Live around here?"

"Naaaw, long gone, Sarge. According to Shelly, he's been AWOL for about a year. That's Army talk, ain't it Sarge? Yeah, dude went *A-W-O-L*. Maybe more'n a year. Shelly'd know for sure. The guy was a regular over there. Plus, all the street scum are buyin' that fancy shit now, Ecstasy and dust, from some pimple-nosed white freak over on 59th Street. Works at a 7-Eleven. You want me to find out more about him?"

"Keep it under your hat for now."

Tinman pulled tight on the edges of his White Sox cap. His bat ears perked up as if he had turned on the radar.

"Listen close. Keep on *this* thing only. You know what Stone wants. Keep the feelers out."

His bat ears twinging as he listened, *Tinman* cast anxious glances at the entrance to *Gi-Gi's*.

"Press the bondage thing. See if anything else comes up. Now get your sorry ass outta' my squad."

"Sure, Sarge," said *Tinman*, saluting, a tired salute from a tired little street mutt.

A man about to enter *Gi-Gi's* watched *Tinman* fumble out of Kolb's squad. *Tinman* kicked the passenger-side door.

"Damn," he yelled. "Okay, then don't buy any of my shit. Go screw yourself."

The man was short with hollow eyes. His cheeks were paunchy and the color of old cream soda. He had that look on his face that Kolb recognized as *street punk variety A*.

"Let's go, Ringo. This piece of shit is wasting my time," said *Tinman*, spitting on Kolb's unmarked squad.

As Kolb walked toward Gi-Gi's, Ringo and Tinman were last seen holding hands. Junkie buddies about to share some scag. They entered a house at the far end of the street, probably their *connect*. We'll hit it on a slow day, thought Kolb. Not now. Let's see what Shelly has to say.

Shelly sat in a booth to the left of the entrance. She was alone, except for a pair of degenerates browsing in the *Chicks-with-Sticks* Section.

"It's a dollar to browse," she informed Kolb.

She was downright ugly, the kind of ugly that begs for euthanasia. Make-up and a good face-lift would be a waste of time, too much to lift and not enough face. Thin to the point of being anorexic, her legs were the circumference of fat magic markers. She had no ass to speak of. And the ass she did have, no one *would* speak of. Her voice was metallic, nickel-plated, and smelled of cheap whiskey, *Jim Beam* maybe. She leaned over the counter, extending an open palm. It was small, red, and dimpled in spots, like a hyena's hide.

"You wanta' browse, one dollar," she said again, more whiskey breath.

"Listen, gorgeous, let's keep this simple," said Kolb, flipping open his wallet, exposing his star.

"Yeah, honey, I like simple. Is that real?"

Kolb pulled back his shirt, which hung out of his pants, exposing his piece.

"Whatcha' need, officer?" said Shelly. "Or is it *Detective*?" she asked.

Shelly's eyes darted back and forth between Kolb and the two men in the rear of the store who were still *browsing*.

"Looking for a guy used to come in here. Kind of a regular. Liked bondage and stuff. You keep a customer list . . . Shelly, isn't it?"

"That's right, Detective . . . . ?"

"Kolb."

"Okay, Detective Kolb. Sure, but just describe him. I've been around a long time. I know all the freaks who come in here. If he's a regular, I'll know him. What's he look like? You got a name or anything?"

"Tell you what, let me see the list and if anything jumps out at me, we'll talk about it. Okay?"

"I'll go get it. Just keep an eye on those two creeps over there. Caught 'em jackin' off in the backroom last week. Good customers, otherwise I woulda' called you guys," she said.

Shelly winked at Kolb. Her left eyelash resembled a broken windshield wiper, as she turned and entered the back room. Moments later she returned and handed a small red book to Kolb. As Kolb scanned the customer directory he jotted a few names of interest on the back of an advertisement for free lessons in anal sex, which lay on the counter.

"These six names," he said.

"Yeah, what about 'em?"

"You recognize any of them?"

"Sure, all of 'em. They're all regulars . . . or were. Except this guy. Haven't seen him around for a while. It's been almost a year."

She pointed to the name *Larry Sternson.*

"What's he look like?" asked Kolb.

"Hmm . . . big guy. Bigger than you. Bad face, scars and stuff. White male. That's cop-talk, isn't it?" she said, batting the other wiper.

"Yeah, and you're doing a hell of a detecting job here. Now what else? What type of stuff did he rent or buy? Or do you remember?"

"That sick, crazy shit. Over there," she said, pointing to the *Bondage* Section.

Kolb tucked the customer list safely in his pocket as she pointed.

"You know, that sado-masochistic stuff. Once a week, maybe more, he'd come in. That's all he ever took. Good customer, though. Always paid in cash. Is he in some kinda' trouble? He was really nice to me."

"Maybe," said Kolb.

"Ah, cowboy boots. Always wore boots and *really* liked leather. Wore leather a lot and bought a lot, too. Over there," she said.

Shelly pointed to some leather masks and restraints that hung from the wall. Things you'd see in a medieval castle.

"Good. You wouldn't have happened to make a copy of his driver's license or credit card, would you?"

"This sounds serious. Is there a reward or something?"

"Your reward, darling, is that I'll allow you to keep this cesspool of a business operating. Okay?" said Kolb.

"I only work here snookums. Gotta pay the bills, know what I mean?"

The smile was gone from her face, replaced by the look of a used car salesman who had just lost a sale.

"I'll get it. It's in the back. Gonna' take a few minutes. Help yourself to a free browse. Over there," she said. "You look like a *big tit* man."

As Shelly disappeared through the beaded doorway, Kolb thought, how perceptive she was. Kolb was tempted but kept to the straight and narrow.

✳   ✳   ✳

She was standing in the doorway waving and blowing him kisses, as he started up the squad.

"Come back any time, *Detective*. I love police talk. It gets lonely here. You can browse for free any time, darling."

A photocopy of Lawrence Roy Sternson's driver's license was neatly tucked in Kolb's pocket.

CHAPTER 17

Squad 6 Area—Chicago FBI

Stone sat at his desk, face down, his credentials staring back at him, and asking him, *How much longer?* Twenty-six years already. Maybe it was over. Maybe it was time to move on and put this *Rivers* business behind him. Let Kolb take over the case. After all, Stone was eligible for retirement. Sure he could tell them to kiss his ass. KMA it was referred to by those surly agents who'd made it as far as Stone had. Yes, KMA sounded pretty damn good right now. But still . . . *Billy Rivers* lingered in his mind like the dregs in a vat of stale beer. This unfinished business . . . this Rivers mess, how much longer could he hold on?

"Here," said Kolb, handing Stone a diet coke.

Stone looked up.

"Thinking again? That could be dangerous, partner."

Kolb took a hit from a can of 7-Up.

"Yeah," said Stone. "Just trying to make some sense of it all . . . this mess."

A half-hearted laugh stuck in Stone's throat like pea-gravel going through a sieve. Kolb caught a glimpse of Stone's open credentials.

"FBI," Kolb said. "Always wanted to be one. 'Nam got in the way. Then Debbie, my first wife. Hell, wasn't smart enough anyway."

Stone read from his credentials.

"*Special* Agent . . . what the hell does that mean anyway?"

"It means you're special and I'm not," laughed Kolb.

The gold bordering on Stone's credentials had turned green. Oxidized over time, the sign of a true veteran. Stone's photograph to the left of the FBI seal depicted a young, energetic man with dark hair, and a determined line to his face. The words, *By order of the Attorney General* were inscribed below the FBI seal.

"Hell, I don't even know the Attorney General," Stone said.

"What?" said Kolb, fumbling with some documents lying in front of him.

"Nothing, John. Just remembering . . . out loud."

Stone closed his credentials case, his likeness of years past imprisoned inside. He tucked the credentials neatly in his coat pocket, out-of-sight. Running his hands through his hair, he continued to ruminate.

"Okay, tell me the bad news. Hell, I know there's no good news," said Kolb.

"Rivers balked. He didn't take the deal. He wanted full immunity on Rita's murder. And the U.S. Attorney said no."

Kolb crushed the 7-Up can in his hand, waited, and then flung a frozen rope at the wall. Kolb and Stone were staring at each other.

"So where are we now?" asked Kolb.

"Well, for one, we're done talking to Rivers. Let the leaves fall where they may on that Lompoc murder. Rivers is on his own now. We'll just have to use what he gave us and try to run down the rest."

"That's a big *rest*, partner."

"We need to find Sternson and . . ."

Stone's voice trailed off like a head linesman's inadvertent whistle on the goal line.

"And?" mimicked Kolb.

"Closure," said Stone.

"You mean nail Sternson's sorry ass, don't you?"

"Yeah, I guess that's what closure means," said Stone.

Stone was feeling old. Really old.

CHAPTER 18

Office of the Assistant United States Attorney (AUSA), Madeline Binder

The manila folder lay closed on her desk. On the cover was neatly printed the name *Lawrence Sternson*, in large, black capital letters. Looking out of the lone window in the room, she crossed her arms. A series of questions darted in and out of her mind, like the ebb and flow of seawater at high tide. She waited, her agenda uncertain, and then the knock at her door startled her.

"Well, good morning," she said.

She glanced at her wall clock, an obtuse monstrosity depicting a bucking bronco and a rider, the rider's arms outstretched in the eleven o'clock position. It was a gift from a DEA agent on a case recently concluded. She adjusted the nameplate on her desk, which read *Madeline S. Binder, AUSA, NDI*.

"Right on time, as usual," she said.

Kolb entered first, then Stone, sheepishly, appearing to feel out of place.

It's good to see him, she thought. Catching herself . . . no. It's damn good to see him. Keep it inside, she reminded herself. Be professional. Remain aloof. The wall . . . the ever-protecting wall, keep the wall up. It would come down soon enough. There was still time, but not now.

Seating themselves across from her, Stone spoke first.

"It's all there," he said, indicating the manila folder. "Everything we know about him. It appears he's overseas now. The United Kingdom, most probably Scotland."

"Edinburgh," interjected Kolb.

"Somewhere over there. We're still checking," continued Stone.

"That makes it difficult," she said.

"Not impossible, just difficult. Murder still is an extraditable offense, isn't it?" offered Kolb, the flat expression on his face appeared *matter-of-fact*.

"Sometimes, Detective. If it's Scotland, we're okay," she said, seating herself lady-like in front of them.

Legs politely crossed, her delicate fingers caressed the file as she spoke.

"It's *him*. I feel it. Call it woman's intuition. Call it what you may. But I feel it."

Her eyes met Stone's, and waited for a response, something, maybe not an answer to her statement but . . . *something*. A connection, she was searching for common ground.

"Still too early, Madeline. We need to find him first. Talk to him and get a feel. Read his body language. We can't trust Rivers' account to be one-hundred percent accurate. You know how it is," said Stone.

"Yes, I'm well-acquainted with your methods."

Her eyes were closed. Thinking.

"When will you leave?" she asked.

"We're making arrangements now. Our Legat in London is coordinating things from his end. We should have Sternson's whereabouts narrowed down by the end of the day. Our flight's tonight, nine o'clock."

"We'll be ready to hit it hard once we get there," chirped Kolb, a narrow crevice of a smile forming on his face.

"After we arrive, we'll notify you of our *point-of-contact* and any other particulars," said Stone, rising, sliding his hands down the creases in his slacks.

Looking up, Stone appeared apprehensive. Madeline read concern in his tired eyes.

"Be careful, guys. Please!" she begged, remembering the file and Sternson's past criminal behavior, violent, bent on sadistic.

"Just get that extradition warrant started. We'll get you the missing pieces," said Stone, motioning Kolb toward the door.

"You think it's *him* then?" she said.

It was more of a statement rather than a question.

Turning, Stone only winked, thinly smiling. His cold, blue eyes remained non-committal. The door closed behind them, as she slumped into her chair. Depressed, thinking of Lawrence Sternson, she opened the file again and began to read, attempting to understand this depraved excuse for a human being. The tears began to well in her eyes, deep sockets that felt like canyons of despair. She held the tears back. The wall. Stone will return, she assured herself. The scar-faced mugshot of Lawrence Sternson stared back at her. *It's me alright . . . and it will be me again.*

CHAPTER 19

Somewhere in Northern Scotland,
United Kingdom

Crouched alone in the corner of the stone cottage, his fingers covered his eyes. The rough scars on his face throbbed with anticipation, the darkness his only friend. His thoughts raced through his mind, trying to sort themselves out, but only confusion remained. More on edge, the precipice he dreaded was in full view, and the decision he must inevitably make was forming in the tangled cobwebs of his mind. He had been here a while. How long, he couldn't remember. It was light then, but now it was dark, a soothing respite from the damned brightness he hated. He coveted darkness, and darkness felt exhilarating . . . nurturing. His thoughts at times were interrupted by the howling of the wind, reminding him of a hound's cry for sustenance, or of lost children stumbling through the moors. The field mice, which scurried across the dirt floor in search of morsels of food, and then scurried back to the safety of their den, were his only companions in this desolate place he so enjoyed.

Yes, safety, he must have safety like the mice, and he felt safe now; now that the darkness had come, along with the solitude it had brought. The darkness did that for him. But his thoughts were still erratic, like a jigsaw puzzle where all the pieces were the same color; thoughts that were unwelcome and disturbing.

His eyes were open now. In the dark they shone like faint pin-points of light. The mice, he suspected, saw them and were eerily attracted to him. They crawled slowly over his legs and ankles, and then back to the darkness of the room, to safety, a safety he envied. Their company was becoming an intrusion, a distraction from his purpose. His thoughts, transparent again, reflected his ever-changing mood. He *needed* to act.

The wind picked up and battered the small cottage from all sides. The groaning of the windowpane pulsated like a festering sore, like so many voices, voices from his past. He never got used to the voices. They were louder now and imploring him. The banging of the shutters, nailed tight, beguiled him and he felt relief, surcease from the insidious and nagging thoughts; but only for a moment, as they seeped back with a vengeance, stronger this time, more concrete, and more graphic. They were bent on defining his purpose.

The fire had died out, the hearth a graveyard of charred twigs and branches, twisted and broken limbs waiting for the next inferno. It was cold and he shivered as the thoughts sorted themselves out. He squatted, listened, but the wind spoke in broken rhymes. It's whining beckoned him. His hands felt like the worn surface of a whetstone. His eyes pooled in disgust, as the thoughts became clearer. He was learning from the droning of the wind, and it's relentless howling. The unmerciful scream of nature was becoming his nature. He was learning and now understanding, not like before, but different this time.

It began to rain, a never-ending banging, a hard, cold rain, a London rain in winter. It was typical of this time of year, at this place; this place he came to for succor, for purpose, for direction.

A small, speckled, brown mouse, the kind he had hunted and captured as a small boy, at this same place, was perched right in front of him. It was still dark but he could feel its presence. He could smell its fear as plainly as he had smelled death. With a darting motion, the mouse was his, imprisoned in the palm of his hand. He breathed easier now, the whipping wind not a factor, the relentless cold rain a forgotten friend. The heaving of his chest had ceased. It was rhythmic and smooth, like gently flowing water caressing glass. The head of the mouse protruded above his grip. At eye-level he held it, and peered into its small iridescent eyes. Biting off the head cleanly, he understood again. Swallowing hard, he felt reborn.

Rising, the tension released itself in a scream within his mind, mimicking the wind. The scream and the howling were now one. The thoughts melted into a limpid pool of solace at the base of his brain. Only one thought remained. Yes, he *must* kill again. After all, he was home.

CHAPTER 20

United States Embassy, London England,
Office of the Legal Attaché (FBI)

The Assistant Legal Attaché (ALAT) was a wiry man whose age was impossible to guess from his looks, somewhere between pubescence and posterity. He had red eyes that squinted in the light, as if he had read small print for hours. His face was small, as was his overall appearance. In fact, the only thing not small about him was his ego. A career diplomat, he couldn't investigate his way out of a piss-soaked paper bag. No, F. Williams Pearl, Princeton educated, was not an investigator like Stone, nor a cop like Kolb. But he knew paper and how to shuffle it, and he was proficient at counting paperclips. And that was why he was in the diplomatic arena.

Pearl spoke in a voice that Stone swore he had heard when elevator music was playing. He was barely visible in his overstuffed chair, along with his overstuffed ego.

"I'll do everything I can to help," he squeezed out of a mouth devoid of expression.

Orders thought Stone, someone's straight-lined this guy.

"Great," responded Stone, seating himself.

Kolb did likewise, not grinning, appearing self-absorbed, thought Stone. Stone knew Kolb was self-conscious around *ALAT* types, preferring cops and cop talk, beer bellies and belly dancers.

"It appears you'll be heading up north. Edinburgh, isn't it?" continued the ALAT.

"Yes, sir. We've traced Sternson to the University. We believe he's working in the chemistry department," said Stone.

"Right."

The ALAT glanced down at the file on his desk and pushed it toward Stone. "Well, it's all there. I hope you can make some sense of it."

Stone picked up the file, bulky, heavy.

"Have you arranged a contact?" asked Stone.

"A Captain William Stevenson of the Edinburgh Constabulary. It's in there. First page," he said diffidently.

Picking up the phone the ALAT punched in few numbers as Stone opened the file and began to read.

"Shelia, I'll send them out. Assist them in their travel arrangements. That's right. There will be two," he said and then hung up.

Rising, the ALAT looked at his watch, as if he was late for a blind date.

"Ah, I'm a little behind. A meeting with the Embassy Committee for . . . well, you know how it is," he said, a half-grin forming.

Kolb rose to shake hands but the ALAT was halfway out of the door.

"Shelia will assist you further. Well, I'm off," he said, disappearing into the hallway, his gabardine sports jacket crinkled in his small hands.

Kolb stared at Stone, as if he were about to draw his piece and K-5 the ALAT.

"Do drop a line and let us know how you did up there. Edinburgh, right?" the ALAT screeched over his shoulder, a quizzical half-smile forming on his face this time, small and boyish.

And then he was gone. Kolb followed Stone through the door. Stone knew what Kolb was thinking. Knew Kolb was glad he was a cop, Chicago's finest. After that performance, Stone kind of wished he was a cop too.

CHAPTER 21

Royal Constabulary Police Headquarters,
Edinburgh, Scotland

"Next slide, please," said Captain Stevenson.

The room was crowded and the heat made the presentation difficult, especially since the air conditioning wasn't working properly. July in Scotland was usually comfortable, but an unaccustomed heat wave had swept in from the Continent and had deposited itself like a wayward uncle.

Stevenson's presentation, *The Criminology of Tattoos / Their Meanings and Identification*, had packed the small lecture hall. As the last slide appeared on the screen, a small man entered from the rear of the room and sat in the last remaining vacant seat.

"This last case I will discuss is by far one of the most interesting I have investigated," said Stevenson, as he focused his attention on the screen.

A forearm of a well-built, dark-skinned man was displayed. Centered on the top of the forearm was a tattoo, which consisted of two serpents entwined about a staff. The heads of the serpents were facing each other, each having a protruding tongue in the form of an arrow. One serpent's head was visibly larger than the other's. The protruding tongue of the larger serpent was wound around the smaller serpent's head. The tattoo was entirely colored red.

"Any ideas?" asked Stevenson.

Stone thought of Rivers, and then wondered what kind of tattoos adorned Sternson's body.

A detective sergeant from Bathgate, a small town located due west of Edinburgh, spoke up.

"Well, it looks like one of them snakes is tryin' to eat the other."

Stevenson hesitated and then moved on.

"Anyone else?"

A policewoman from the City of Glasgow raised her hand and was acknowledged.

"It looks like the color red is important. Blood and fire, as you spoke of earlier."

Stevenson waited and when there were no other responses, provided his analysis.

"What you are looking at is the forearm of a serial murderer who is no longer with us."

A slight rustle filtered through the room, then soft laughter. Gallows humor thought Stone, probably executed, the police subculture at work again.

"He was executed in the United States, Florida to be exact, earlier this year. We believe he was responsible for between ten and fifteen deaths, though he was only convicted of one."

One. That's all we need to fry Sternson. One. Rita. Stone's gaze wandered, catching Kolb fiddling with his pencil and paper, drawing something, rapt in thought, analyzing. When Kolb was onto something, he became cocoon-like.

Then the man in the back of the room caught Stone's attention. The man was leaning over his chair, intent on following Stevenson's presentation.

Stevenson continued, "The color *is* important. Yes, blood and fire come to mind, but more importantly, the concept of competing emotions is indicated here, deep emotions tearing apart the individual. Strong emotions, which oftentimes lead to unyielding and, oftentimes, violent behavior."

Violent images of Sternson unleashed invaded Stone's mind.

"In this particular case, these emotions manifested themselves in serial murder, all of the victims being young women between the ages of twenty and twenty-five."

Stone thought of the file prepared by the ALAT at his request, all unsolved murders within the past two years in the United Kingdom, all women, all young. The victim's were about Rita's age. Fifty-six victims made for a thick and heavy file.

"But the color itself can't always lead you to the identification of the suspect," said a large, portly officer, with unkempt, ruffled dirt-brown hair.

The officer was seated in the front row. His uniform, old and worn, didn't match anyone else's in the room. Probably some obscure village constable who'd been around for a while, thought Stone.

"Yes, alone the color is not indicative of a particular trait or habit, but must be considered along with the entire aspect of the tattoo. We must look to the remaining features of the tattoo, and couple the meaning of the color with the other symbols."

Stevenson pointed to the larger of the two serpents.

"Yes, it does appear that one serpent is devouring the other. Good over evil, or evil over good? Let us look first past the serpents themselves to the overall meaning of the design."

What type of *design* did Sternson choose? He had to have tattoos. Rivers did, swastikas, animals, *Born to fuck*, but what about Sternson? Kolb still fiddled, drawing something.

"Two serpents entwined around a branch or a wand depicts a caduceus, which has been known since 2,600 B.C. However, in a true caduceus, the serpents are of equal bearing and define a symmetrical relationship, unlike here. Here, the larger serpent is dominant. In a true caduceus, opposing forces, good and evil, are balanced and cancel each other out. A balanced duality, if you will. But here we are dealing with a bastardized caduceus where the forces of good and evil are . . . out of kilter. Evil is dominant over good. Self-control ceases to be a factor."

Kolb's hand shot up.

"Yes, our guest from America, is it? I was told you'd be attending. Mr. Stone or is it Detective Kolb?"

"Kolb, sir. But the meaning . . . he's out of control. That's what it means," said Kolb, smiling as if he'd discovered relativity.

"Exactly. Out of control and bent upon violence."

Another arm was raised, as Kolb, sketching, slouched down in his chair.

An elderly man in a three-piece suit identified himself and spoke.

"But how did you find him? I mean, I follow the analysis, but just how did you catch the sorry bastard?"

Subtle cop laughs permeated the auditorium.

"Further analysis of the tattoo is necessary. The caduceus is presently used as an insignia of the Catholic Bishop of Ukraine. This fact alone directed me to look for someone having a relationship to Ukraine. As it turned out, the murderer, whose forearm you are viewing, is one Josef Brusilovski, a Ukrainian immigrant to the United States. Brusilovski was employed as a caretaker at a Ukrainian monastery located in St. Augustine, Florida. Several of the murders occurred in the St. Augustine area. One victim who had escaped had given a description of her assailant, along with a description of the tattoo you are now viewing. This information, along with other evidence, mostly circumstantial in nature, assisted us in profiling the murderer and ultimately leading us to the monastery."

Where would Sternson lead them? Stone wondered, as Stevenson nodded to the attendant and the screen went blank.

"That concludes my presentation and I thank you for your attentiveness," said Stevenson.

As the hall began to empty, Stone and Kolb approached the podium where Stevenson remained. Kolb's sketchpad was tucked under his arm. But the man who had entered late remained in the rear of the hall.

Stevenson was gathering up his materials as the little man approached, sweeping past Stone and Kolb, his hand held tightly to his breast.

"Excuse me, sir. Please," he begged.

He was a fragile little man, and looked as if he would break in two if someone dropped him. His hands were delicate and soft, like a woman's; certainly not workman's hands. No, the little man worked in a bank counting money and deposit slips, thought Stone. In his late fifties, or thereabouts, his frail face beseeched Stevenson for answers.

"Yes," simply said Stevenson, looking up, somewhat perplexed.

"Sir, I know I was not invited. I'm not a constable or anything like that," the little man panted.

Used to dealing with police detectives, not civilians, thought Stone, as he focused on Stevenson's face, which was devoid of emotion.

The small man collapsed in a nearby chair, catching his breath. He spoke rapidly, as if the hourglass was about to be turned over.

"But I just thought you could help me. I read about your presentation in the newspaper. I need your help. Please . . ."

Distraught and losing his composure, the little man slumped into a ball, his wrinkled tweed suit so out of place on such a warm day. He began to sob in little gasps that reminded Stone of a small child.

"If I can help you, I will," reassuringly said Stevenson. "But what is it *exactly* that I can do for you?"

Reaching into his coat pocket, the little man removed a small, discolored envelope, which, it appeared, he had been carrying with him for some time. He handed the envelope to Stevenson who removed the contents, two photographs.

Stevenson froze. The expression on his face reminded Stone of man who had lost his car keys. He hesitated, pondering the photographs, before addressing Stone.

"Mr. Stone, maybe you can make something of these. I would have preferred a more formal introduction, but . . . here we are," Stevenson said, as he handed the two photographs to Stone.

The first photograph was of a young woman, possibly in her twenties, having blonde hair and blue eyes, and being fairly attractive. It appeared to be a student I.D. from the University of Edinburgh. Stone studied it for a moment and then handed it to Kolb. The second photograph was particularly striking. It appeared to be the same girl, but this was a crime scene photograph, which showed her dead. At least Stone presumed it was her. The corpse was headless, like Rita. On the small of her back was a tattoo of some sort that Stone could not quite make out.

"Your daughter?" asked Stone.

The little man nodded, wiping his tears on his sleeves. Turning his reddened face up toward Stone, he implored with painful eyes.

"Will you help me?"

CHAPTER 22

Royal Constabulary Police Headquarters,
Edinburgh, Scotland

Alone in the small interview room, Stone immersed himself in the file of Mary Agnes Robinson provided to him by Captain Stevenson. Kolb had volunteered to run down some leads at the University to determine if Sternson was employed there, trying to corroborate information Kolb had obtained from the University of Chicago, Sternson's last employer in the U.S.A. Stone agreed, needing privacy to sort out the mess that was Mary Agnes Robinson. The file itself was not nearly as thick as the one given to him by the ALAT, which Stone had pushed off to the side. And this was as good a place to start as any, with Mary Agnes Robinson, just another unsolved murder.

The file contained only four photographs, including the one Stone had previously been given by her father, now known to Stone by the name Sean Robinson. The remaining three photographs showed different angles of the wooded crime scene where Mary Agnes' body had been discovered. Setting the photographs to the side, Stone began reviewing the background section of the file.

The body had been discovered by two hunters two days after Christmas of last year. It was a wooded area located approximately halfway between Bathgate and Edinburgh. Hunters, Stone thought, why was it always hunters? Secluded dumpsites, wooded areas, and hunters . . . dumpsites, hold that thought. Just like Rita, killed somewhere else and dumped at another location. Stone read on, his mind cycling the information of Rita and Mary Agnes on the same wheel of despair. Looking for similarities, links to a killer. The body was nude, and almost completely intact, except that the head had been severed from the body and remained missing. The body, lightly covered with brush, appeared to have been left in haste by the killer. There were no signs of sexual assault on the body, and forensics was negative for hairs and fibers. *He* was very careful, reasoned Stone, almost in a scientific sort of way. Neither seminal fluids, nor DNA was detected, and the search of the crime scene was negative. Time of death was estimated at 24-48 hours prior to discovery, based primarily on the fact that the body appeared fully intact, having only moderate discoloration, and little evidence of carnivore activity.

She could have been murdered on Christmas, Stone thought. Significant? Maybe? Maybe nothing? Rivers, tattoos, Sternson . . . no solid connection, not yet anyway.

Stone read further. Positive identification of the body was made by the victim's father, Sean Robinson, a self-employed jeweler / antique dealer, and former bank teller from Dunvegan, Isle of Skye. Mary Agnes Robinson was listed as Sean's only daughter, age twenty-two, and a second year nursing student at the University of Edinburgh.

Stone grabbed the bulky file provided by the ALAT and pulled it toward him. Its weight reminded him of the gravity of the situation at hand. Thumbing through the index he searched for Mary Agnes' name. Nothing, how peculiar, he thought. It appeared the ALAT missed this one. Were there others or was this just chance luck that they had stumbled onto Sean Robinson, or him onto them? Luck and police work, they were married in an odd sort of way. Yes, luck was involved with police work and Stone, for some inexplicable reason, began to feel lucky.

Stone continued reading the small file. There was some minor evidence of postmortem damage to the hands and feet by small carnivores, probably scavengers. The cause of death was listed as blunt trauma to the back of the neck and spinal cord area. A small cylindrical wound at the base of the neck, just above the shoulder blades, was noted. The manner of death, it was further postulated, could have resulted from a sharp, cylindrical object, like an ice-pick. The mode of death was concluded to be homicide.

Stone continued to thumb through the file until he came upon the section marked *miscellaneous*. There, the tattoo was described. It was located centrally in the area of the small of her back. It was described as a half-moon, blue in color, surrounded by the numbers 6, 7, and 8, all of which were colored red. A handwritten note in the margin of the file indicated that the tissue surrounding the tattoo appeared recently traumatized, indicating that the tattoo was recent.

How recent, thought Stone? Did the killer place this on her after the murder? Or was it more bizarre, possibly occurring *during* the murder? Or did she have it before, maybe some sorority prank? Too many unanswered questions, the prominent one being, why was this case absent from the ALAT's file? And why hadn't Stevenson, an expert in tattoo analysis, been called to render an analysis? After all, this was Stevenson's own backyard. Somebody had dropped the ball.

Stone closed the file, but continued to look at the crime scene photographs. They all showed the same thing, a bludgeoned to death nude woman, lying among leaves and branches, and having a strange tattoo on her back.

Stone gently placed the photographs back into the file jacket, noting that on the cover the file was marked, *Unsolved: Pending-Inactive*. The investigator assigned to the case was listed as Detective Sergeant John Reamington, Homicide Unit, Bathgate Royal Police.

It was now July and unseemingly warm, but the murder had occurred in December when it was cold. Almost seven months and no leads, it wasn't looking good. But there was that damned tattoo, and tattoos had meanings. But what hidden meanings did the curious tattoo hold? What was it keeping back, hidden in its colors and numbers? Maybe the investigators had missed something at the crime scene, something the spring thaw may have revealed that nobody took the time to look for. Too many new cases, not enough manpower, there were always excuses. But something was surely there, waiting for an epiphany. Maybe nothing on the surface, but it was worth a try. Stone needed to go to the crime scene. And he needed to go with Detective Sergeant John Reamington.

CHAPTER 23

Shearington Forest, Bathgate, Scotland

"There," said Reamington, pointing to a spot just a few yards in front of them.

Stone stared and then focused where Reamington was pointing.

"That's where she was found."

It was a flat area. A small brook meandered through the place in the shape of a lazy *L*. The brook was a sickly greenish color, with streaks of brown appearing slightly below the surface. It was rather shallow, and in spots the shale bottom was visible. One side of the brook had a steep bank. It was rock-filled, the other side was flat and littered with fallen leaves and tree limbs. An occasional, odd-shaped, moss-covered rock was visible near the spot where Reamington stood.

Glancing at the greenish muck, Stone surmised that one could easily navigate it. Perhaps that's what the killer did . . . to get the body to this point. He glanced down at the silent ground, beseeching it with sad eyes to give up its secrets.

Above them the canopy almost fully enclosed the site. A large, oval-shaped boulder, several feet in height and having the diameter of a small sitting room, jutted out at the point where the brook disappeared into the thicket of woods. It was located at the far end of the crime scene. The boulder was covered with red-brown moss and was completely shaded. Mushrooms were growing there. The boulder's reflection graced the surface of the stillborn stream, resembling a whale with its mouth open. Several other rocks jutted out at various angles, orphans from some long ago landslide, and littered the raised streambed that led to the boulder. It gave Stone the impression that he was inside of a pinball machine. The rocks were speckled with mucus-colored moss and blue-green fungi, and resembled turtles' heads, which pointed directly across the brook to where Reamington was standing.

"We searched everywhere. Couldn't find it . . . her head. Excuse me, her skull. Didn't find a bloody thing. Of course, it was winter then and there were spots of snow on the ground. Not much, but certainly quite different than . . . here. No footprints either, just not enough snow, only a spattering. We get it every Christmas."

Reamington continued to survey the ground below his boots, as if he expected to find something. He was uniformed, his gold sergeant stripes gleaming in the trickle of sunlight that purloined its way through the canopy. Larger than Stone, and quite a bit younger, Reamington still exhibited an enthusiasm for the chase that so many others in their profession had lost.

"The scene must have looked considerably different then," remarked Stone, focusing on the large boulder.

"Quite different. Yes, sir."

"None of these around," said Stone, as he kicked his boot in the direction of Reamington.

A small cricket, the color of ochre, was propelled from the toe of Stone's boot. It landed where Reamington stood. Righting itself, the cricket continued on its journey.

"No, sir. Certainly none of them."

Stone wasn't listening, losing himself in the crime scene, imagining. He was now standing next to Reamington, absorbing what the scene would tell him, slowly, methodically, like a connoisseur considering a rare wine, first smelling the bouquet, then swirling the glass, and finally tasting. Slowly, ever so slowly . . . the scene was now giving up some secrets. Stone smelled death . . . felt the pain. His soul filled with anxiety and fear, as he knew he was close; living it, as *they* had and dying it, as *she* did. The killer and the victim, good and evil, the guilty and the innocent, blended into a myriad of thoughts and suppositions. Seeing, hearing, interpreting, all was eerily quiet. Stone was endeavoring to get to that place that few ever ventured. The killer's mind taunted him to enter.

Stone's train of thought was derailed by the crackling sound above him. A crow, the size of a small cat, was perched in an ash tree directly over Reamington. Its beak, shaped like a fishhook, held something. Stone couldn't make it out. It was small and was quickly gone, down the crow's mouth. Its existence ended as surely as Mary Agnes' had on that December day. The crow was flying now, wings spread, floating like dead leaves in a gentle breeze. It rose above the canopy, hung motionless, and then disappeared.

Reamington looked up, and then across at Stone.

"Funny thing, isn't it? One of those was here when we found her."

What did the crow know? What had it seen? This place knew, and it would tell Stone.

Stone circled the area where Mary Agnes was found. Using a large tree branch, he disturbed the forest debris that carpeted the ground. He knew that what he was looking for would not be here; not here at the *drop-site*, but he needed familiarization, a point-of-reference. Circling in the opposite direction, he began again to drink in the contents of the scene like a thirsty traveler. Reamington was saying something, but Stone wasn't listening. The crime scene was communicating with him, belching up bits and pieces in a chaotic dance, directing him, teasing him and ultimately confessing.

Reamington stood motionless, his hands clasped behind his back, as if he were at parade rest. The temperature suddenly dropped, giving Stone a chill as he made his way toward the large boulder, away from the dumpsite, maybe a new crime scene, or an extension of the original. Reamington shifted, his eyes following Stone's movements, like those of a seamstress sewing a silk dress.

The large boulder almost shut off the flow of the brook. A small trickle of greenish scum made its way in and out of ruts and crannies that formed the streambed. The ground was flat here, good for lying down, resting, watching, remembering. The ground at Stone's feet was littered with dead things, mostly plants. But some insect casings were strewn about near a small hole where some animal lived.

Using his branch, Stone began to flick the dead leaves about. Leaning his arms on the slippery topside of the boulder, he felt that he was at the right place. Sensing something, Stone peered at the spot where Reamington stood, and then crouched behind the boulder for safety. This *was* the location. There was something malevolent about it. He felt it inside of his gut, like an intruder. Here, the event could be relived, time and time again, the morbid fantasy absorbed into the sociopath's musings, like a towel wiping up a spill. The actual dumpsite was too open, too exposed. But this spot insured safety, seclusion, privacy. The killer could come and go and not disturb the dropsite, just in case someone like Stone came back looking for clues. No, no one would look *here*, a safe distance away. Months after the murder who would look here? No one, except the person who understood, except Stone.

"Mr. Stone, how much longer? The temperature is dropping. Could be rain on the way," yelled Reamington, now sitting on a flat rock, pulling up his collar.

Before Stone could respond, the crow was back. Above Stone, hovering, cawing, cackling, as if to tell him that he was right. Its blackness was stark and depressing. Its penetrating eyes resembled small, red ink blots. This black cat of the sky hung motionless in mid-air as Stone tried to relive the scene.

Back, back, back, deeper in thought, trancelike, the vision came to him. *He* watched from here, after it was over. And then again months after that, several times maybe, but certainly he had returned. Crouching here, resting here, he had pleasured himself *here* as the fantasies had returned; pleasured himself as he had when he had killed her. He had felt relief here, and safety. Stone disturbed more ground with the branch, first, slowly, and then more vigorously. Something *is* here. The crow knows. Stone looked up, but the bird was gone. The sky, ever darkening, implored Stone to get on with it. Then, near some beetle carcasses, he saw it. Then more, several discolored . . . somethings stared up at him. Stone leaned down and smelled. Removing his buck-knife from his back pocket, he probed with it, speared the thing and then brought it to nose level. The faint odor of cannabis lingered on darkened paper. It was a small find, but then more of the same. The sweet smell of marijuana, remnants of a killer, pieces to a puzzle, the smell of death was back.

"Mr. Stone!" yelled Reamington.

Stone looked up over the boulder.

"I'll be right down."

The crow circled above, its wings like mainsails.

"Find anything?" asked Reamington, spying the small plastic bag Stone clutched.

"Yes," Stone said, holding up the evidence bag. "He's a smoker, marijuana and maybe something else. We need to get this to the lab."

Reamington's face resembled a spent cartridge as he took the bag from Stone.

"I'll take care of it right away," he said, appearing embarrassed for having missed finding the evidence.

Stone paid no mind, was drifting again, trying to make the pieces fit. But there were too many round holes, and too many square pieces. Where was *her* skull? Where was *Rita's* skull? Maybe . . . with *him*. Maybe with Sternson.

Stone looked up. The crow, once a solitary sentinel, was now joined by several of its friends.

"Better check and see what Kolb came up with," Stone said, pondering the possibility of similar *M.O.'s*.

Stone looked up. The sky was empty.

CHAPTER 24

University of Edinburgh, Pembrooke Hall,
Chemistry Laboratory

He stood above the Bunsen burner, the yellow-orange flame inviting him in. Drawing him ever closer, as the heat radiated against the jagged scars on his face, nurturing them. Adjusting the height of the flame, the orange color yellowed, matching his irises. They were one now, the flame and his eyes. Pinpoints of despair set in a sea of gloom, his eyes danced and flickered in and out of a reality he had created; a reality he endured, but strayed from time and again. Taking the straight glass rod, he placed it at the zenith of the flame, the hottest part. Twirling it rhythmically, he removed it, and with the motion of a gymnast, bent it. The glass responded, forming itself into the shape he desired, a perfect *V*, a match for the scar below his left eye, self-inflicted. He placed the glass rod on the lab bench in front of him. Hot glass was to be respected. The pain it inflicted was infinite and wonderful. He speculated for a moment on the pain, his surroundings fading into a cloudless vision of delight, encompassing him. Alone with the pain, he touched the glass. Exhilarated, the blister formed in seconds. He watched the redness grow to the sharpness he coveted, emanating from the center of the burn like crystals growing. He was amused, the pain a fleeting friend. But it would return again, his confidant in his life's work.

He took clean white gauze from the first-aid kit and covered the burn, then taped it. An annoyance, but it would heal in time. The pain would be remembered infinitely . . . and cherished.

He often thought about the others. How they reacted to the pain. Not like him, some begged. Others wept, whimpering like small, insecure children. Many screamed hysterically. There were many, if he included all the animals. And there would be many more, hopefully, he thought.

He never tried to understand it all. The meaning of evil was for the *so-called* professionals, the doctors and criminologists, and of course, the police. He knew they would catch him at some point. The impulses were too great now, and came too often. He had become less cautious over the past few months, more daring. Possibly it was a death wish, but daring was more rewarding, the high more stimulating, and less fleeting, like burned flesh. Rita Suarez invaded his thoughts. Remembering, he got aroused. Yes, that was quite an evening. It was picture perfect. Billy saw to that.

Ah, Billy boy, and his idea of luring Rita to his apartment. Billy hated her father and wanted revenge. Billy got her there but *he* did the rest. Or most of the rest after Billy was done with her. And the dumpsite was Billy's idea, Wolff Lake, their old stomping grounds when they were teenagers. The well where they had dumped all those dead cats, that was Billy's idea. The cats Billy had set on fire and the dogs he had bludgeoned to death were there too, tongueless. Billy did that. He understood the beauty of the blade even then. The tongues were part of it, a kind of rite of passing from one level to the next. Again Billy's idea, and once ingested, Billy said, they would have the ability to communicate with animals and control them. It was all about control, then and now. *Control.* He really didn't believe it, but felt that the idea had some merit, at least as far as bonding with Billy was concerned.

Dead dogs, dead cats, oh, yes, he had come a long way since those days. The others included in his journey darted in and out of his psyche like a wobbling strobe light, Karla, the redhead from Maine, the twin sisters from Champaign and his favorite, Rita from Chicago. But then there was Mary Agnes, right here from Scotland, his birthplace. Yes, they were all with him now.

Certain events, he knew, were seared in his memory and aroused by specific stimuli, like the smell of burning flesh. He looked at his bandaged hand, imagining the scar that would form underneath. He remembered the tongues of the dogs that he had eaten, burned black, coffin black, and roasting on a stick over a fire built near the well. Yes, Billy's well and Rita's grave. He would go back there again but not now. They would never find her. She was with the dogs and cats, forever entombed.

Too bad Billy was back in jail. But Billy was careless, would always be incarcerated somewhere, for something, the result of too many drugs. But *he* would not be that careless, at least not yet.

He turned down the flame. It faded away slowly into the hollow tube, disappearing into nothingness. Gathering up the odds-and-ends that lay on the lab bench, he reflected on the time. Class would begin promptly in one hour. He needed to prepare the lab for the lecture. His mop and bucket awaited him.

Exiting the lab, he flicked off the light. The taste remained in his mouth, a distant memory. Salty, dog tongues always tasted salty.

CHAPTER 25

University of Edinburgh, Administration Building, Office of Employment

"Sorry, he's not employed here," she said brusquely, her back to Kolb.

She was a short, stout woman, with a face that looked like the inside of an empty closet. Her ears were floppy and sagged like dough improperly kneaded. Her ruddy complexion was in stark contrast to her milk-white arms, probably too much booze, or not enough. Either way she was a real man-hater. Too many failed relationships, it was in her eyes and in the lines on her face, which Kolb read like a cheap magazine. The lines intertwined, forming a spider-web of abuse. Her eyes were marble-like, black and devoid of compassion.

"When did he leave?" asked Kolb.

"Like I said, he doesn't work here and never has," she quipped, her back still turned, filing something.

Kolb was immune to man-haters, had met them routinely doing police business. And this one, maybe a little coddling might work.

"Well, I'm sure a woman like you has a good memory for details and figures. And not a bad figure, yourself," Kolb lied, trying, but not too hard.

Not turning, she continued to talk directly into the file cabinet where she busied herself.

"December, last year, the end of the term, it was. Just before Christmas, we received his application. But he never showed up for the interview. I never met him, just saw his picture," she said, turning slightly, a half-smile on her face.

Kolb thought, yes, more coddling.

"Well, that was his loss . . . not getting to meet you, I mean."

"And he left no forwarding information either. No friends were listed. No associates, just his references from his former employer. But you know that already, the University of Chicago. That's all it says here," she said, waving a 3x5 card at eye-level. "Didn't even enter it in the computer."

"No local address? Nothing around here? He had to live somewhere."

"Just this," she said, handing Kolb the 3x5 card, her fat fingers touching his.

Her fingers were rough, like a miner's. Not much tenderness there, but that could be fixed. Fixed, if he needed more information.

A small passport-type photograph was taped to the back of the card. It was Sternson alright. It matched identically to the photograph Kolb had viewed in the University of Chicago file. He was even wearing the same shirt. Typed on the front of the card was an address.

"Last known address," she said, pointing to the card. "That's police talk. Used to date me a constable once." She winked, her sagging eyelids clamping down suture-like over the black marbles.

Before Kolb could thank her she was gone. He looked down at the card and the address. Bathgate, interesting, Stevenson should know. He checked his watch, 11:00 o'clock. Stevenson should be back from the Chemistry Department soon, having checked out that angle. Bathgate, hmm, interesting.

CHAPTER 26

14 Regishire Way, Bathgate, Scotland

It wasn't much of a house, a small cottage at best. Rundown with broken shutters, the eaves were askew, twisted from the wind, no doubt. It was isolated from the surrounding, far-off buildings by large trees, and difficult to see from the road. It stood like an errant sentry, set back from where the mailbox stood about a hundred yards or so. It beckoned them like a lonely vagrant looking for a handout, desolate and tired. A strange place to live, reasoned Kolb. As they made their way down the dirt path, the wind picked up, swaying the trees rhythmically, sensually, in cadence to the whistling tinny sound emanating from the drooping eaves. Kolb felt the eerie presence of stale air, felt the heat from the sun beating down on them as they approached the cottage. Stevenson, prodding slowly, led the way, his gun-hand gently flipping back his coat, exposing the butt of his revolver. Kolb, unarmed, followed. Damn these laws. Kolb felt naked.

"We've no warrant," Stevenson said, eyeing Kolb cautiously. "We just want to have a little chat with the bloke."

Kolb nodded, knowing the extradition warrant for Sternson would arrive soon. Feeling a little ill at ease for not having checked in with Stone first, Kolb followed gingerly in step behind Stevenson. Kolb's trepidation dissipated as they climbed the front stairs. This was Stevenson's jurisdiction anyway.

They stopped at the front door. No activity. Deserted, thought Kolb, then the creaking of old lumber and the occasional hum of bees, their hive somewhere under the porch. The smell of the air had a strangeness to it, as Stevenson braced the cottage door.

Stevenson whispered, "Looks empty. Like no one's been here for a while."

Kolb glanced at his watch, 12:00 o'clock sharp.

"I'll give it a bit of nudge. See if anything happens," said Stevenson, his grip on the butt intensifying.

The door was not locked, and swung on its hinges like a tired gymnast on the uneven bars, as Stevenson's slight push jarred it. Sunlight struggled through its splintered surface, dust motes dancing in and out of the disjointed light. Another push and the door was fully opened. The light from behind them formed a funnel on the ground, exposing rotted boards. The planking on the porch, mildewed and spongy, sucked in Kolb's feet, as the bees hummed. Stevenson was inside now. Kolb followed, creeping softly, as if not to wake the dead that awaited them. Empty, not a stick of furniture. There, in front of them, on the floor, lay an old rug, matted and covered with discolored animal hair. Kolb kicked at it. It moved slightly. Kolb kneeled down as Stevenson approached from out of the dark, shining a small flashlight on the rug. Kolb grabbed the frayed ends and lifted, the odor of damp decay assaulted his face. Under the rug was a door with a handle. A cellar of some sort, thought Kolb. Stevenson edged closer. Removing his revolver from his belt, Stevenson caught Kolb's stare. Stark. Intense.

"You give her a yank, and I'll point," said Stevenson, as the business end of the service revolver pointed over Kolb's shoulder.

Kolb grasped the handle of the door, thought of Stone and pulled hard. The door was up, dust floating everywhere, on his clothes, in his eyes. Stevenson was wiping the detritus from his own eyes when the first dart hit him, square in the middle of his forehead. Stevenson was down, paralyzed, the drug taking effect immediately. Not moving, his bulky torso hindered Kolb, as he searched for the revolver. The air was muffled and fetid, vacuum-like, as the second dart found its mark in the back of Kolb's neck. The two bodies lay together, entwined in some type of macabre dance, a tango of death, motionless, yet embracing.

The square, black hole to the cellar was lit only by faint red pinpoints, the tired eyes of the sociopath. They reflected crimson light, absorbing all other colors of the spectrum like a greedy scavenger. They appeared as tiny dots, approaching out of the gloom, pulsating with relentless contempt. Growing wider, swollen with hatred, fear was their copious companion. Kolb struggled vainly to rise. His limbs were lifeless, dead weight. The circles of despair were darkly crimson now, fiery, and near Kolb's face. Hot, fetid breath assaulted him. Kolb saw the scars . . . the scars . . . the scars . . .

CHAPTER 27

14 Regishire Way, Bathgate, Scotland

Kolb awoke to pitch black. The effects of the curare were wearing off but his legs and arms felt like heavy iron. He lay flat on his back on a table of some sort. Hard. Wooden. His thumb and forefinger scratched the surface looking for answers. The feeling was coming back into his hands. Slowly. He heard groaning. Stevenson?

Kolb's eyes searched the blackness. He strained toward the murmuring. Saw nothing, the darkness cloaking him like an insensitive coffin. He could not penetrate the colorless void. He tried to speak but was cotton-mouthed. Nauseous. Remembering, clouded images scattered themselves aimlessly in the deep crevices of his mind. The pieces did not fit together at first. But then . . . the cottage. The concealed entrance to the cellar. The sharp, cutting pain in the back of his neck. And the face . . . the scars. Sternson.

Kolb was thinking clearly now, Stevenson's groaning his only companion in this dark sepulcher of hopelessness. Then a creaking sound above and scratching, like rats scurrying across a wooden floor. A swath of light cut through the darkness. Growing wider. The trapdoor was open now. Legs descending. The light hurt Kolb's eyes. How long he'd been down here, he could only guess. He squinted but his eyes were desert dry. More light. The tread of heavy steps getting louder.

The light was on Kolb's face. Then away from him. Onto Stevenson strapped to a wooden table. Like him. But Stevenson was unconscious, breathing irregularly. The light was back on Kolb, clinging to his face like frozen rain. Then clinking, metal on metal. Keys? Louder as the footsteps approached. Then grinding. Kolb could see clearly now, as Sternson sat on an overturned bucket, a lantern on the floor beside him. Sternson was massaging the blade on a whetstone in a circular motion. Soft, rhythmical grinding. The light reflected off of the blade and onto Kolb's face.

The cutting edge was close to Kolb's neck. Next to his face. The light danced off the serrated metal, as Kolb saw his reflection imprisoned on its surface. It blinded him momentarily, as the blade touched his chin. Cold. Hard. He thought, the end. He felt the air move upward as the blade was lifted. Darkness around him as the light found Stevenson. The swift, heavy blow struck just below Stevenson's chin. A clean cut. A muffled thud, like ice breaking, as the axe found its mark. Stevenson's head rolled away, as if it no longer belonged to his body. It rolled, Kolb thought, forever. Until it fell off of the table, hitting the soft, damp dirt floor with a squish, like a melon being squeezed too hard.

The light was in his face again. And then Sternson spoke. Guttural, rough tones, like marbles rolling over broken glass.

"I hope you'll do better than your friend. He told me nothing I didn't already know. No use for him now."

A noise. The swish of a leg kicking stagnant air. Sternson's heavy boot hitting Stevenson's head with full force. The head propelled into the darkness, lost from sight, hitting a wall.

"It's your turn now. Detective Kolb, isn't it? Or so, Constable Stevenson said."

Kolb tried to talk but couldn't. His mouth was dry. His stomach nauseated. A cup of water was poured on his face. Cold. He licked violently, attempting to get the droplets in his mouth. Some relief now. The words began to form slowly. His jaw hurt as he coughed them out, and sucked in stale air.

"Sternson . . ." he stuttered.

"I must apologize for the curare. Bamboo curare to be specific. It's a muscle relaxant, but in potent quantities it can paralyze and be quite deadly. I happened to make your dart a little stronger than his," he said, pointing to the darkness where he had kicked Sternson's head. "That's why you were out longer."

Kolb tried again, but the words would not form.

"Well, Detective, you tracked me here, all right. I congratulate you for that. Good work. I suppose you want to know who I *am*? Hmmm?" he said as the axe blade fell. Cool air engulfed Kolb's face, as the blade embedded itself in the wooden table next to Kolb's chin.

"Any more questions?" he laughed. An ugly, deep, spastic laugh.

The sweat on Kolb's face pooled erratically, forming lakes of exhaustion. Kolb had vomited when the blade hit the table. Sweating profusely and covered in vomitus, he tried to clear his throat, spitting blood, choking on dead air.

"What . . . what do you want?"

The words formed slowly, crippled by fear.

"Just simple answers. Simple answers to simple questions," he said, schoolboy-like.

Kolb was muttering incoherently, struggling to mask the fear. Fear his enemy. Sternson's back was to him now. Dark and large. Moving away into the darkness. Kolb struggled to free himself. More feeling in his arms and legs. But, still . . . useless. Rattling, clinking from the darkness. Coming closer. Louder, like *things* moving. Quick movements, scurrying, small animal noises. Louder now. Closer. The light was blinding him again. In his eyes. The heat from the lantern fell on his face with malice. The odor was closer. Overpowering. The nausea returned in waves as he saw the cage.

It was metal and rectangular. One side was completely solid, having no bars. Inside, three, maybe four . . . *rats*! The acrid smell of feces and urine violated his senses. The incessant scratching, jumping. Some on hind legs. Some biting metal, each other. Long, ugly tails. Snakelike, whipping back and forth. Hungry.

"Ahhh . . ." Kolb muttered, as Sternson pulled Kolb's shit away from his body, exposing the flesh of his soft belly.

Then the excruciating cold of metal on flesh. Freezing. Penetrating. Icelike. The solid side of the metal cage was placed on his stomach. Then clamped down onto the table, as if it had been used there before. For this . . . this what?

"My friends will help interrogate you," laughed Sternson, almost convulsing.

The rats prodded, ever restless, scrambling hideously for an opportunity. The stench from the cage floated in the lifeless air in layers, encompassing Kolb's face, causing him to choke, dry-heaving as he searched for words. The vomitus stuck in his throat. Silence. But Sternson wasn't listening anyway. He appeared consumed with his *friends*.

The light was now on one of Sternson's hands. A rope of some sort. No, an electrical cord. It hung loosely in his grasp. He played with it, as if it was the tail of a kite. The light assaulted Kolb's face as Sternson spoke. Low, dreamlike.

"Did Billy talk? Did he tell you anything about *me?*"

"Billy who?" Somehow the words came out. Half-formed.

"Yes, Detective. Billy Rivers. Did he confess? That's what you were doing with him all that time, wasn't it? Getting him to confess? The interrogation of Billy Rivers?"

Silence. Muffled air. Rats moving but Kolb didn't hear it any more. Kolb was a dead man and he knew it. The inevitability hit him like a sucker punch on a Saturday night. Time floated endlessly as Kolb prepared himself. Reaching inward to the only place he knew. The Army, Special OP's, had taught him that. Back to his childhood. Memories of his father. A good man, a charitable man. Hardworking, a steelworker from the mills in Joliet. Baseball on Sundays at Kiwanis Park near the mill. Pancake breakfasts with the Boy Scouts. Other things. Things Sternson wouldn't understand. Fishing for carp near Braidwood. Him and his dad. Good times. Long ago.

Kolb was drifting now. Thinking of the Police Academy. His good friend, Rusty. Dead now. Saved his life during a live-fire drill when another cadet's gun jammed. The rounds just missed Kolb as Rusty dove, pushing him down. Taking the rounds meant for Kolb. Good ol' Rusty. Loved his beer too. Drifting, drifting, more thoughts. More memories. His first wife. It was his fault. Too many late nights out with the boys. It happened to all cops. But it happened to him too often. She was happy now and that's what mattered. He was calm now. Getting to that special place where they couldn't hurt him. Drifting. In another world. Not thinking about Sternson. Sternson didn't exist. Time was irrelevant to Kolb. Time didn't exist.

"Damn you," he said, flicking the switch on the small generator.

The sound of the generator gently hummed in Kolb's ears as he floated. Floated backward in time. Backward . . . backward . . . .

The cage began to radiate heat as the rats scrambled up and down the metal bars. One trying to cling to the top, upside-down, clinging with all fours. Kolb was jolted back to reality as the heat intensified, causing red blotches to form on his stomach. The pain pulled him back to the present. To now. To Sternson.

The solid metal door was removed, exposing Kolb's stomach. The rats scrambled for a way out of their heated prison, finding solace in Kolb's flesh. They were biting now. Eating through Kolb's stomach. Biting at each other. Flesh and blood everywhere. Biting as they went. Inward. Fresh meat. Raw and bloody. Away from the heat. Kolb's screams drowned out the gentle humming of the generator as Sternson turned up the heat switch.

Sternson moved away. Into the darkness. Returned with an oblong container. Another metal box. Took one last look at Kolb, and began making his way toward the stairs.

Kolb shrieked, "Rot in hell, asshole!"

Sternson looked back as the rats frantically ate their way out. Smiled. Looked away, toward the stairs. Toward daylight. Up there. A daylight Kolb would never see again. The box was heavy. After all, it contained five heads.

CHAPTER 28

4330 South Dresden Avenue, Apartment 3A, Chicago, Illinois

Special Agent Thomas Reynolds, a slender man with the personality of a curious docent, held the crime scene photos obtained from Rivers in his hand. Comparing, analyzing, looking for common ground. The colors on the walls didn't match, probably painted over. He'd have to scrape. The carpet in the photographs was an ugly green mess. It was hardwood floors now, as he looked down. Seepage from the carpet into the floor? Maybe. Probably not. Too much time had expired. Any of Rita's blood would have been contained in the carpet that was no longer here. Walls and floors, that's all Reynolds had to work with. Empty walls at that, and a carpet that didn't exist. At least not here. Not now. As for the creep in the photos, that was Stone's domain. Reynolds was here for the physical evidence. And there didn't appear to be much to go on. Best-case scenario was a fresh scene. This scene was years old. Needle in a haystack? Damn, this was a grain of sand on the beach.

"They's gonna' be back at 5:00, so's you best hurry it up. And the Missus said don't make no mess," said the building custodian, a short, drab man with the face of an old watch, and a tick-tock matter-of-factness about him.

He wore olive green overalls, like the *Boston Strangler* had, that dragged on the floor and covered his boots. His hands were large and fleshy. His clock-face sallow, as if he hadn't laughed in years. The pass-key for Sternson's former residence dangled from his left hand, swinging back and forth like a pendulum. Befitting for the clockman, thought Reynolds.

Looking up from the photos, Reynolds motioned for the team photographer. "Shoot the shit out of the place," he said.

Turning to the clockman Reynolds asked, "Has anyone lived here recently?"

"Peoples come 'n go, you knows. Noboby's livin' here right now. Them walls been empty for a while. I'm still cleanin' up, though. Fixin' to rent her out any day now. But some peoples moved in right after that guy yous been lookin' for. Sternson, ain't it? But they's gone now."

"What makes you think we're looking for anybody?"

"Word gets around. On the street. You know what I mean," he said.

Reynolds looked away. Thought of *Tinman*. Yeah, *Tinman* spouting off again. Trying to hit pay-dirt. Reynolds looked back at the clockman, the gentle tingling of his keys the only sound in the apartment.

"So what happened to the carpet, Mr. Johnson?"

"You's can call me Hank. Lookie here," he said, as he pointed to the embroidered name *Hank* on his shirt pocket.

"Okay, Hank." Reynolds waited as Hank shifted his weight, appearing embarrassed.

"The carpet, well . . . I didn't steal it or nothin'. Landlord, he told me get rid of it. So's I just yanked 'er up and threw 'er down yonder. You know, the basement," he said, pointing straight down toward the floor. "Was fixin' to use 'er at my summer place up north, now that the kids is all growed and all. Been plannin' to really fix the old place up. Hell, it was all stained and raggedy as hell, you know. Guess that's why Cowboy wanted it out."

"*Cowboy*?" asked Reynolds.

"Yeah, that's what I called him. You know with all them ropes and shit he had layin' around. Boots too. Leather stuff. Yeah, Cowboy liked that name. I gived it to him."

Reynolds was focused now. "What do you mean stained?"

"I'll show ya'. Ya' all can see fer yerselves. Went to hardwood floors after that. Sanded real nice like. Refinished too. Paid for it all hisself. Told me I could keep it, the carpet, I mean. Said he had a party and spilled all kindsa' stuff all over it. Beer, wine, food and all. Lotta' purple-like blotches and stuff on it. Told 'em I was gonna' clean it up real nice like. You knows how parties is," said Hank, real hillbilly like.

Parties? No, Reynolds didn't know. Reynolds worked evidence. And on his days off . . . Reynolds worked more evidence. But he nodded anyway, just to keep Hank in the fold.

"I need to take a look at it," said Reynolds, his 6'4 frame towering over the clockman.

The photographer continued his work, methodically going from one room to the next, as Hank led the way to the basement. The remaining ERT members followed in single file.

The basement smelled of diesel fuel and old newspapers. It was dark and musty, and the absence of light gave Reynolds the creeps. Reynolds was afraid of the dark as a kid, and, quite frankly, never outgrew it. But only Reynolds knew that, his skeleton in the closet, so to speak, and quite apropos for an evidence man, he thought.

"Over there," Hank pointed.

Hank's flashlight illuminated a large rolled-up carpet pressed against the cellar wall. Dust particles danced in the beams, as if beckoning Reynolds forward.

"Been meanin' to fix the light down here, but you know," he said.

Shit happens, thought Reynolds.

Beams from several flashlights from ERT members were now shinning on the carpet. Reynolds moved closer, his rabbit ears vertical, sensing the mother lode. Maybe, just maybe, they'd get lucky.

"Let's get it out of here," Reynolds ordered.

ERT members moved in and began the heavy lifting.

"We'll look at it downtown. If it appears promising, we'll send it back to the lab."

The carpet was covered with dust, but what was inside should be preserved, thought Reynolds. Not pristine after so many years, but still there was a chance. Bloodstains, semen, hair, spit, a roadmap of terror. The mosaic of a demented psychopath. Or was it a sociopath? Reynolds never could understand the difference. Reynolds worked the evidence; let the others work the criminal mind.

"Yeah, never got around to it. Too much goin' on with the Missus and kids. You know how it is," said Hank, his half-smile showing 4:00 o'clock.

Reynolds didn't know. Didn't really much care. Had what he came for, and that was that.

"Agent Jenkins, have our friend, Hank, sign the release form and waiver," said Reynolds, as he directed a flashlight just below Hank's chin, four o'clock changing to 9:15.

The grunts of the ERT men struggling with the bulky carpet filled the soundless void of the murder house, as the clockman signed with an X.

CHAPTER 29

3959 North Sedgewick Avenue, Chicago, Illinois

He sat alone as he often did, now that Rita was gone. His wife had died years earlier. Carcinoma of the liver, or so they had told him. It was ironic. She was a non-smoker and he enjoyed his pipe every night. The kind Freud smoked, a gift from a friend from Zurich. He tapped the stem of the pipe on the ashtray. Speckled flecks of charred *Sir Raleigh*, Rita's favorite blend, floated downward blanketing the table. Rita would scold him for his messiness, yet she loved the aroma. The tobacco pouch was half-open, its sharp aroma gently wafting toward him like a specter, her specter, as he cherished the memories. The pipe filled, he gently set it down, the aroma reinventing the image of her. Days past, gone forever.

Judge Antonio Suarez spent most of his evenings alone. Mostly reading, the Bible had become his nightly companion. He vowed to himself to read it until he understood. Understood how an all-knowing, all-loving, perfect God could take from him, first his wife, and then his only child. What had they done to merit such punishment, while he remained alive? The bitterness was past; however, and now it was the *understanding* that he coveted.

He placed his bible on the nightstand, its usual place. It was the *King James* version, handed down from his maternal grandfather. The black cover was almost gray now. Worn in heavy spots. He could almost see handprints where his grandfather had held it. Large hands. Strong hands. Worker's hand. His father was a *picker*, right out of *The Grapes of Wrath*. A poor, migrant worker from Sonora, who eventually made his way to Chicago, *the Promised Land*, searching for a better life.

The Judge placed his hands on the ghost prints, imagining. Tying to feel his grandfather's thoughts, his advice. Childish, of course, but he *wanted* to believe in miracles. A miracle was all that he really had left. And so he waited but . . . nothing. Just a worn out Bible and a worn out man.

Time and again he searched his mind for answers. What exactly *was* he searching for? Closure? He hated the sound of the word. Had heard it too many times in victim-impact statements. Revenge for her murder. Early on, yes. But now he sought only meaning. Peace. But that, he knew, would only come with the identification and capture of her murderer. Revenge returned with a vengeance, and revenge was in the Bible. He had memorized *Revelations 2:16*, and now he opened his Bible again to the page he had dog-eared. Found the glassine envelope containing several fronds of Rita's hair from childhood, and read the verse again. Remembering. Closing the black coffin, her hair was sealed deep inside, keeping companion to the verse. He would try again. Tomorrow.

His insignificance made him a prisoner of his thoughts. He struggled to comprehend, but the fronds of Rita's hair played on his senses, as if a conductor was incessantly tuning a viola. And soon the viola *was* tuned. The music sweet and soothing. Making him feel real again, as if she was with him. But he did not know . . . could not know the significance these simple fronds of hair would play in this murderous endgame.

CHAPTER 30

Chicago FBI Evidence Processing Room

The ugly, green carpet lay unrolled only halfway due to its size. Underneath was spread a clean sheet of butcher's paper to catch the debris. The photographer was again busy as Agent Reynolds called Stone.

Stone answered the call, as if roused from a deep sleep.

"Sorry about that," said Reynolds. "Forgot about the time change."

"Go ahead, Tom. I know you wouldn't have called unless you had something. Just tell me the good news." Stone was getting his bearings.

"Well, I'm staring at it right now. The carpet from the murder scene. I hope."

The news jolted Stone like a sucker-punch.

"Are you sure?" blurted out Stone.

"Pretty darn sure. We got lucky. The janitor at the building removed it at Sternson's direction. Put it in the basement and was planning to use it for himself. But he never got around to it, though. And now we have it. Dumb luck, I guess. It's the closest we'll get to a fresh scene. Stone, I think we have an opportunity here."

"Damn. How's it look?"

"We're photographing it right now. It's only half open. You know the size of our evidence room. We can't get it completely unrolled all at once. But from what I see, well, it looks like there's lots of discolored areas. Could be anything. Food, wine spills . . ."

"Blood?"

"Exactly . . . at least I hope so."

"Try the luminol."

"You read my mind, partner. We'll spray, and if we get a hit, we're sending the whole kit-and-caboodle back to the lab with an armed guard."

"Will the length of time be a factor?"

"Well, a fresh scene would be optimum, but . . . if blood is still there, we may be able to coax it out."

"Call me as soon as you know something. Either way."

"You got it," said Reynolds, as he closed his cell-phone and clipped it back on his belt.

Proceeding toward the gray, metallic evidence locker that housed the chemicals to prepare the luminol, Reynolds, a devout Catholic, prayed to Saint Anthony. *Good Saint Anthony, come around. Something's lost and must be found.*

Returning to the carpet, now lying half-exposed, its dull, greenish color reminding Reynolds of dying evergreens, he motioned the photographer to leave the room. Reynolds always worked alone. Moving quickly, Reynolds sprayed the carpet with the luminol mixture he had prepared; the photographer banished, but ready to take photographs of the after-effects, if needed. Reynolds knew that if he got a *hit* with the luminol application, the other half of the carpet need not be tampered with. It would go back to Quantico, signed, sealed and delivered by the ERT men who waited outside of the room.

Anticipation hung in the air like an early morning mist on a Canadian lake, as Reynolds sprayed. Flipping the light switch off, Reynolds waited in the somber gloom of darkness. If blood was present, the blue-green chemiluminescence would reveal itself in a matter of minutes. The colored patches, not necessarily indicative of blood, would indicate the presence of iron. And iron was contained in hemoglobin, and so Reynolds waited, knowing they would be only halfway home if he got a *hit*. But halfway was better than *no-way*.

Like fireflies in the night twinkling their golden light, areas of the carpet began to emit faint glows. But the glows were blue-green and Reynolds' heart almost pounded out of his chest, as if he had just won the lottery. Then more emissions. And then . . . a footprint appeared where only ugly, green had been. Large blotches and assorted pinpoints randomly developed, as Reynolds leaned back against the wall watching the chemistry of death recreated. The surface of the carpet was now aglow with a greenish-blue panorama of chemical magic, as Reynolds tapped on the door to indicate that he needed the photographer.

As the photographer began his systematic approach to preserving the mosaic of mayhem on film, Reynolds stepped back and considered the puzzle before him. Yes, he had his *hit*. And yes, they did get lucky. And as Stone always said, luck always *was* a part of it. And Stone was usually right. Looking down again at the colorful emissions that, on another day might remind him of glowworms and fireworks, he considered the possibilities. Blood? Maybe. But whose blood? Now it was up to the lab to nail the *son-of-a-bitch*.

The luminol, it appeared, was now played-out. Its story told, at least on this half of the carpet. Several smaller, partial footprints were now visible. Rita's, Reynolds thought. And still more . . . blood. Rita's blood . . . maybe. Tears of despair welled up in Reynolds' eyes. They always came, as Reynolds fought them back.

Alone in the room now, the photographer finished with his methodical documentation of the dregs of hell, Reynolds worked. He read the carpet, the glow. Feeling the presence of the *players*, he traced the mayhem, footprint by bloody footprint. At least two men. Rivers and Sternson. The footsteps reminded him of dance steps in a book he had once read. But here, grisly, a dance of terror. More pinpoints of glowing green appeared, late arrivals, as if their story was redundant or cumulative. Reynolds leaned against the wall, the darkness encompassing him like a funeral shroud. He sank slowly to a sitting position, watching the eerie glow before him. The ERT men, outside, waited. Reynolds knew they would understand. They always did. Reynolds would remain in the room. In the dark. For as long as it took. Reynolds worked evidence. And Reynolds always worked alone.

As the flecks of debris fell from the ugly, green carpet, the evidence technician in the Hairs and Fibers Section at the FBI lab in Quantico wondered if a known sample of Rita's hair existed.

CHAPTER 31

Metropolitan Correctional Center (MCC),
Chicago, Illinois

The incessant hum of the overhead light was Rivers' only companion. He waited, handcuffed to the bench. Waited to be moved from General Population back to the *hole*. A minor scuffle with Inmate #1094, he didn't know his name. A dispute over Jell-O pudding, chocolate, his favorite. The sticky Latino got a slap on the wrist, while he got the damn *hole*. But the Latino also got ten stitches just below his chin. Sometimes plastic forks can be dangerous, chuckled Rivers to himself.

He jingled the handcuffs, the sound reminding him that he had fallen out of grace with *them*. Stone and the others. Lost his edge. That's what happens when cooperation isn't forthcoming, when the whole story isn't told. That's what happened to him, Billy Rivers, esquire.

Esquire. He saw it somewhere. Remembered it and liked it. Liked the sound of it next to his name. Some sleazy attorney's business card. One of his many burglary busts. But he didn't have the faintest idea what it meant. But damn, it sounded good.

The room was small. A holding area lined with lockers. Ugly, institutional orange. He faced them, tinkering with his constraints, as if they magically might fall off. Wondering what was in the lockers. The square grid on the face of each locker allowed a glimpse inside. A glimpse into the soul of the owner.

A picture of a female body-builder, tan, nice biceps, adorned the first. A girlfriend or just a fantasy? He never liked them muscular. Liked them small and supple, submissive.

Easy to dominate. To control. It was all about control. That's the first thing he taught Larry. Control. First control, then everything else would follow.

Nothing on the second locker. The third locker had a lapel button taped on it. It read, *Tact is for people who aren't witty enough to be sarcastic.* Tact wasn't one his strong suits, he thought. Witty, of course. He was good at parties. Cunning, definitely. Sarcastic, hell yes. Whatever it meant.

He was just about to consider the fourth locker when the guard came in dragging an inmate behind him. The inmate could barely walk and tried to shield his eyes with his sleeves, his hands cuffed behind him. His neck was puffy, the flaps of skin hanging down, forming a fleshy ruff. He coughed and wheezed and made whimpering sounds, as he was shackled to the bench adjacent to where Rivers was secured.

"Ya'll just sit there a spell, and let the light get used ta' ya' again," said the guard, a hillbilly from Tennessee.

The whimpering diminished into soft sobs as the guard approached Rivers.

"Yer turn, puss-face," said the guard, as he eyed Rivers up and down. "See that little prick over there, a week in the *hole* and he's whinin' like a damn little punk."

Rivers looked away. Knew what was waiting for him. Been there before. Many times.

The guard, a large man, with large, rough hands, produced a piece of paper from his pocket. Waved it under Rivers' nose and let out with a thunderous laugh that sprayed Rivers' face with droplets of spit. Tobacco stained. A pouch of *Redman* chew was tucked in the guard's back pants' pocket.

"You done won the lottery, shithead. You got the big one, thirty days in the *hole*. What'd ya' do, piss off some judge?"

He'd never done that much time in the *hole*. And he was older now. Thirty days . . . down there. He began to sweat, as if he was in an oven with the door closed. His knees weakened. His breathing stalled. Thirty days . . . maybe he should tell them. Tell them where the other bodies were.

CHAPTER 32

1415 West Brwyn Mawr Place,
Chicago, Illinois

The knife's edge pressed against her milk-white flesh, just below the nape of her neck. His face, concealed by the nylon stocking pulled tautly over his head, she could only imagine. The pressure on her neck increased and his free hand pressed hard against her, his thumb leaving a reddish circle just above the cut. His hands were gloved. Surgical gloves. And the blood began to ooze snake-like from the ever-widening gash in her neck. Trickling down. A faint sensation of warmth. Slithering like a worm down the blade, its crimsonness encompassing the handle of the knife and his gloved fingers. Lifting up the nylon stocking, he tongued the red mess, appearing to enjoy the coppery taste, as he smacked his lips rhythmically. His heavy, shallow breathing became deeper and more pronounced. She felt herself drifting, somewhere, limbo-like. The stocking mask was off now, his face exuding an expression that he was in a world melded between pleasure and pain.

She wanted to scream but the gray duct tape that sealed her mouth prevented her. The pain increased, as did the pressure from his thumb. A long, rough thumb, with a jagged edge for a nail that cut into her flesh. He moved the knife back and forth in a seesaw manner, ever so slightly, the wound increasing in depth with each maneuver. Her bound wrists held tight. Her legs, taped to the chair legs, prevented any movement. She sat upright, totally immobile. Except for her eyes, wide open, which followed his every move.

She wanted to shut her eyes. Have it over with. But she couldn't. He had dilated them and stretched rubber-bands over her forehead, pinning her eyelids open. Forcing her to watch. Controlling her, she thought. To look at *him*. That was part of it.

The knife cut deeper. Hollow, dull pain. Her eyes ached. Throbbing and pulsating in rhythm with his panting. His free hand was fondling himself in a pallid cadence with his moans, and the seesaw motion of the knife. A macabre melody of evil.

She wrestled to free herself and lost control of her bodily functions. His expression was now one of dominance, appearing to have expected it. He breathed in deeply, exuding his invincibility. She felt him stealing from her all essence of herself, her weakness, and her soul. His breathing increased, erratic, deep. Violent, as blood gushed with the lurching of his lower body. All went black.

Entangled in wet, rumpled bed sheets, she bolted upright into a sitting position. Panting like a dog in heat, her salty perspiration burned her eyes. Swollen. Red. Her head felt as if someone had crushed ice with a hammer inside of it. Her body was frozen. She shivered, trying to orient herself. Her heart thumped, as if trying to fly out of her chest. She couldn't swallow and coughed up bloody phlegm. A small pool of blood dripped down the front of her nightgown, a slight oozing from her nose. Then it was over. Her senses returned like a wayward child. Confused at first, then frightened. Worst of all, frightened.

She had often tried to imagine how Rita had spent her last moments. Now she had a glimpse into the possible hell she had endured. Had a glimpse of the horror, of the madness. Of the *madman*. The face of Lawrence Sternson would never be erased from her memory.

Lonely, frightened, she needed Stone. But Stone was chasing the *madman*. And Stone needed her to be strong. To do her job. She would not tell Stone of the nightmare. She would not burden him with it. No, she would deal with her fears alone.

The unfinished extradition murder warrant for Lawrence Sternson lay on her desk. Now that she understood Rita's hell, it would be easy to finish. She turned on all of the lights and sat in silence. She would not sleep this night. She sat down at the desk and began to write.

CHAPTER 33

14 Regishire Way, Bathgate, Scotland (Crime Scene)

Stone recognized the smell instantly. Death. The stench was overwhelming as they descended. Downward into the belly of the beast. Tracing *their* steps, they had come to this place. Observed the empty police unit parked in front, doors still open. And they knew the inevitable. This place . . . this place of silent horrors.

The Scottish authorities were there first. It was their domain. Two young constables in their early twenties. Had *they* ever smelled death? Stone thought not, but they would learn. As he had. Now, Stone waited for his turn to descend, to discover the truth. The truth about his friend, Kolb. And the truth about his assailant, Sternson. The god-awful, gut-wrenching truth. The all-encompassing, all consuming truth. Damn the truth, he thought, as his feet found the stairs, which were illuminated by Detective Sergeant Reamington's flashlight.

"Prepare yourself, Mr. Stone. It's not a pretty sight," said Reamington.

Stone followed several beams of light to the execution tables. The young constables, pinching their noses, stood zombie-like, as Stone approached. The buzzing of flies, bluebottles, the only sound.

Kolb's face was distorted, as if he had died painfully. His eyes bulged out of their sockets like over-ripe grapes. The rest of him was a mess. The cage was still hot even though

Reamington had made sure the connection to the generator was disconnected. Two of the rats were dead in the cage, apparently from the heat or attack by the other rats, two of which had survived. They lay on their sides, engorged with Kolb's intestines, inside of Kolb's midsection. They moved ever so slightly as the flashlight beams from trembling hands bounced erratically off of them, their red eyes aglow, beacons to the carnage they had created. A portion of Kolb's entrails was strewn, spaghetti-like, across the table. Results of the feasting frenzy, Stone imagined. Noticing that he was standing in a small pool of liquid, Stone quickly moved away, distancing himself from what he imagined to be Kolb's blood. He repositioned himself, as the beams moved slightly to the left where Stevenson's head lay on the floor.

The electrical cord from the small generator, having been removed by Reamington, was being re-coiled by one of the constables. The cord moved, spastic-like, as he tried to control it with shaking hands. More buzzing of the flies filled the room. And then Stone saw it, the headless corpse of Stevenson, a hatchet sunk into the table where the head had once been.

"Mister Stone, I do think it best if we move out of here and let the young officers secure the scene. There's a lot of evidence to process here," he said, indicating the constables at work, as if they had seen death before.

But Stone knew differently. Knew how those who had seen death acted in cases like . . . *this*. No, these constables had not seen death like this. Stone moved away. Couldn't think. Couldn't talk. Only . . . nothingness. Then the truth crept in, slowly at first, like a lost friend returning in the night. The truth about Rivers and the truth about Sternson. Damn the truth.

CHAPTER 34

*Basement Apartment, Brownson Hall,
University of Edinburgh*

Sternson was a master of disguise. That's how he got the night janitorial position in the Chemistry Department without anyone guessing his true identity. The long, shaggy, blonde wig helped. His primped eyebrows were dyed the same color as the wig and the molded buckteeth fit snugly in his mouth. He even altered his voice mannerisms, leading to his transformation into a dim witted, shoe-shuffling, stuttering *mopper-upper*, as he termed it. But the scars, that was another challenge. Even the heavy make-up, at times, did little to hide them. Too pronounced. Too many.

Glancing at his watch, he noticed that the time had gotten away from him. His shift at the lab would start within the hour. Too much time dwelling on the events in the cellar . . . with *them*. But still, just enough time.

As he massaged the flesh-colored paste around the edges of the scar, small specks of dried paste dropped onto the newspaper he was reading. Yesterday's. The headline read, *Bizarre Murders—Two Officers Found Slain*. As he read on, he realized that the article revealed little of what truly happened down *there*. In the cellar. His cellar. Yes, he understood police-work. Understood that they never gave away all their . . . secrets. The need to discourage all those unfortunates seeking publicity, or a sense of self-worth, who might confess, but lacked specifics. The need to hold something back to rule out the pretenders and trap the . . . well, trap him. Nothing was mentioned of the rats, or of the cage. An old trick of the *Okrhana* he had learned about while researching the Russian Revolution years ago. The key was keeping the rats fed just right, so they wouldn't eat each other.

He looked in the mirror. The transformation was complete, a transformation that would allow him access to the chemicals he needed and the prey he hunted. Prey, not victims. *Prey* made it sound sporting. Like a contest or a game. His game.

He pulled the blue janitorial sweater over his head. Over the front pocket was emblazoned the name, *Billy*. He tucked the sweater neatly in his dark blue work trousers and spruced up the wig just a little bit more. Satisfied, he strolled out of his drab, little apartment and began the thirty-minute walk across the campus to the chemistry lab.

Billy, he thought. *Billy Rivers*. He touched the nametag on his sweater and thought, tonight *we* will see her again.

CHAPTER 35

Crime Scene—Mary Agnes Robinson,

Shearington Forest

Stone felt Sternson would return. *When* was the real question. And so Stone waited. But returning was always a part of it. Reliving it. The fantasies and the power. The control. Stone knew it was Sternson now. The lab analysis had confirmed cannabis and ecstasy found on the evidence Stone had retrieved from the very place where Stone now waited. The same drugs Sternson was selling around the University of Chicago when Rita was murdered. It was Sternson, alright. Same M.O.'s. Headless corpses and psychedelic drugs. If he didn't kill again soon, he would return to this place, his last conquest. And so Stone sat in the dark, crouched behind the boulder shaped like a shoulder's helmet. Alone in the cold. Waiting.

It was after midnight now. Stone glanced at his watch, as condensation crept along its face in streaks. The moon, a lone sentinel, was almost full. It cast its light like a tired beacon on the spot where May Agnes' body had been recovered. Strangely marking the spot, daring *him* to come. To return and relive the horror.

Maybe not tonight. It was only a hunch that gnawed at Stone, like so many pesky gnats. And so he played it, hoping for an opportunity. But it was only days since Kolb's murder, and maybe Sternson's passion for blood had been satisfied. Maybe he wouldn't come, but Kolb's and Stevenson's murders were not the same as the others. They were murders born out of necessity. Not the type of lust murders Sternson craved.

Lived for. Sadistic, yes, and the result of aggressive drives, sexual in nature, that bonded at an early age, and melded into traits exhibited by all true sadists. But the victims just weren't right. And so Stone waited, praying for a chance.

Stone pulled his jacket collar up around his neck. Set the flashlight, unlit, on the ground next to him, and listened to the night sounds. Waited for footsteps or the crackling of a twig, the rustling of underbrush, foreshadowing the emergence of the intruder. Anything that would indicate the sociopath had returned. Stone strained to hear, but evidence of the unwelcome guest was not forthcoming. Nothing . . . no, the forest did not want him back. The iridescencent eyes of the night creatures in the trees shone like small lanterns of watchmen keeping vigil. The only sounds heard were of crickets, their endless chirping, melodious and sententious.

Stone caught himself half-dozing. Looked at his watch. 2:30 a.m. The glimmer of light from the moon soon faded, dark clouds the culprits. But only for a moment. The light was back in eerie strips, dripping through passing clouds. Stone refocused.

Hunkering down, the boulder sheltered him from the wind. His fingers were numb as he gripped the handle of the revolver, a *gift* from Reamington. Smooth metal. A welcome feeling in this unfamiliar place.

Silence and darkness. Nodding in and out of restless sleep. And then Stone felt a presence, but couldn't put his finger on it. Tasted it in the air. Smelled it. Something . . . foreign. Not like before. The cacophony of the crickets continued unabated, while the feverish wind in the trees overhead rustled lyrically in tune. Probably just the wind, Stone reasoned. But the strange feeling inside of him wouldn't subside, like an itch that had to scratched. It played continually on, like a tune one couldn't get out of his mind. A presence, somewhere. Out there.

CHAPTER 36

Crime Scene—Mary Agnes Robinson,
Shearington Forest

He crouched about a hundred yards away. Stone's back was to
him. Motionless. The inky blackness was lit only by the faint
light of the moon, now engulfed by clouds. Sliver-like, the
light fell on Stone intermittently.

Sternson studied him. Knew now that Stone was different
from the others who had hunted him. This one understood
him. Knew that he'd return to this place. His place. Sternson
was frustrated, the scars on his face pulsating with hatred
for Stone. Stone, who had prevented him from re-entering
his fantasy world. Stone, keeping vigil. Sternson took some
solace in the fact that he had outguessed Stone. That he had
been right, when he feared Stone would be here, in this place,
his place. Little consolation, when the scars were throbbing
for relief, for sustenance from the past events, whose last act
played out here. But Stone could have been careless like the
other two. *Careless* is what got them dead. No, this time he'd
be patient, testing his theory about Stone. And this time he'd
be right.

A pale cloud passed in front of the moon, blocking its
light. All was black. Sternson was at home in the black, and
the surcease it gave him. He strained to keep sight of Stone,
the binoculars useless now in the pitch black, and knew that
he must leave. Stone was too close, and knew too much.
Understood too much. About him.

As he adjusted the night vision goggles, Stone edged away. The orphan cloud passed, revealing the full moon, its light returning to the motionless figure crouched behind the boulder. Stone, he was sure, would wait. And would return again, until Stone understood. Recognized the inevitable. That this time he, Sternson, had won.

CHAPTER 37

Metropolitan Correctional Center (MCC),
Chicago, Illinois

Somehow feeding pigeons had always put Stone at ease. It was something about them that fascinated him. Maybe because it was immediate positive reinforcement, seeing them gobble up brown-red kernels of corn into hungry mouths. Corn that he threw among them as they skittered across the cobblestone mall in front of the MCC. Their different colors a magnificent display of diversity, yet they were all alike. And the way they wobbled back and forth in front of him, with fat, protruding bellies. The way they huddled in protective masses under the EL-tracks, waiting for the next handful of kernels to be tossed their way. Stone a silent docent to their needs.

Yes, feeding pigeons always put Stone's mind at ease. So he sat on the tired, rust-colored bench that faced the MCC, feeding his friends, and deciding if he should navigate the unforgiving waters of seeing Rivers just one more time.

It was almost two years since he had returned from Scotland, a defeated man, with Kolb's body stuffed in a military coffin, complements of the Scottish government. Two long years of soul-searching, dead-end leads, and no sighting of Sternson. A cold case now gone frozen. The case remained open, but only theoretically. Pending-Inactive was the police term. The case files, Rita's and Kolb's, sat on lonely shelves clustered with those of other forgotten victims, begging for new leads, new information, that would justify the manpower required to continue.

So Stone sat, deciding whether to enter the sociopath's realm one more time. To do battle with the tainted ego of Billy Rivers. Deciding whether to climb the steps that led to the entrance of the monstrosity known as the MCC that faced him, taunting him to try once more. To get Rivers to confess.

Stone pulled out his FBI credentials and looked at them. Much younger then, he thought. Looked back at the stolid face of the MCC. For over two long years Rivers had been incarcerated there, and now, from somewhere inside of the concrete beast that hid many sins, Stone felt Rivers beckoning him. Stone looked back at his photograph on his credentials, just below the inscription FBI. Putting his credentials back in his coat pocket, he tossed the remaining kernels from the brown paper bag onto the ground in front of him. The two white pigeons inexplicably hobbled away. Crumpling the bag in a ball, he tossed it aside and walked toward the FBI office.

As Stone walked the methodical path from the MCC to the FBI office, Rivers was being processed for the short trip to *The Farm*, where, according to the communiqué held in the fat guard's fat hands, he was to be put to death by lethal injection upon arrival.

CHAPTER 38

Paris, France

Changing his name and his appearance, Sternson had made his escape across the Channel to Paris as a deckhand on a fishing trawler. It was there in Paris that Sternson encountered his new master. A chance encounter at that, when Sternson had answered a newspaper advertisement for work as a welder at Rue #10, St. Moritz, a clearing house and supplier for medieval artifacts and antiques used in the entertainment business. And it was there that Sternson apprenticed for over two years; welding drawbridge parts, metal restraints and medieval weaponry, and other curious devices used in 14th century torture chambers. And that is also how he entered the strained and twisted world of the *Tattooed Man*.

CHAPTER 39

Terre Haute Federal Prison Camp
(The Farm), Terre Haute, Indiana

Rivers' attorney had exhausted all appeals, and within twenty-four hours Rivers would be put to death by lethal injection. The final nail in the coffin for the murder of James Tokar, a Bureau of Prisons guard at the Lompoc facility where Rivers had previously been incarcerated.

The letter had been faxed by Rivers' attorney, as Rivers had requested, and now he waited for Stone's reply. His last chance to cheat death. This was his last card and he played it straight up, as if he were in a poker game in a Deadwood saloon. He didn't have time to bait Stone as before, and pull away. No, it was *aces and eights* now and Rivers knew it. Stone *must* come, he reasoned. He'd bet his life on it, because that's all he had left.

CHAPTER 40

Squad 6 / Chicago FBI Office

The fax was hand-carried to him in a sealed envelope by the teletype clerk. It was marked *Immediate*. Stone had been listening to undercover tapes from an old insurance fraud case that finally was making its way to trial. Just beating the statute of limitations, typical of the U.S. Attorney's office.

Stone took off the earphones and placed them on top of the recorder. Picking up the envelope he felt a twinge, as if it contained bad news. He hesitated, and then opened it. The message was short and to the point. *There are more bodies. Come and I'll tell you where. Billy.*

Stone had been down this path with Rivers before. The false hopes. The dead-ends. The constant carrot-and-stick maneuvering. Usually, the results were negative and inconclusive. So far all it had accomplished was to get Kolb dead and let Rivers walk on Rita's murder. Just not enough hard evidence. Too circumstantial. He had heard it all before. And Sternson was still out there. Lurking somewhere. Waiting. Killing. But Rivers had bought the farm on the Lompoc thing, and that was good. But with Rivers gone, the probability of finding Sternson approached zero. But at least the mess that was Billy Rivers would be gone. Gone forever. That was enough for Stone, or though he convinced himself.

He read the fax again and knew that he must go. All leads *must* be covered. All opportunities *must* be explored. He owed that to Rita and the Judge. He owed it to Kolb, as well. And if he could not verify the supposed forthcoming information from the sociopath, at least he would stick around and watch the pathetic excuse for a human being breathe his last breath. *Fry*, so to speak. But that was an inappropriate euphemism, one used when the death penalty was administered using *Old Sparky*, the electric chair. But that was then, and now the choice of execution was lethal injection. Yes, he would go and observe the so-called painless execution, if need be. No burning scalps. No lingering, shaking and convulsing. A simple drug overdose administered by someone who on other days would adhere to the *Hippocratic Oath*. And not exactly an *eye-for-an-eye* punishment that Rivers' crimes warranted. Just a deep, deep sleep, never to wake up from.

Stone stopped himself in mid-thought. No, he mustn't think about that. He must go to Terre Haute and confront Rivers. After all, the coins were in his pocket now. Hopefully, they were lucky coins as the clock continued to tick on Rivers. He was a dead man now and if Rivers was telling the truth, the murders were Sternson's work. And that would generate more leads; leads that might result in Sternson's capture. He folded the fax and tucked it in his coat pocket. Stone glanced at his desk calendar. Tomorrow's date had been circled long ago, an *X* drawn through it. Rivers' execution date, a date that Stone had etched in his mind indelibly.

One last time to confront the beast, Stone thought. To descend into the horrors he had tried to repress over the years dealing with Rivers. One last time to maybe get it right. One last time, he thought, as he dialed up Padino to tell him. More bodies . . . but how many more?

CHAPTER 41

Terre Haute Federal Prison
Camp, Terre Haute, Indiana
(Death Row)

It was a small room, but Rivers' presence seemed to make it larger, as if he were insignificant. The guard remained outside of the cell, fully armed, as Stone entered Rivers' pathetic little world. They sat across from each other, a small plastic table separating the sociopath from his adversary. Staring, not talking, time was on Stone's side. Time a runaway train carrying Rivers to the gurney.

Rivers broke the silence that surrounded them like a thick fog.

"I knew you'd come," he said, a slight grin struggling from his mouth. A nervous tic Stone had seen many times before.

Stone lit it, then offered the cigarette to Rivers. The sociopath took it, cuffed hands trembling, just as Stone had anticipated. Knew now that Rivers was his. More silence as Rivers inhaled, coughed a spastic cough, the smoke enshrouding his dogface. The cigarette dangled from Rivers' hand, ashes falling on his slip-on, blue prison sneakers. Generic, the K-Mart variety, stenciled with *Bureau of Prisons* in white lettering. He flicked the ashes away in disgust with a kick of his leg and refocused on a silent, waiting Stone.

"I knew you'd come," he said again, more confident this time. The old Rivers.

"You already said that, Billy," Stone coldly replied.

"Yeah, well, if you want what I got . . . and I got a lot, man, all you gotta' do is stop this shit," he said, as he waved his hands at the clock on the wall. A quiet ticking. 3:15 p.m.

Rivers was scheduled to get lit up at midnight. Plenty of time, thought Stone, to get it all out of him. The second hand moved slowly as Stone waited and eyed the clock, playing chess with Rivers. Stone's queen was bearing down on Rivers' unprotected king, as Rivers' furtive glances at the clock on the wall told Stone to wait. Just wait him out. Checkmate was in the balance. Rivers' move now. Would he castle into checkmate? Or would he simply resign?

Stone held a pat hand as the minutes ticked away. Then Rivers blurted out, "You want it or not you crazy bastard?" Smoke fuming from his nostrils. Blue smoke.

"Sure, tell me what you have, Billy. And no need to keep looking at the clock. It's not going to stop. At least not until you puke your guts out to me. Now, do we understand each other, shitface?"

Stone eased back, trying to make the uncomfortable prison issue chair conform to his torso. Rivers was right where Stone wanted him. Desperate and without options.

"What do I got? Shit . . . I got everything, man. But you gotta' stop it. Promise me, man. Promise me you'll stop it. I'm givin' ya' two bodies, man," Rivers begged. More furtive glances at the time bomb ticking on the wall.

"Oh, I'll stop it, *Billy*, but only if the information is plausible, good information. You know what that means . . . plausible? It means no more bullshit," Stone said, staring into Rivers' eyes. Dead space. Hollow.

"Okay, man. You want Sternson. I know it. Know all about it. He wrote, man. Not in his real name. You guys woulda' found that out. Not him, exactly, but some bitch he was seeing. Probably offed her too," he chuckled nervously.

"From where?" asked Stone.

"Champaign, Illinois. You know, U. of I. Probably hangin' around there. Don't know the exact address, but he's down there, man. Wants to see you."

Stone waited, his heart picking up beats. It was a race now.

"Yeah, had this bitch write the letter. She's just as fucked up as him. Always on something, man. You know, that psychedelic shit," he said, inhaling more smoke, coughing.

Stone waited.

"I know, man. I know what he did to Kolb with those fucking rats. It was all over the newspapers once you got back to the States. Not his name exactly, man. But his style. I knew it was him when I found out Kolb bought it. Dude told me how he used that trick before. He called it a trick, man. So when I read about it, I knew it was him. You want this shit or not?" He barked in a gravely voice, sucking in more smoke.

Rivers tapped his fingers on the plastic table, the swastikas on his knuckles moving rhythmically with the tapping in a hypnotizing way. Stone stared at Rivers' forehead, doing the best he could do to control the adrenaline rush set off when Kolb's name was mentioned. This was pay dirt. He hadn't expected Rivers to mention Sternson. Had anticipated other things. Tangential things, but not Sternson, *per se.*

"Two bodies, man. Both of 'em if you want 'em. Got 'em both, man. Never told you about it, but I got 'em, man. Know where they're at. He told me. Shit, you gonna' help me or not, man?"

Stone felt like he was sitting on needles. Wanted to get right to it, but knew he had to make Rivers squirm and give it up. He couldn't appear to be begging for information. Stone sat motionless, giving Rivers the FBI eyes, as greasy sweat pooled in the crevices of what Rivers called a face.

Then Stone spoke. "Okay, Billy, here's how it's going to work. You tell me everything. I'll evaluate it and then we'll see where we're at."

"No fucking way, man. You promise me now. Right now!"

Rivers' shouting brought the guard to the cell door as Rivers smashed the cigarette butt into the plastic table. Palm down, squishing it like a bug in his proverbial street punk style.

Stone rose to leave and called for the guard to open the cell door. Rivers froze, Stalingrad-like, and appeared not to be expecting this. Several darting glances at the clock, ticking fast now, and then yelling at Stone.

"Awright, man. Awright," a slight laugh. "Just testing 'ya, man. I'll give 'ya everything I got. Just slow down. Sit," he said, breathless, panting, his dog tongue, jaundiced and serrated, hanging low from his mouth.

Stone turned and motioned the guard away. Sat down and faced Rivers. Waiting, as the second hand ticked away Rivers' sorry excuse for a life.

"Okay," Rivers said. "There's two. Sisters, I think. Maybe twins. Don't know for sure. Did 'em both in a quarry down there. Champaign area. You know, by where he used to work. Colleges and stuff. He told me, man. I know it's good. Check it out."

"Who are they?" Stone asked. "Names?"

"Students, man. That's all he ever did. You know, when he was teaching. Bitches, man. From the dude's classes or something."

"I need specific information. Exact directions."

Rivers produced a small envelope from the bible that lay on the table. Tossed it to Stone saying, "Right there, man. It's all there. Written in his own fucking hand. Mailed it to me hisself. Not from that bitch. This one's different. No, from him this time. Got it last week. Fuck him. Why'd he wait so long?"

"Because he's an asshole, just like you," said Stone, grabbing the envelope.

Not looking at the contents, Stone tucked it in his pocket.

"Where's Sternson?" Stone asked.

"You ain't even gonna' look at it!" Rivers snapped, doglike.

"Oh, I'll look at it. But first, where's Sternson?"

"Fuck, I don't know. Just read the fucking letter. He wants to meet you, man. He's a sick fuck."

Stone moved toward the cell door as the guard slid it open.

"Everything, okay?" asked the guard.

"A-okay," replied Stone, patting his coat pocket which contained the letter, and winking at Rivers, as if to say, *gotcha' motherfucker*.

Panting, Rivers gasped, "Get back to me, man. Tell my lawyer I helped you big-time. Stop this shit, man!"

Stone turned toward Rivers and did something he rarely did.

"I'll tell your lawyer *and* the warden that you're cooperating," he lied.

Rivers smiled. Searched for the cigarette butt.

CHAPTER 42

Terre Haute Federal Prison Camp,
Terre Haute, Indiana
(Execution Chamber)

He was lying on the gurney, twisting, as they wheeled him in. Two guards, one small, one large. *Tom-and-Jerry* like. Rivers' pathetic dogface was white with fear. His eyes, colorless and vacuous, were still. He appeared to be in a self-induced trance. Stone watched from behind the glass window along with the usual entourage. Some bereaved family members of the slain guard were present, along with a few paid witnesses. A death penalty protestor here and there, sprinkled among the hardliners, the obligatory Bureau of Prisons officers. And, of course, the news media, including several reporters from the local newspapers, no doubt anxious to write their bleeding heart editorials. No one from Rivers' immediate family was present.

Rivers' attorney was there. A federal defender, newly admitted to the capital bar, Stone recognized him as a liberal to the nth degree. Unseasoned, gullible, naïve . . . and those were his good qualities; his pallor was grayish, resembling dried clay. He spoke in spurts, spitting out the words like drips from a broken faucet.

"Well, we tried," he said. "I guess that's all we could have done, considering the circumstances, that is." He smiled half-heartedly.

Stone looked past him. Didn't have time for this foolish gibberish. Focused on Rivers, as the medical attendant calibrated the IV that would deliver the lethal cocktail containing sodium pentothal, the first of the triad of opiates that would send Rivers to the netherworld, Stone breathed easily.

Shaking his head, the attorney faced Stone and whispered, "In the name of Jesus . . ." Kind of an Orson Welles on the *Jesus* . . . "He lied to me. He lied to all of us. He promised me that he was going to tell you about some other murders. Too bad he didn't . . . confess. It may have saved his life, and stopped all of this."

"Yeah, too bad," said Stone, watching Rivers, as the drip, drip, drip from the IV methodically progressed.

No one spoke as the clock ticked. Rivers' clock. The sociopath's eyes were glasslike now. Dreamy, as his muscles relaxed under the influence of the drugs. The heart monitor was near flat-line. It would be over sooner than Stone had anticipated, his sense of timing way off. He'd been daydreaming. Thinking about the senselessness of it all. But Rivers was gone now and Stone felt no remorse. Like putting a rabid dog down, it had no effect on Stone. No exhilaration either. Just a passive relief.

"Yes, too bad he didn't tell you anything," the attorney said, head bowed, shuffling aimlessly.

"Yeah, too damned bad," expounded Stone, thinking *too fucking bad.*

Turning toward the door, Stone took one last look as the medical attendant closed the curtains on the mess that was Billy Rivers.

CHAPTER 43

Terre Haute Federal Prison Camp,
Terre Haute Indiana
(The Mortuary Room)

The room was cold and smelled of damp limestone. Antiseptic came to Stone's mind. The limestone walls, a reminder of just how old the prison was, held many secrets, most of them bad. The medical assistant, a smallish man with a deep voice not indicative of his frame, ushered Stone into the room.

"Over there," he pointed.

The gurney was empty now, devoid of the evidence of death. Rivers' body lay on a cold metal table, face-up, awaiting the autopsy. A clean white sheet covered him from the waist down. Stone approached, breathing shallowly. An unexpected reaction. Death again. A deserved death. A good death. But still . . . death.

Rivers' body was a patchwork of scars and tattoos, scalds, burns and other marks. Stone had seen most of them before. A hard life, Stone thought. A criminal's life. The signs of a non-repenting recidivist.

The smallish man spoke. "Doc said he's gonna' start in about an hour. You can stay and watch if you like."

"No thanks," said Stone, leaning over Rivers and gently lifting the death shroud, as if Rivers was only sleeping.

"Makin' sure he's dead? Huh?" The little man laughed, his little teeth clicking like staples coming out of a stapler the wrong way.

Stone said nothing. Was thinking about Sternson.

"Yeah, happens every time. You don't believe in ghosts, do you? Boo!" He shouted, startling Stone.

The little man then laughed a tired little laugh, and then frowned, his tiny hands raised above his head, as if to say he was sorry.

Stone replaced the sheet in its original position, half covering the tattoo on Rivers' belly. A unicorn, deep red in color, was only half-visible. Just the head and horns were showing.

"Damnedest thing I ever saw," the little man said, prodding Stone for a response.

"And what's that?" Stone asked, taking the cue from *Tom Thumb*.

"All those tattoos," he said.

"Well most criminals have tattoos. It's not out of the ordinary," said Stone flatly.

"Yeah, but aren't tattoos meant to be seen? Don't they signify something. Guys like him . . . ." He pointed to Rivers. ". . . don't they want people to see them?"

"I suppose so," said Stone.

"So what about the ones on the soles of his feet? Huh? Nobody's gonna' see 'em down there. Doesn't make any sense, does it?"

Stone stopped dead in his tracks. Returning to Rivers, he lifted the sheet exposing Rivers' lower body. On the sole of each foot was the same tattoo, a tattoo Stone had seen before, but not on Rivers. It was the same mysterious symbol Stone had observed on Mary Agnes Robinson.

CHAPTER 44

The Holiday Inn, Rural
Route #8, Champaign, Illinois (outskirts)

The letter was open, lying on top of the envelope. Stone had read it several times, arriving at one course of action, and then just as suddenly, discarding it for a different approach. He leaned back in his chair, massaging his temples like Madeline did, and casually sipped his bourbon and water. He read the letter again.

> *"My friend, Billy, please make sure you give this to Agent Stone. It may save you from being executed. Sorry I took so long, but, as you know, I am a busy man. Agent Stone should believe you because by now you have already spoken to him about me. Mostly half-truths, I suspect. But that's understandable. Jealousy is a funny thing, isn't it?*
>
> *Anyway, tell Agent Stone that the other bodies, two of my former students, are waiting for him in a quarry near Champaign, Illinois. I'm sure he can figure it out and, perhaps, we will run into each other when he comes searching. I'm hoping he comes alone. That's important. I don't like crowds. I am rather looking forward to a one-on-one with him, if you know what I mean.*
>
> *P.S. When they start the IV, don't hold your breath. It only prolongs the inevitable.*
>
> *Your friend."*

Spread out in front of Stone was a map of the Champaign area. He had noted several locations where limestone quarries had been operating before they were closed down. He reasoned that Sternson had utilized a quarry that had been deserted for some time.

This was Stone's mission now. Not the FBI's. Not anyone else's. Stone had come alone as Sternson wanted. Now it would be just the two of them to finally put this thing to an end. He had told Padino that he was taking a few days off to go fishing. To clear his mind after all this Rivers' business. He had told Madeline that he needed some time alone. And so he had come here. To this place. Come to find Sternson and to exact justice and to kill him if necessary. And have it done with forever.

Stone knew that if he involved the Springfield FBI Office it would get too messy. Too much paperwork and red tape, and by that time Sternson would be gone. Sternson was too smart for that. He'd been successful in eluding the law for years, and it wasn't just all luck. No, Stone reasoned, he just didn't need those distractions. Not now. He'd go it alone, knowing full well that Sternson was probably watching him now. Yes, Sternson was good at what he did. Watching. Waiting. Killing. And then disappearing. Yes, Sternson was a devious sociopath, an organized killer, a manipulator . . . and he wanted Stone alone. And that's what he would get.

Stone had pieced it together. Little by little. It had taken time, but now most of the pieces fit together. He knew that Sternson murdered Rita. As far as the murder of Mary Agnes Robinson, the tattoos on Rivers' feet confirmed that Sternson was responsible for that, as well. Stone was sure that Sternson had the same tattoos somewhere on his own body. But that was for later. The simple truth was that Sternson would kill again if not stopped. A true sociopath with a narcissistic personality, a need to control and manipulate, and a penchant for inflicting pain and death would certainly not stop on his own. No criminological theory had been proposed expostulating that view. No, Sternson needed to be stopped. Needed to be dead.

It wasn't a game with Sternson, as he wanted Stone to believe. That was Hollywood stuff. No, Sternson simply needed Stone out of the way because he knew that Stone understood him, and feared that Stone would eventually catch him. And now two more bodies. Two more unsolved murders to deal with. Stone simply had had enough of this degenerate's trail of death. Had had of enough of sleepless nights and endless nausea. Had had enough of Sternson and his inherent constitutional rights that he would avail himself of if apprehended.

It was simple now. No due process. No reciprocal discovery. No depositions or *Miranda* warnings. No trials. No hearings. No appeals. No stays of execution or proffers. It all would soon be moot. Stone had come to Champaign for one reason, and one reason only. To kill Mr. Lawrence Sternson. Plain and simple.

CHAPTER 45

Winnman's Quarry, Old Frontage
Road, East Champaign, Illinois (Day 1)

It ran along the old railroad tracks to a large tunnel-like opening in the side of a cliff. It was a narrow path and Stone had to go slowly so as not to trip over the tracks as he approached the opening. The tracks ended abruptly, having been pried up in an attempt to disengage them from their supports. Some of the rails were missing. Scrap metal scavengers, no doubt, thought Stone. Other rails were bent, twisted and remained partially in place.

It was nearing dusk and Stone, fatigued, approached the entrance. It had taken all day to locate the tracks which led to this place, and now it was getting dark. Everything within him told him to stop. To return tomorrow and start again when he would be fresh. In the daylight, when he could focus. But the entrance beckoned him on, begging him to enter, like a hawker at a carnic sideshow. Motioning him forward, tempting him to enter the bowels of the quarry. Into Sternson's womb of evil.

Stone felt for his sidearm and was relieved to feel the reassuring, smooth metal cylinder of his .357 Magnum. He inched forward as nervous energy took over. Strapped to his ankle, inside of his boot, was the 5-shot Chief Special revolver. Just a precaution if things got out of hand. Stone pulled the flashlight from his knapsack and entered the tunnel.

The dank, musty odor of damp earth penetrated Stone's clothing. Moisture was everywhere, dripping from cracks and crevices in the walls, like sweat from a fat man. The air was thick

273

and pasty and smelled of rotting vegetation. The walls of the tunnel were home to a slippery moss, brownish, and clammy to the touch. As Stone made his way further inside, the hollow sound of his own footsteps startled him. The muffled noise echoed in the silence beyond, fading in the distance where Sternson awaited him. Waiting to kill him.

Stone was not afraid. Was way beyond that. And even though the daily nightmares had taken their toll, somehow Stone felt immune, like a severely injured burn victim who feels no pain, though it's there and ever present. His career flashed before his eyes in increments, like pulses from a laser. Bursts of light from a strobe depicted scenes of past events, piecemeal, and in sections. Unconnected and disjointed. Not making sense, and waiting to be pieced together in some form of semblance. Stone's head buzzed incessantly as the images bombarded him.

The faint light at the end of the tunnel was barely visible now. Sternson, he thought, removing the .357. The light in the distance glowed eerily as Stone crept along, clinging to the vines growing on the walls of the tunnel. Rubbing up against the edges of jutting rocks and wet moss. Stepping in muck. Breathing in the stench of living things that littered the fetid limestone walls, some of which clung to his boots, making it difficult to move.

It wasn't about Stone anymore. He had tried to do it the right way. The old fashioned way. *Wear-a-Tie-Catch-a-Spy* FBI way. But now the only way left was to kill *him*. Kill *him* for Rita. For Kolb. For the Judge. For Madeline and . . . yes, for himself and all of the other victims. Like lancing a boil. Excising a wound. Just like killing a rabid dog, nothing more.

He felt the soft rush of cool air flow past his left ear, and then felt the hand on his shoulder before he could react. The last thing he could remember when he woke up was, "Hello, Agent Stone, nice of you to come. I . . . ."

The blow from the shovel to Stone's neck had laid him out cold. Upon gaining consciousness, Stone awoke coughing, spitting out dried phlegm and crusty blood, and convulsing. His mouth tasted as if he had been tear-gassed.

"Oh, I'm sorry," said Sternson, referring to the obvious distaste in Stone's mouth. "It's the same stuff you guys use in your pepper spray. I make it myself. Here."

Sternson shone a light on a wooden workbench containing various chemicals and pieces of glassware, as he smiled at Stone, tied to a chair. He then removed the vial from under Stone's nose, sealed it, and placed it on the wooden bench behind him.

"And so sorry about the shovel. You caught me in an awkward moment. I wasn't expecting you so soon. I was planning on using the stun gun but . . ."

"Shut the fuck up you sick bastard."

"Feisty, are we. So much for offering you any water then."

Stone continued to cough up phlegm and dried blood. His eyes were watery and scratchy from the pepper spray substitute used on him by Sternson. He tried to rub his eyes but found that his hands had been secured by duct tape to the arms of the chair in which he sat. His legs, immobile, were secured in the same fashion.

"Welcome to my world," Sternson said, a fractured smile on his placemat of a face.

Stone's head began to clear. He was becoming accustomed to the faint light that surrounded him.

"I was happy in Scotland, but you and your partner forced me to leave. It's all your fault, Agent Stone."

Stone's mind was buzzing. He had let Sternson gain the advantage. Now this . . . problem. All seemed lost and wasted. Despair entered where it seldom tread. Stone had told no one where he was. He was alone and he was desperate. But maybe it was a game with Sternson, after all. Stone sensed Sternson wanted to talk. As long as Stone could keep Sternson talking, the game would continue. It was a mental contest now, but death was in the offing. Stone's death. Must keep him talking and somehow get to Sternson's inner self. His real self. It was now *one-up-man-ship* with a deadly ending.

Sternson was facing away from Stone. Tinkering with something in the dark. Small noises in the distance alarmed Stone that what was next would not be pleasant. Stone's truncated thought process, caused by his unconsciousness and partly from the inhalation of the pepper spray, was interrupted by Sternson's movements. Closer. He was carrying something toward him. A cage shrouded with a dark cloth. A funeral cloth.

"Stole it from a priest once. The cloth, that is. It's purple. Something to do with Lent, wasn't it? Hmm. Who cares. I hate those hypocritical bastards. Anyway, I thought we'd try it out," he said, placing the cage on the small table in front of Stone.

A slight fluttering of something inside broke the silence, like fans waving in stiff air. Stone's heart approached arrhythmia, as he thought of how Kolb had died; how Sternson had killed him with rats in a hot cage.

"This is an extrapolation on a theme. Rats for Kolb. Bats for Stone," he proclaimed, as if he were reciting a haiku.

Sternson continued to chant, rhyme-like, as he removed the purple death cloth from the cage, exposing the bats within. Three of them. Ugly. Hanging upside down from the top of the cage. Small rat faces. Rats with wings, Stone's mother had always said. Red eyes. Fluttering, webbed wings. Stone, half-retching, struggled with his constraints. The duct tape held tight, as he tried to free himself.

"I think they'll do just fine," said Sternson.

The scars on his face, bulbous and blood-red, pulsated as he spoke, as if they were about to implode. The bats were becoming agitated as Sternson plugged in the electrical cord that ran from the cage to the generator located near his workbench.

"The Okrana were a curious bunch, don't you think, Agent Stone? Ingenious people. Experts at interrogation.

Interrogation? Isn't that what you did with Billy? Isn't that your specialty?"

Stone sat stiffly upright, but continued to move his left leg in a circular manner. The tape began to budge.

"We'll just heat this cage up a bit and open the door on your soft belly. It is soft, isn't it . . . or have you been working out?"

As Sternson continued to hum and mumble to himself, Stone continued to try to free himself as subtly as he could without arousing suspicion. Sternson turned away and grabbed a propane torch from underneath the workbench. Adjusting the oxygen flow on the nozzle, he lit it. The bright orange-yellow light illuminated the battlefield of scars on his face. At the edges of darkness and light, Sternson's face took on a dogmatic look, as if he were about to enter a confessional from the priest's side. As Sternson slowly approached Stone, Stone's .357 was tucked in a leather belt that hung loosely from Sternson's waist. A large hunting knife was removed from its sheath and held up to the light for Stone to inspect. Feeling a slight warmth from the propane torch that Sternson held in his left hand, the flat part of the blade was pressed against Stone's pulsating neck.

"This would be too easy. Besides, you're not a girl anyway. It just wouldn't be the same," he said stoically, flipping the cold blade over and roughly massaging the area where Stone's hyoid bone was located.

Stone tried hard to swallow, but the knife was pressed so deep into his neck that he struggled to breathe.

"Ah, yes, don't worry. I'm not going to snap your hyoid bone. That's for sissies like Gary Ridgway who strangled helpless women. The *Green River Killer* . . . you know about him, don't you? No, your death will be much rougher. Feel assured, Agent Stone, when they find you your hyoid bone will still be intact. As for the other parts of your anatomy . . . well, let's just leave that to conjecture. Hmmm?"

Thinking came in spurts as the coldness of the knife blade pressed against his worn skin. Abruptly the pressure was gone and the blade was ripping his shirt away from his chest. Torn to shreds by savage strokes of the sexual sadist. Some minor cuts on Stone's abdomen began to bleed haphazardly, as if to inquire . . . *will there be more?* Then shallow cuts on Stone's forearms began to appear in the flickering light as Sternson adjusted the flow of the gases into the propane torch. The cuts were not lethal, though blood flowed sporadically in tiny copper rivulets, just enough to arouse the mercenaries of death in the cold cage that weighed down like so many bricks on Stone's chest. Then the fluttering of bat wings became incessant, as Sternson had apparently cranked up the heat in the cage.

"Thermal conduction is a wonderful concept, is it not, Agent Stone?" asked Sternson, looking first to the revved up generator growling in the hollow void of the cave and then back to the metal bars of the cage, which were taking on an iridescent orangish glow.

"Oh, them . . ." Sternson stared into Stone's darting eyes. "Those are vampire bats, *Desmondus rotundus.* But you know your *phyla*, don't' you, Agent Stone? Studied biology in college. Wanted to be a physician. I did my homework. I know *lots* about you. And you know they *do* like blood. So let's just make a few more little cuts, shall we?" Sternson continued, as if addressing school children.

Sternson adjusted the metal cage that now had dug deeply into Stone's rib cage. Rigid flesh had slowly turned into serrated strips of raw meat. The solid metal door of the cage was now flush against Stone's midsection. It was secured tightly around Stone with several bungee cords. Sternson then positioned a copper, foot-long rod parallel to the cage and clamped it onto the metal bars with a copper cleat. The propane cylinder was next. He placed it inches from the copper rod, allowing its flame to impinge on the rod's tip, causing an orange-blue glow.

"We'll just use this as a catalyst, so to speak. Heat transfer again. You understand the principle. They taught you that at the Academy, didn't they?" Sternson laughed, his face close to the flame, sucking in its painful emanations.

The fluttering inside of the cage began to escalate. Soon, Stone hoped, the bats would begin to attack each other if they couldn't find a way out.

"The copper tube is heated and then the heat is transferred to the metal bars of the cage . . . here." Sternson gently taped the cage bars with the blade of his hunting knife. "Then my friends get a bit fussy . . . edgy might be a better description. You see, they haven't eaten in days. Then slowly sliding the metal door away from your abdominal area and, well, you know, the heat and all, it get's a bit messy. You can figure out the ending, can't you, Agent Stone?"

Stone searched the innermost part of his mind for a way out. An answer to an unsolvable problem that was happening in *real time*. Not some algebra word problem to ponder over, or some existential exercise to dwell on, but simply life or death in the balance, and to be decided in microseconds.

"Shall we continue," he said, pushing the blowtorch closer to the copper rod. A brighter flame at the point of impingement now. It's blue-white color temporarily blinded Stone as he focused on the glowing point of contact. Everything was slow motion now for Stone. His speech was labored. He strained to see, the dark edges of the cave walls closing in on him, as if he were being buried alive. Fighting the salt and sweat that assaulted his eyes, the only thought that came to him was . . . *keep him talking.*

"Where are the other bodies?" Stone blurted out, half-knowing what he asked, coughing up blood as he spoke.

Finger to the side of his head, like the professor he was, contemplating a question, Sternson said, "Oh, they're here. Over there. Buried. That's what the shovel was for . . . the one I hit you with. But anyway, I like to keep them close to me. The heads, I mean. But you wouldn't understand that. I just keep the heads. Dahlmer kind of had the right idea, keeping body parts. But he just got carried away. C'mon, leaving body parts in your refrigerator. Anyway, he preyed on little boys. That's not my style. But I like this spot. It has so many, well, memories."

Sternson put his left index finger close to the point of impingement. Stone saw the red welts forming. Saw Sternson's penciled slit for a mouth upturn slightly into a sadistic grin.

"Yes getting hot now. Hot! Hot! Hot! What made the Hottentots so hot? *Wizard of Oz*, wasn't it? Off to see the Wizard, aren't you, Agent Stone? *Who* is your Wizard . . . God or the other one?"

The light from the blowtorch was at such an angle that Stone could clearly see around Sternson. Sternson's sadistic little playground. His props. His gadgets. His accoutrements of torture. Stone focused clearly now. Sternson was completely dressed in black leather. He wore boots, black, pointed. A thick, rhinestoned, black belt was around his waist and held Stone's .357 and the hunting knife.

"I think we're ready now," he said. "Just hot enough to give them a good head start, don't you think?"

The point of impingement was now pumpkin orange, as Sternson babbled on and Stone, summoning the last of his strength, tried to free his leg. The duct tape on Stone's left leg was giving. If he could only get Sternson close enough, he might be able to trip him. Do something. Anything. His mind groped for ideas. Finally hitting on insults. Yes, insult him. Insult the control freak that sought domination and cowering. No cowering now. *Fuck this bastard.*

"You are one ugly motherfucker, you know that. Those scars make your face look like raw meat, asshole," Stone laughed, belying the pain that engulfed his very being. A controlled laugh he learned as a hostage negotiator.

Sternson was caught off-guard. The bats were panicking now, snapping at each other. Drawing blood. Sternson approached Stone, reaching for his knife. The propane torch, glowing eerily, was now in his left hand.

"Maybe a little of this in your face, and you can have some scars to!" He screamed.

The flame was near Stone's face, the savage heat causing blistering under his eyes, the pain excruciating. Sternson's hot, fetid breath assaulted Stone's face. Goat-like and salty. Sternson's eyes, pale and malignant, paralleled the flame in a sickly dance. His scars, Martian-red from the glow of the torch, pulsated erratically, a fleshy tango of death and mutilation. He breathed irregularly, deeply, and then leaned forward, exposing jaundiced and fragmented teeth. Thick words rattled out in a macabre melody.

"Fuck *you-uuu-uuu*", Mr. FBI man.

Stone marshaled all of his strength. Spitting in Sternson's face, blood and crusty phlegm hit its mark dead center. Sternson's left eye closed. Stone kicked savagely with his left leg and the duct tape gave, ripped shards of tape flying in all directions. Stone's leg was free now, as a blow landed in Sternson's groin. Sternson lurched forward, attempting to balance himself, his face contacting Stone's. Stone bit hard, like a rabid dog, breaking an incisor, and sinking his teeth deeply into Sternson's left cheek. A clean bite. Cobra-like. Sternson's flesh that surrounded the wound was ripped and flailing in the air. Stone spit chunks of bloody flesh back at Sternson, as Sternson grabbed at the gash. Thrashing about in pain, Sternson inadvertently knocked the bat cage loose from Stone, just enough to release the bloodsuckers. Two were on Sternson instantly, attracted to the fresh blood gushing freely from Sternson's swollen cheek. Then on his hands. On his shirt. He swiped at them with his free hand, the other hand attempting to cover the gash and stanch the flow of blood.

The propane torch, dropped by Sternson, during the struggle, lay on the ground near Stone's feet. A hungry vampire was picking at the open wounds on Stone's chest. He kicked with his free leg and the chair rolled over. The bat was propelled off of him as Stone fell. Sternson continued to fight off the other two bats, but they were relentless to feed on blood. Biting. Attacking. In Sternson's eyes, now joined by the third one freed from Stone.

Stone twisted, contorting himself like a gymnast. His taped wrist was now near the flame of the torch lying on the ground on its side. Burning, cutting through the tape on his left wrist. Welts. Big, ugly, red welts began to appear along his wrist, but his hand was now free and throbbing with pain.

Sternson kicked at Stone as he wrestled with the bats. Grabbing one with a bloody hand, Sternson bit the bat's head clean off. That left two. And Stone struggling to free himself. Stone grabbed the blowtorch with his free hand. Still taped partially to the chair, Stone brought the blowtorch up to Sternson's ankle, forcing him away screaming.

Stone had time now. Sternson was injured, struggling, his face a bloody mess. Stone frantically freed himself. Blowtorch in hand, he limped toward Sternson. His right eye was completely destroyed by the vampires that now lay on the ground, crushed by Sternson's big hands.

Stone held the blowtorch at shoulder level, illuminating Sternson's face. The hunting knife had dislodged from Sternson's belt during his foray with the bats. It lay on the dirt floor of the cave next to a pile of bloody flesh. Stone's .357 was nowhere in sight, another casualty of the struggle. Sternson eyed the dormant knife with his good eye.

"Don't even think about it, asshole," said Stone, flashing the blowtorch forward, prodding Sternson back.

Sternson was one-handed now. His other hand was busy stanching the flow of blood from Stone's vicious bite.

"You taste like shit, asshole," said Stone, spitting the remnants of Sternson's rotting flesh from his mouth.

Stone motioned with the blowtorch and Sternson crept backwards away from the light. Away from his props. His things. His world. Into the further reaches of the tunnel. Obeying, as he clutched his disfigured face.

"Keep crawling," ordered Stone.

"How far?" asked Sternson, appearing oblivious to the pain.

"Just keep going. All the way to the end. You know where. It's on the map. Get up and walk to the shaft!"

Sternson struggled to rise. Gaining his balance, he limped pathetically further into the belly of the beast. Into the darkness, thirty or so yards later he stopped. Turned and looked down.

"It's the end, Agent Stone. It's a hundred foot drop straight down," he said, resuming his stare into the dark pit with his one good eye.

Stone fought off his own pain. The open cuts on his forearms. The welts from the burned flesh. The bat bites on his chest and abdomen. The burns on his legs and arms stretched and pulsated with a devastating agony, as he maneuvered Sternson into position

"I could rush you right now," Sternson threatened, the hollow socket where his eye had once been sucking in snippets of light from the wavering blowtorch in Stone's shaking hand, like a black hole at the end of the universe.

Stone pointed the blowtorch at Sternson at eye-level.

"Do it and I'll put your other fucking eye out!" He shouted.

Stone, remembering, reached down into his boot and retrieved the 5-shot Chief revolver from his ankle holster.

"Forgot about this, didn't you?" Stone said, pointing the revolver at Sternson's K-5 area. His kill zone.

"You can't kill me, Agent Stone. You know that. That would make you just like me. A common criminal. Remember, fidelity, bravery and integrity? All that good stuff they taught you back at FBI school? Hmm? Remember? And my constitutional rights, Agent Stone, you're obligated. You know that."

Sternson trying to manipulate. Distract. Control. No, Stone was way beyond that now.

"Criminology 101," Stone said.

"What?"

"Criminology 101. I taught it at the Academy. Didn't you do your homework?"

"So . . . maybe I . . . ?"

"Sexual sadists, like yourself, have the highest recidivist rates of all criminal offenders. You're an incurable sociopath. There's only one place for you now."

"You've got to take me back, Agent Stone. You know that, and then go through all that legal mumbo-jumbo shit. And I'll still make your life miserable. You might win in the end, but you *will* suffer. You and all of your pathetic colleagues. You can't do it. It's against your training, your ethical standards. It's against what you are supposed to be. Besides, you don't have the guts!" Sternson barked.

Stone had stopped listening several minutes ago. Had only watched Sternson's lips moving. Stone was in that special place that Kolb had educated him about. Stone was there now. Alone. Sternson was no more than a simple annoyance, an unwanted fly on the wall, a wrong number soon to be hung up on. Stone heard only Kolb's voice, clear and convincing, *Kill the motherfucker and let's go celebrate.*

Stone cocked the revolver. A metal click echoed through the cavern.

"You have two choices. You can do it or I can do it. Jump, motherfucker, or I'll blow your balls off."

"Agent Stone, we're alike. Warriors . . . but with different agendas. You won and I lost. Now I deserve a warrior's outcome. I'm your prisoner," said Sternson, hands raised, surrendering, attempting to limp forward.

Stone's finger on the trigger began the slow squeeze that preceded discharge. Sternson inched forward, away from the edge of the pit. His large hands were outstretched, imploring Stone for forgiveness. Palms up, Stone saw them. The strange markings that lingered in his mind. On Rivers' feet. On Mary Agnes Robinson. And now on *him*.

Stone hesitated, but only long enough to regain the sight picture. Slow trigger pulls. Three. Breath held. Smooth as glass. Slow. Textbook. No flinching. Steady. Three shots in his kill zone. Sternson's body slumped, felled by three point blank .38 caliber rounds. Dead weight now. Motionless.

With his good leg Stone kicked Sternson forward to the edge of the abandoned mineshaft. Then, kicking as hard as he could, Sternson's body fell the hundred or so feet to the bottom of the abyss. A muffled sound, like a distant splash, a body being buried at sea, echoed back. Sternson was gone.

Stone, on the edge of the pit, looked down and spit into the darkness.

CHAPTER 46

Winmann's Quarry, Old Frontage Road East, Champaign, Illinois (Day 2)

Stone awoke in a stupor. The cuts on his chest had somehow clotted on their own. Dried blood was everywhere. He strained to remember but his head pulsated with pain, as if a runaway train was running through it. Somehow he made it to his car. Passed out. Slept there all night.

It was dawn now and the sun shinning through the windshield had awakened him. His throat was parched, as if he hadn't had water for a week. A grimy gray crust had formed around his eye sockets above the red welts left from the propane torch. It was coming back to him in spurts now. The pain did that. Reminding him. Taking him back. It seemed like forever ago, but it was less than 24 hours. In there, he thought, as he gazed toward the tunnel entrance. It was completely shaded now, the entrance barely visible.

Stone sat upright, gingerly, positioning himself behind the wheel. Needed to get away from here. Get cleaned up. Then it hit him like a jackhammer on dried asphalt. Sternson was dead. A calming feeling came over him. Something he hadn't experienced in years, since it all had begun. He relaxed and looked at the clock on the dashboard. 7:30 a.m. She'd be at her office by now, he surmised. He opened the glove compartment and retrieved a spare cellular phone, his other one lost somewhere in there. He glanced toward Sternson's sepulcher and then back at the cellular phone he held in trembling hands. He dialed her private number and waited. Three rings and she was on the line.

"Yes," a soft voice.

"Hi, stranger," he choked out.

"Who is this?" She demanded, not recognizing Stone's voice.

"It's me, James."

"James, for Godsakes, where are you? You said that you were going to call every night and then . . ."

"I'm fine, really . . ."

"You sound awful."

"Yeah, well, I had a hell of a night. I guess I just need some more time off. You know fishing can wear you out."

"When are you coming home? I miss you. I like fishing too," she said. A soft voice. A gentle voice.

"Listen, darling, I'm going to the Keys for a few days. You know, Kolb's old place. His brother thought I should have it. Haven't been there since . . ."

"I know. We talked about going."

"Well, I'm heading down that way. Going to catch a flight today. Just sit on the beach, count the waves, and feed the pelicans."

Silence. Then, "Okay, honey. Just call me when you're ready. Please . . . just call. I need to hear you. It's hard at night. Those . . ."

She couldn't say it. Stone finished it for her.

"Dreams?"

"Yes."

"Rest assured, things will be different when I get back. We'll put all of this behind us. Believe me, I have things to tell you, but . . . well, I just need some time. Okay?"

"Okay."

Silence.

"Love you," a soft voice, but he was gone.

CHAPTER 47

Springfield FBI Office,
Springfield, Illinois

"Whatcha' got, rookie?" asked Agent Williams, a 25-year veteran who would be retiring within a month.

"Ah, an anonymous caller. Something about some bodies at a quarry down near Champaign. Should I write up an FD-71 or just call it into the RA?" asked Agent Meade.

"Do both. Write it up as a legit complaint and then I'll call Timmerman down at Champaign. He handles that kind of stuff down there. How many stiffs and where?"

"Three altogether. Two buried in a cave and one at the bottom of a hundred-foot mine shaft. Ah, Winmann's Quarry. Ever heard of it?"

"Sure, use to rock hunt there as a kid. Arrowheads. You know, Boy Scout stuff. Made Eagle, too."

Agent Meade continued to type.

"Well, maybe I'll take a ride down there. Haven't seen that fat ass Timmerman in a month, anyhows. Wanna' tag along, kid? Might be interesting."

"Damn straight," said Meade, reaching for his holster and making sure the sidearm was still there. Satisfied, he said, "Soon as I get this complaint form typed up. Okay?"

"Sure, kid."

Williams was on the phone to the RA as Meade tidied up the complaint form. Filling in every box, dotting every *i*, crossing every *t*. A masterpiece, a thesis. A beginning for a rookie right out of the Academy.

Stone sat near the telephone booth from where he had placed the call. The rental car that he had rented in his undercover alias had been returned hours ago. Paid in cash. No loose ends. Now he waited for the shuttle bus that would take him to the United Terminal and his non-stop flight to Miami. O'Hare was just waking up. It was about 8:00 a.m.

He was cleaned up now. Not exactly spic-and-span, but presentable. He'd be in the Keys in a few hours with all of this behind him. By that time, he thought, the Springfield Division would have found the bodies; and would have started trying to piece it all together. At least some of it, anyway.

His .357, unfired, was in his knapsack. He had stumbled over it on his way out of the cave. On the ground, near the dead bats. His 5-shot Chief Special was strapped to his ankle. Two rounds remained unfired. The other three were in the sexual sadist. Untraceable. Bullets found in a drug raid years ago. Bullets saved by Stone for an emergency. An emergency like Stenson.

CHAPTER 48

Squad 6—Chicago FBI

"It's the Champaign RA out of Springfield," said Kathy, the squad secretary.

Padino looked up from the pile of papers on his desk, a file review with one of the Investigative Assistants assigned to his squad.

"Okay, I'll take it in here," he said, shooing away the IA who had been getting grilled.

"Padino, Squad 6," he answered the call.

"Hey, shit-for-brains, you still work for us?" asked Williams.

Recognizing the voice, Padino responded, "Williams, you homo, how the hell are you? Haven't heard from you since your partner got drunk at the Sox game and puked all over his wingtips. What was his name?"

"Fuck him. He's KMA in Knoxville working copyright cases. Got a new partner now. Kid right outta' the Academy. A real go-getter. Still polishes his shoes. Know what I mean?"

Padino looked down. Scruffy brown wingtips stared back at him.

"Yeah, great. Now you can sit on your fat ass and let the kid do all the work. How much more? Two, three months?"

"Less than one, brother. And I'm counting every fucking day. Hey, Dave, listen. We found three stiffs down here. One of 'em's yours. A Lawrence Sternson. Positive I.D. Extradition warrant outta' Chicago. Your squad. Ran NCIC and found he's listed as a fugitive. UFAP-murder. Ring any bells?"

Padino froze. Dumbstruck, as if an uppercut had knocked him into no-man's land. Something came out, but he retracted it and tried again.

"Yeah, he's ours. Damn, are you sure?"

"Positive I.D., Big Daddy. Dead as disco. Three shots to the K-5 area. Real nice grouping. Real tight. Somebody K-5'd his sorry ass. You got the picture?"

"Any idea what happened?"

"Well, for starters we found two other bodies. Had to do some digging, though. Buried, but not too deep. Cadaver dogs sniffed 'em out. Lots of dope, too. That psychedelic shit from the '70's. Made the dogs goofy. Had to shoot one of 'em. Was tryin' to eat his own damn tail. Anyway, found the bodies in shallow graves. Seemed like they'd been buried, dug up and buried again. Ground was disturbed. Weird, man, like something going down on queer street."

"Yeah, Sternson was into that shit. I follow you."

"Got a positive I.D. on both of 'em. Twin sisters. Disappeared from the university down here about a year ago. No leads. Until now."

"Headless?" asked Padino.

"Damn, how'd you know that?"

"Sternson's M.O."

"Yeah, we found the heads in the cave, too. Not buried though. He kept them preserved in some chemical solution like a damn bio-exhibit. Dogs found 'em by the dope."

"Right. The creep had a chemical background. Worked around labs and stuff. Anything else?"

"Yeah, well, we found 'em. Made the I.D. Ran NCIC and bingo . . . got a hit on your guy, Sternson. The LEADS message said to contact Agent Stone. Must be James Stone. Only Stone in Chicago I know. On your squad, right?"

"Right."

"Radio room said they couldn't locate him. Extended leave or something like that. They routed me up to you, partner. What's next?"

"Good work, young man."

"Young man, shit. I'll be 55 next week."

"Join the club. I know, asshole."

They both laughed. Had gone through MAP together.

"Where's Stone, anyway? asked Williams.

"Fishing."

"Fishing where?"

Padino hesitated. Didn't really know, though he should have. Trusted Stone. Then said, "Shit, I forgot. I'll have to check his locator card."

"Well, we got a lot of good spots down here. Tell him to call me when he gets back. We'll talk some fishin' and headless corpses," he laughed, gallows humor settling in.

"Will do, and thanks. In the meantime I'll send a couple of agents down to assist."

Williams signed off and Padino hung up the phone, thinking out loud, calling for his secretary.

Handing Padino Stone's locator card, Kathy said, "Couldn't help overhearing." She then smiled and returned to her previous eavesdropping position.

Written on the locator card were no telephone numbers or addresses, no motels or hotels, just . . . *Southern, Illinois—Gone Fishing*.

Padino sunk his chin into his hands, elbows secured on his desk. Thought hard for several minutes. He took the locator card and walked to the shredder. As the machine grumbled, the locator card disappeared into nothingness, as did Padino's memory of it.

CHAPTER 49

Rural McHenry County, Illinois
Mile Marker 135

He sat alone listening to Vivaldi's *Four Seasons*, her favorite composition. The melody played in his head assuaging the despair that lingered there. She had played it on the violin many times for him. Now he listened and thoughts of her filled the void. The void between then and now. Past remembrances and . . . this.

The bible lay on the seat beside him, opened to *Jeremiah* 30:12; *For saith the Lord, thy bruise is incurable, and thy wound is grievous.* Her fronds of hair marked the passage. The fronds had been returned to him, as he had requested, after the positive identification had been made by the FBI Laboratory. A friendly call from a female lab technician late one afternoon. A friendly voice, but he couldn't remember her name. She informed him of the DNA match between the hair and some of the assorted bones found in the well. And then had expressed her condolences. A nice voice. A friendly voice.

He began to drift as the music came to an end, and the despair crept back like an unwelcome neighbor. Slowly at first, then overpowering him. He glanced at the bible for solace, but it had ceased to help long ago. Endless silence, and nothing seemed to erase the memories of her murder. He had read the case file over and over. Padino had seen to that. Violated FBI rules. Had hand-carried the file to him in his chambers whenever he requested it. And once at his residence when the loneliness was overwhelming. Padino, a good man. A family man.

The file was a mosaic of two madmen. One was now dead, executed. The other, a Federal fugitive, was hiding in dark places. Waiting. Waiting to kill again. Rivers was gone now, and became a non-factor as far as providing evidence against Sternson. So that meant it was going to be a circumstantial case. And those cases were difficult to win.

He had studied the file from a legal perspective. Like a scholar. And had come to the conclusion that the evidence was too weak without an eyewitness. Without Rivers. Sternson's counsel would lay everything on Rivers and the Government would strike out. Sternson would never testify, assuming he would ever be caught. No, the evidence was just too weak. No witnesses, no witnesses, no . . .

He awoke, having dozed off at the wheel, still clutching the bible. A lifeline. He tried to piece the puzzle together again. The positive I.D. of Rita's remains from the well. But no one could put Sternson there. Only Rivers could, but he was dead. The evidence from the carpet showed three blood types, Rita's, Rivers' and one that was inconclusive. DNA from the blood matched Rita's and Rivers', but Sternson's DNA was not on file to match. He'd have to be apprehended first . . . but where was he? Even if the blood turned out to be Sternson's, he lived there. It was his apartment. It was still arguable, but was it concrete enough . . . beyond a reasonable doubt . . . to secure a conviction? Reasonable doubt. No witnesses. No Rivers, only his lies to the FBI. Impeachable at best. Falsehoods at worst. Just too much ammunition for a sharp defense attorney, the Johnny Cochran type. He had seen them before in his own courtroom. Twisting the evidence. Turning lies into the truth.

Rivers was dead and that was good. It brought some relief, but Sternson was still out there. Still waiting. The thought stuck in his mind, festering like an open wound. Tormenting him and urging him to end the pain.

The engine was running. Had been for nearly an hour, ever since he had come to this spot, a deserted railroad crossing. The only sound was the hum of the engine. He glanced at his wristwatch. 2:30 a.m. Funny, the sky was clear and they had forecast rain. He cracked his window, and sucked in cold air. He hoped that it would rain. It would make it look more like an accident. But the sky was clear, and the stars many, like when he was a boy at camp. Laying flat on the ground and looking up at the heavens. He believed in Heaven then. Watching the shooting stars. Comets they called them now. Really only rocks and ice leaving a tail of debris. He felt like counting them again but . . . no. He *must* do it.

The faint whistle of the train in the distance brought him back to the present. He shifted into drive and the Lincoln Navigator lurched forward onto the tracks, just before the gate went down. The blinking red lights on the gate began to mesmerize him. His headlights were shut off now, as the train sped closer. A freight train, the rumbling louder. Maybe a coal train, he thought, like when he was boy. Slipping back again. No, no one used coal anymore.

The train's whistle was deafening as the Judge clutched the bible close to his chest. There *must* be a Heaven. They're both there and I will be there soon, too. Tears were everywhere. He felt them on his cheeks. Reminded him of her. Soft tears on his shoulder. Thoughts of his grandfather. A good man. He would understand. The pain was too much. He would forgive him.

The blinking red lights of the cross-rail faded to nothingness as he closed his eyes for the last time. The train was upon him, the whistle deafening, as the face of Billy Rivers kept intruding. The whistle, high-pitched and shrieking, signaled the end. The Navigator was cut in half and dragged down the tracks. Metal on metal drowning out the shrill of the train's whistle.

*   *   *

Death was instantaneous, a final respite from his earthly torments. The bible was flung from the vehicle at the point of impact. It lay open a hundred yards down the track. Its pages fluttered in the gentle breeze, finally settling on *Proverbs* 17:7; *The just man walketh in his integrity, his children are blessed after him.*

CHAPTER 50

Kolb's Summer Home
Marathon Key, Florida

It was late August and hot. Stone was healing slowly from his wounds. Getting stronger physically, but mentally the struggles continued. He'd killed in cold blood and it gnawed at him, slowly at first, but now a persistent, silent executioner.

He'd been here for several days. Drinking. Sleeping. Lying on the beach. Drinking. Mostly drinking. He wasn't really much of a drinker, though. And that was the irony of it all. Solace in drinking, something to which Stone was unaccustomed. But now he drank until the memories began to fade. The memories of pain and fatigue, of all the shattered lives . . . of Rivers . . . and of Sternson.

With both of them dead, he should be able to move on and right things. Start over. But it wasn't as easy as he thought. And so he lay on the white sand sipping bourbon and water from a plastic cup, and trying to forget.

Padino would surely understand. Would protect him if it came to that. Retirement was a fleeting thought that was soon dispelled, but just sitting on the beach and feeding the pelicans *was* appealing. But Madeline was back in Chicago, so hell with the pelicans.

He glanced over his shoulder at the old house. He didn't need more. A little fixing up and it would be fine. Maybe a transfer down here. Hell, he had enough time on the job for that. But would she come?

He lifted his glass and was about to swallow the last dregs of comfort when a small boy appeared on the beach from behind a mound of cattails. He carried two small puppies. One was black with a white face, the other solid bone white. Mutts.

The boy appeared to be about ten years old and smallish for his size. He wore a tattered white shirt and faded blue swim trunks. The puppies were nipping at him, trying to get free. Finally, the bone white one succeeded and fell to the ground yelping. It righted itself and bolted straight for Stone.

Stone had seen the boy before. He lived in a trailer park down the road. White trash. Yellow hammers. Sad names, yet fully descriptive. The puppy nipped at Stone's toes now as he bent down to pick him up.

"Ain't got no name yet'," grinned the boy.

"He needs a name," said Stone, casually petting the white ball in his hands.

"He's yours now. You name 'em," said the boy, turning and running down the beach, holding the other puppy with both hands.

No name had imploring, sad eyes. Stone had seen sad eyes before. Many times. Madeline had had sad eyes way too often, and Stone had suffered through it, but that was over now. Stone held no name to eye level. Small whimperings. Tongue patting in every direction. On Stone's face. Salty. Stone looked down the beach in the direction to where the boy had run. Empty. He picked up the bottle of bourbon, empty, and flung it into the ocean. Time to start over and it appeared that no name was his responsibility now. He would be all right. He would call her. He would wait for her. And there would be no more sad eyes. Never.

CHAPTER 51

Padino Residence, Oak Lawn, Illinois

He attacked the green beans with a vengeance, one stab after the other, muttering to himself. Thoughts, half-formed, jostled around in his mind like marbles rolling downhill. The mashed potatoes were next, and then the meatloaf when his wife put an end to the blitzkrieg.

"You're talking to yourself again, Dave," she said, her hand pulling away his plate.

His fingers played an unfinished symphony on his lips.

"Stone?" she asked, smiling. A beautiful, caring smile.

"It's that obvious, is it?"

Getting up from the table, Padino grabbed a beer from the refrigerator and then retreated to the living room to his comfortable chair, his only possession in the house that was off-limits to the boys. She shooed them away and they scattered like chickens in a barnyard during a twister. She then seated herself, ladylike, on the small footstool in front of him.

"We should talk about it. I think you need that," she said, smiling. A different kind of smile. Inquisitive, yet not intrusive.

She was a good woman. A Bureau wife. Padino had been married to the Bureau for 27 years and she had been married to him. Same difference. The late nights, the never-ending phone calls and interruptions, the missed ball games and birthday parties. The bonuses at the end of the year that never came, compliments of the public sector. The ups-and-downs, the mood swings, and best of all the government pay. Yes, it all added up to one *helluva* woman.

"Yeah, I guess I could use a sounding board," he whispered in between sips on the longneck.

She listened intently while he explained his suspicions about the death of Sternson and Stone's unexpected and unexplained fishing trip to Southern Illinois.

"Hell, he doesn't even know how to bait a hook. Took him out last year with Bobby and little Tommy and he damned near took off his thumb. Ten stitches, remember?"

She nodded. A simple nod. An understanding nod. Rising, she said, "You're probably right. You usually are. And I'm sure you'll figure out what to do."

She called for the boys to get to bed. Looking over her shoulder her eyes met his. Gentle eyes.

The answer was evident to Padino. He would simply do nothing. Not a Goddamn thing.

CHAPTER 52

Hyde Park, Chicago, Illinois

It was lightly raining. It usually did when he needed a fix. Must have something to do with air pressure and barometric readings, things he really didn't understand, but thought about anyway. It was always late at night when the urge would hit him. A subtle tingling in the joints at first. His throbbing fingers forewarned him. Then the toes, and his fingernails began to itch. And ending with sharp flashes all over his body, like pins being stuck in him and then pulled out slowly. Repeated over and over again. His teeth hurt, too. The teeth that he had left, anyway. But one thing was always the same, he ended up calling Stone. But Stone would never come. It was always Sarge. A phone call from Stone probably forcing Sarge's hand. But the *Tinman* never knew. Never really cared as long as he got his medicine. The *edge* he called it. Just taking off the *edge*.

But now Sarge was dead. And Stone hadn't answered. Probably out of town or something. Gone somewhere. Somewhere important. Not like him, stuck here in this cesspool of misery and pain. But this was life-or-death now. *His* life or *his* death. And so he reached in his pocket and pulled out a sorry excuse for a wallet. Cowhide once, but now worn, dirty and crumbling. He fished out some small bits of paper, yellowish. Phone numbers were haphazardly scribbled on them, some incomplete. What good did that do, he complained to himself in between jolts from the pins he felt now embedded in his knees. Damn, where was that number. Frantically searching he found it. Emergency numbers. Yes, there . . . Nirvana. Hands shaking, he traced the number with numbing fingers. It was scribbled under *stash house—Westside*. Remembering Stone's cautionary warning, *Call him if you can't get me or Sarge. But only if it's an emergency*. Damn straight, this is an emergency. So, the *Tinman* dialed Padino's number and waited as the rain dripped off his Cubs hat, which was pulled down tightly over his bat ears. Endless ringing, as the *Tinman* held out his hand. It was trembling uncontrollably. He stuck it in his pocket and fumbled for more coins.

The *Tinman* had met Padino only once. Stone had explained that his supervisor was required to personally meet all of the informants assigned to agents on his squad roster. He had been reluctant at first, but now maybe it would pay off. He tapped his fingers incessantly on his watch, hoping the stinging would go away. But it never did. The phone continued to ring as the *Tinman* strained to make sense of the clicking monstrosity that now weighed down his wrist and was changing colors from deep purple to bright red. Damn that psychedelic shit. Going back to straight weed this time. His watch had stopped dead at 11:45 p.m. No matter, Padino was on the line now.

"Hello?" Padino warbled, like a walrus being awakened from a long sleep.

"Sir, it's me. The *Tinman*. Stone said I could call if . . ." He stuttered, coughing out the words staccato style, as the cold rain formed an odd pattern on his face. ". . . if, if he wasn't around."

Silence. Years of Silence for *Tinman*. Seconds for Padino, shaking the cobwebs from his brain.

"And he's not around. Not answering. So . . . I'm calling, asking . . . got some stuff. Real good stuff for 'ya. But . . ."

"You need some cash?"

"Yeah, cash. Cash would be nice. Real nice. And I got . . ."

"Where are you? Exactly, *Tinman*."

The *Tinman* always got a rush when the feds called him by his code name. Damn, he picked it out himself. Liked the sound of it when it rattled out of his mouth, the syllables trickling off his remaining, jaundiced teeth like a runaway train going downhill. *T-I-N-M-AAA-N*. Yeah, the rush was always good, but not the same rush he'd get from the smack he now needed to take the *edge* off.

"Ah, phone booth. Right at the place I met you the first time. Remember?"

Silence. Padino remembering. The *Tinman* dying a thousand silent deaths.

"Yeah. Got it. About an hour or so. Don't go anywhere else."

"I'll be right by the phone booth waiting, boss," he said, keeping one eye glued to his shopping cart located just outside of the booth.

"Hundreds would be nice. Sarge always brought hundreds and . . ."

But Padino was off the line and the *Tinman* would just have to wait and pray. And make up something good. Real good. Something Padino would bite on. So he racked his brain for falsehoods about to become solid, reliable and valuable street intelligence. The *Tinman* was good at that. Prefabrication. That's what Sarge had called it when he'd caught the *Tinman* in a series of lies awhile back. But he had learned and this time he'd come up with something real good for Padino. He racked his tired brain for subject matter as a short tramp pulling a shopping cart like the *Tinman's*, except it was empty, approached the phone booth. Within seconds, the exchange had been made and the tramp was scurrying down 57th Street with the *Tinman's* cart of assorted treasures, several hubcaps spilling out.

Seeing the theft, he yelled but the tramp didn't stop. And the *Tinman* couldn't pursue. The dilemma presented itself matter-of-factly. He must wait at the phone booth. Must wait for the money to get his medicine. Just to take the *edge* off. So he waited and it continued to rain.

CHAPTER 53

Kolb's Summer Home, Marathon Key, Florida

The house was small, set back from the road a hundred yards or so. Pine trees lingered nearby. It wasn't difficult to find after she had located the gravel road that wasn't on the map. A little help from a County road crew clearing underbrush in the area didn't hurt either.

Perched on a rocky prominence on one of several small inlets that projected, fingerlike, backward toward the road, the house appeared in disrepair. It was vine-covered and badly in need of a face-lift. A good project for someone with time on his hands. Someone like Stone.

She parked the small rental car, a compact Dodge Stratus, directly behind the lone vehicle already parked alongside the house. Stone's probably. A convertible, top still down, and wet inside. Must've rained last night, she thought, as she noticed a moss-covered tarp half-slung over a small camper nearby. It appeared to have been there for some time.

She wanted to surprise him, so she softly shut the car door, leaving her things inside. Except the over-sized *Coach* beach bag. It was hot and humid, but the occasional soft breeze from the ocean side of the Keys was a welcome respite from the heat.

Then, over the small ridge that flattened out to the beach she saw him. He was sitting in a beach chair near the water, white foam washing up around him, lapping his legs. A red Cardinals' baseball cap, tilted down, covered his sunglasses. As she approached, the pattern on his Jimmy Buffet shirt became clearer. Several pink flamingos standing on one foot. The backdrop could have been this very beach.

He wore cut-off jeans shorts. Old and tattered. A radio was next to his chair. Something about baseball, but she couldn't quite make it out. A small cooler was nestled under the beach umbrella behind him, secured in the sand by a large rock. He was motionless, appearing to be asleep.

She ducked behind the old camper, which was hidden by some tall, tufted grass on a mound of sand. Pussy willows were growing there along with some red flowers. The transformation from business attire to lover in bikini took only a moment. Tight fitting, the white bikini showed just enough cleavage to be interesting. Her long legs, not yet tanned, were muscular in a feminine way. Runner's legs.

Her clothes were stuffed into the beach bag, which she carried in her left hand. The sunscreen, in her right hand, was nervously gripped as she made her way through warm sand to the beach. Several feet from Stone she tossed the bag. It landed near the radio with a soft thud, startling him. He jerked his head around clumsily, falling out of his chair.

She held out the suncreen and coyly said, "Wanna' help me?"

Half-tripping over the leg of the beach chair, Stone bolted toward her, not saying anything, and smiling as if he had just won the trifecta when the mortgage was due. Their embrace was awkward, all arms and some legs. They fell to the ground tangled, the sunscreen lost in the struggle. They rolled back and forth kissing. Deep kisses and bone-crushing hugs. Until they were sand-covered. Exhausted.

Stone rolled on his back, no name licking his face. Sunglasses askew, he smiled a beggar's smile, pointed and said, "No name. He's mine."

She laughed as Stone picked her up effortlessly, no name licking his ankles, and walked into the water. Warm and soothing. They sat like Indians around a campfire. Touching, kissing, not talking. The only sounds the sea waves massaging the beach and no-name's occasional yelp. Suddenly Stone rose and pushed back his wet hair with both hands. Helping her up, he brought her to eye-level, her tiptoes barely touching the water.

"I knew you'd come," he said.

They were in a small boat now. Fishing equipment lay in the bottom. Rods and pails. A red tackle box. Bread crumbs were scattered about. She listened but he didn't speak as the boat made its way out to sea. The house was barely visible when he cut the engine. Silence now, floating on placid sunlit waters. Calm, like smooth glass. He had that forlorn look in his eyes. She had seen it before, mostly at funerals and wakes. But now she welcomed it.

He opened the tackle box and removed his 5-shot Chief Special revolver. He stood now, back to the sun, gun in hand.

"I killed him with this," he said.

Stone emptied the barrel. Two rounds spilled into his hands.

"Thought about using them but . . ."

Silence. Except for a pair of gulls in the distance diving for fish.

"But?" she asked.

"Then he would have won and I would have lost . . . you."

He threw the rounds as far as he could. Silent splashes in the distance. On any other day it would have been fish. The gun was next, flung overboard further away. A splash. The evidence gone forever. Lost among the ever-widening ripples.

They returned to shore, her hands held tightly around him. Her head resting on his broad shoulders. The sun cast a subtle shadow on the floor of the boat, their backs to the horizon.

"I read about the Judge," Stone said.

"Let's save that for another time," she replied, tightening her grip, nestling her head among the thick muscles of his neck and shoulders, as they drifted toward shore. He nodded slightly, strong arms now around her waist.

No name was waiting when they beached the boat. Panting anxiously, she picked him up and let him excitedly lick her face.

"That looks like fun," said Stone.

"I have a better idea," she said, no name under her arm, as she grabbed Stone's hand. "But first he needs a name."

"Umm . . . okay, you choose."

There was no hesitation as he carried her from the beach to the small house. A silent conspiracy of love.

"Sarge," she said. "We'll call him Sarge."

CHAPTER 54

San Blas Islands, Panama
(The foreboding of things to come)

The path was worn down. It wound like a lazy pretzel, finally coming to an abrupt end where, on a clearing, stood a lone building. The structure was block-like and made of stucco. Originally white in color, it was now streaked with shades of yellow and brown from the vegetation growing on it. It appeared in disrepair. Having no windows and only one door, it resembled a small barn.

The solitary figure was busy with the needle, putting the final touches on several severed fingers. Other assorted appendages lay on the small table waiting their turn. Each would bear the distinctive mark. His mark. A blue half-moon surrounded by the numbers 6, 7 and 8. He would save them and place them with the other treasures. Down below. Below where no one would see them.

Except for Pequeno, the *Tattooed Man* was alone on this small, insignificant island. And Pequeno was busy preparing the boat for their trip to the mainland. And their eventual destination, Paris. They would leave soon, as dusk lingered like a lost child on the horizon.

Time was really of no importance to him as he continued his work. Massaging the lifeless joints, freshly severed, the blood vessels were hardening now. But he persisted, concerned only that he had not heard from his prized student in some time. But time was really only a fleeting entity in his life, his real concern being the fingers and how they would fit into his plans.

Maybe Sternson would be in Paris when they arrived. Time would only tell. He motioned to Pequeno, returning from the pier. The handful of poison darts were secreted in the small canvas knapsack that hung from his shoulder. Pequeno signaled that all was ready. Somewhere on the mainland, the *Tattooed Man's* next victim was waiting.